For Reuben
enjoy!!!

The Cosmic Lottery

BOOK ONE

Apocalypse Grin

Brian Sheehan

Cheers! 08/06/11

Acknowledgements

For Mimi and Frannie, my "godmothers". There can be no greater debt than what I owe to them.

For my father, who is bigger than life.

For Tommy Bradshaw, the inspiration behind "Saint" Germaine.
Rest In Peace, My Friend.

For Justus Rosenberg, professor, mentor, and dear friend. He outwitted the Nazis, and took a young, unpolished writer under his wing. I can think of no greater honor.

Special thanks to my artist, Rick Holland, whose patience and skill rival that of Dorian. And that's saying something.

Table of Contents

Chapter One

A Reasonably Decent Day to Die

It was profoundly ironic that he now found himself deposited into this 15th century mud-pit nightmare. Even worse, the locals were just moments away from burning him alive for heresy. Somebody somewhere had a perverse sense of humor.

Over the millennia, his interactions with Catholics had never been very good. It was widely rumored that, back in his own relative space-time, the Uber-Pope had issued a secret religious decree calling for his assassination. Therein lay the most ironic aspect of this whole painful misadventure - it wasn't a sleek, hyper-advanced New Vatican hit-squad dressed in neat-looking black optical camouflage suits that was about to do him in this time, rather it was a bunch of peasants whose greatest technological development was crude by even the most generous of standards.

He had been reduced now, his face driven into hay and excrement while his body was carried in the back of a horse-drawn cart, an unlit pyre in the middle of town waiting to take him into the next life. The whole affair was so twisted that he could weep for joy at the sheer mad scale of it all, if only there weren't those guards with their damned hot pokers.

Life was certainly filled with surprises, his life more than most. However when his matter-transference beam got knocked off course and he wound up in 15th century France, six hundred years from his intended target, it was not a very welcome sort of surprise.

He'd been stuck in this century for quite some time now, and he wasn't very happy about it. After two months of sheer boredom in a time-period and location he openly despised, he began drinking quite heavily and quite regularly at the public house, and other less than reputable spots. He'd also begun to hang out with the 15th century version of a 'bad' crowd. The drinking was to be expected, hanging out with the more desperate and colorful inhabitants was certainly to be expected, however the sheer misery of total, unrelenting boredom that had engulfed him over the last two months was simply more than he could bear.

For the last two weeks he had been in a foul mood. He had been itching for a fight, philosophical, spiritual, or otherwise. His brain was literally starving for some sort of discourse that transcended the idiotic, superstitious ramblings of the monkey-descendents. Three days earlier, during a highly spirited and wholly ignorant conversation concerning certain articles of faith, he lost his filter and threw himself headfirst into controversy. He had been sitting at a long table with a crowd of miserable drunks. There in the reek and filth of the public house, amid the flickering candles and droopy, soapy-eyed faces, he muttered the simple words: "You know, the Pope shouldn't have really started the Crusades."

His argument was simple and not entirely without merit, and it wasn't possessed of even a trace amount of sentimentalism. He reasoned that there were terrible costs involved in maintaining these sorts of foreign excursions, and that these costs would mostly be paid for with taxes, which, in turn, would invariably give rise to the pestilence of the tax attorney, and his related ilk. The whole of civilization could only go downhill from here.

What was his effort at a comedic provocation, however carefully crafted, did not fall upon sympathetic ears. The claws of orthodoxy and impenetrable dogma reached out in the form of several grimy hands, and he was quickly deposited into a nasty, dank, rat-infested dungeon, subjected to various tortures, as obscure as they were obscene.

The charges were brought to the local constabulary, an overworked, underpaid bureaucrat. Following a review of the facts, an event that transpired in under three minutes, he was sentenced to die in a most horrific fashion. Needless to say, the 15th century judicial system was fairly violent by most relative measures.

Admittedly, he should have known better. The Enlightenment was still percolating like a teapot on the cusp of a final boil. Scientific rationalism didn't even exist to be persecuted yet. It was a crude era filled with cruder solutions. Freedom of speech certainly was not a luxury enjoyed by the masses. So it appeared that he would be just another in a long line of people with a poorly timed sense of humor who ended up paying the ultimate price for what amounted to an excess of personality.

It had been quite some time since he'd actually pondered his mortality, the possibility that one day he would be no more. It was a thought better entertained in private, not in front of a leering crowd as he was now. Even in his wildest and darkest fantasies he could never have envisioned that he would go out like this. Such was fate, utterly capricious and perfectly unkind. So be it, he thought. Whatever else could be said on the subject, he'd had a good run, a good long run. His life had been one wild ride, and he was smart enough to appreciate the unique privileges afforded by his wealth and radical choice of lifestyle. It seemed only fair that he get unlucky eventually.

The ride into town in the back of the cart was relatively uneventful. Alongside the broken path leading into the dour little village there was a growing crowd of gnarly faced peasants with sun-beaten, wrinkled skin and violently lit-up eyes. They were scowling and screeching with murderous intent. It was a sort of anti-parade. They spat at him, and cursed him viciously as he passed by. Many of them held their hands up, fingers curled into an O like shape to ward off his 'evil eye'.

These were a simple folk who were quite simply enjoying the pleasure of submitting oneself to mass hysteria around a commonly shared source of hatred. As an additional bonus, the weather was very nice for a family outing.

As he had never attended his own execution before, he had no idea what was the proper protocol. There was the old-fashioned, stoic "Go quietly, man, show them your dignity to the end" routine. Then there was the "Screw it! Might as well tell them what dirty, horrible little creatures you think they are!" And, of course, there was the terribly unattractive, repentant approach where he would beg for forgiveness, offer his life to become a mendicant, reflect upon his wicked ways and dream only of good things for a good Earth. Poofah, he thought. None of these options were appealing.

He sighed as he took it all in, the crowd, the assault of noises, all those expectant faces waiting to dance wildly around his dying embers, the spit, the pokers, and all those sleek sounding French curse-words.

Now that he seemed near to his death, part of him wondered if there was a girl at all at the heart of this mysterious matter, or whether it had been just a story to lure him to this planet, to lure him to his doom? If so, it was the by far the cleverest ploy he'd ever encountered. Even if he'd suspected a trap, he'd have come to the planet anyway. He had to find out whether or not the girl really existed. If a Nephyr had arrived in the universe and was being imprisoned on Earth, he had to take a chance and rescue her. He'd always wanted to meet one of the creators of the universe.

For the moment he was stuck in the wrong century, and it didn't look like he would make it out alive. There was no one around who was literate enough to record the final moments of his life, just a ritual extermination with no more than mindless, rabid spectators. Where was a Jesuit when you actually wanted one, he sighed.

The cart grumpily, noisily came to a stop in the middle of the town center, a dilapidated enclave of weather beaten, wood and stone structures surrounding a decaying gray-stone trimmed well. The church, the hub of intellectual activity, stood a few yards away from the pyre. The bell in the tower was ringing, but there were no clergy present. Pity, as he would have liked to tell them what nasty creatures he thought they were. Turning the other cheek and burning someone to death were incompatible directives. Somebody had gotten it all cocked up somewhere down the line, and he figured quite logically that it had started with the clergy. It usually did.

The guards brought him roughly to his feet. He was forcefully lifted up and more forcefully tossed off the back of the cart. With his hands wrapped in twine behind his back, he landed on his face. All the while, two words kept ringing in his mind, reflecting off the backs of his closed eyelids like a neon advertisement. The two words were:

'Room Service'. He could really go for a Shiatsu massage followed by an hour in a steam room, then a light dinner someplace ritzy with a witty, sexy companion. He wanted grilled chicken with a gingery peanut sauce but he was in the wrong time-period, and on the wrong planet for really good Thai food.

Two pairs of grubby hands lifted him up and lashed him to a pole with twine. He looked up in the sky above. It was a beautiful, clear day. The sky was as wide and blue a sky as he had ever seen. Whatever else one might say, it truly was a reasonably decent day to die.

With his end only moments away, he suddenly felt a rant would not be out of order.

"You simian bastards!" he yelled out over the din of the crowd. "You'll get no screams out of me, you monkey-offspring."

His French was rudimentary at best, and the word 'Monkey' was a sound without much currency in a 15th century French village. Feeling as though they had been lobbed some unknown curse, the locals responded by tearing at his clothes, scratching at his skin. They were shrieking wildly. With no ability to react, he could only endure.

The guards fought the crowd off while the pyre was lit. Fumes of smoke were quick to envelop the scene. It was a noxious, acrid scent. Flames licked at his lower legs singeing the short hairs and giving off a sickening vomit smell.

"This is not going to be fun," he muttered. "I suppose being a militant atheist, I had this coming."

As the flames began to envelope the wood pile, a bluish light appeared atop the scene. At first it was only a dot, a tiny marble, but it quickly grew in intensity and size. Soon a grayish blue cloud of energy-discharge the size of a football field appeared over the entire area.

He knew what that blue meant. It meant freedom. It meant rescue. And if things occurred with some alacrity, it could mean significantly less time in the burn ward.

A scout ship appeared suddenly in the center of the rumbling cloud of energy discharge. It was shaped like a large bronze egg, eight meters in length, as wide as double-trailer, luminescent in the sunlight.

The villagers fell to their faces in fear, prostrated on the ground in utter confusion and terror. They weren't above a little idol worship, particularly when one hung dangerously above their heads. The guards were bewildered, more brawn than brains and not much room for creative thought. They looked like they wanted to pound the daylights out of something or someone. It was their natural response to most situations.

"Yeah, yeah, fear Satan, you illiterate simians, fear evil!" he yelled out over the roar of the vessel's engines. He stuck out his tongue and gave the crowd a big raspberry.

The ship shot out a beam of energy that encapsulated him just before the fire could. Within a split second he evaporated into thin air. The vessel then flew off at an incredible speed, hitting mach sixty and disappearing before the villagers could react in any sensible fashion.

As he materialized onto the metal floor of a high-ceilinged chamber, his body reinitiated its relationship with pain. He was a mess. He smelled of burnt hair. He had two week's worth of a nasty beard on his face, and his breath was as devastating as a blow-torch.

"Come on, Captain, we need to get you to sick bay," a familiar voice stated.

"I'm all right," he responded. "Just a little scorched around the edges. I think I'll tan nicely."

"We followed your transponder through the anomaly five seconds after your beam was diverted. How did you manage to make yourself the object of a witch burning so fast?"

"Huh. Five seconds. That was the longest five seconds of my life, and nearly my last," he answered. "I was trapped on Earth for two months, Capoella. 15th century humans are cracked-out of their tiny minds."

"You started that mess down there, didn't you?" Capoella replied.

"Of course I did," he answered innocently.

"Why do you always start trouble like this with the locals, Captain?" she asked.

"Why does anybody do anything? The role of free will in the events of history is completely indeterminable," he shrugged. "What's our exposure on the main nets?"

"Not a whisper," Capoella responded. "We've re-cloaked. We'll be back aboard the Cortez in a few moments."

"All's quiet, that's strange. I would have thought somebody would be monitoring this place. Somebody booby-trapped the planet, after all" he grumbled, brushing bits of burnt hair from his calves.

"If any encrypted signals were being transmitted, Doja would have picked up on them. There are no discernible patterns in any radioactive output across the spectrum."

"Does our little Doja have any rough calculations on the energy it would take to knock my mat-trans beam off course so quickly, and so precisely?"

"More than the Cortez can generate," Capoella said. "That says a lot. She doesn't think the Bureaucracy is behind this incident and neither do I. Our temporal shift tech is way more advanced than their top military grade, but even if we towed in a dwarf star for a power source, we'd have a hard time pulling something like that off without cooking your molecules in the process. I think this is one intrigue we may need to walk away from."

"Which intrigue, the booby-trap or the girl?"

"Both."

"Well, things have certainly changed, but I can't think we should abandon the mission."

"Matching wits with the Bureaucracy is one thing, but dealing with an enemy more advanced than us is generally problematic."

"It's a challenge, that's all. Why are you so pessimistic?" he asked.

"Doja doesn't think we should go after the girl. Not after this mess. "

"Doja's never liked the idea of this mission. She's worried she might lose her status as the greatest enigma aboard the Cortez," he stated.

"Doja's motivations cannot be comprehended," Capoella replied flatly.

"Look, how about I rescue the girl and then we can continue this conversation?"

"You want to continue this conversation because you know where this is headed. We both know who messed with your energy beam. Our pact with the VD means we don't interfere with their business."

"Nonsense. This is a legitimate mystery. Besides, I really don't think the VD are behind what I just endured. Let's just get back to the 21st century, and we can do this the old-fashioned way. No mat-trans beam. I come in fast, cut the girl loose, and we get the hell out of this star system."

"Why do I get the impression that you're happy that things have worked out like this, and that you can now go down to that miserable little planet and apply brute force to the situation?" Capoella asked.

"What are you talking about?"

Capoella shook her head disapprovingly. "You're gonna go down there and wreck the place."

"That's absurd. I'm not going to wreck the place," Germaine replied.

"You're gonna wreck the place."

"No, not a chance" he protested. "I absolutely will not wreck the place."

"You're going to wreck the place."

"Well, yes, probably. So what? I want to wreck the place. Big deal," he confessed under the pressure.

"You *always* want to wreck the place."

"Well...I *always* have a good reason. And that's important. Besides, it's not a very nice place she's trapped inside. I suspect it deserves to be wrecked."

After the scout ship docked with the Cortez, the larger vessel broke free from Earth's atmosphere, and soon it moved out of the magnetic field.

Capoella and Germaine entered the bridge after arguing for several minutes while they made their way through the winding halls. The bridge was a wide open area with regal red carpeting and a large video monitoring screen. There were only a few consoles as most operations were conducted via encrypted telepathic interface. Within a few seconds, the ship's exotic particle generators were charged. Capoella monitored the energy field as the generators initiated a graviton pulse towards the space in front of the ship. Although a thousand variables were at play and a million horrible deaths were possible should she miscalculate, she remained calm, constant. This was her gift. Germaine had chosen her well.

Capoella possessed the enviable quality of being able to monitor and comprehend the situation when all the laws of physics had been thrown into disorder, when the particles behaved like schools of silvery fish swimming through the turbulent, mostly invisible ocean of space-time, diving in and out of dimensions, appearing several places at once. Capoella saw the truth for what it was, that all was possible, all that could be imagined; that the laws of space-time could be whipped about, torn through, often simply disregarded by renegade physicists from a billion advanced species, each one aiming for the same goal from discrete, unique vectors. The laws, such as they were, were nothing more than placards on the side of a cosmic highway, speed limits to be ignored, scribbles of mathematical symbols on whiteboard programmed into magnificently complex, and ultimately irrelevant computer models. The universe was, to the consternation of many, a bizarre and thoroughly lawless place.

Capoella calibrated the high-energy particle pulse as it tore a localized rift in the fabric of space-time just off the bow of the Cortez. Within a few nano-seconds the vessel crossed over the blue fire of the event-horizon of the singularity just as it formed, and thirty nano-seconds after that the vessel was on the other side of the rift and in orbit around 21st century Earth, a decidedly different look at the same planet they had just left. The previous view of the planet had revealed no industrial development, almost nothing that could be recognized from space. That image had shifted. The ship was now in geostationary orbit hanging several hundred miles above the western hemisphere during its night cycle. The coastal regions of the continents were lit up like elaborate, misshapen Christmas trees. There were so many artificial satellites and fragments of discarded trash, that the orbit around the planet was suddenly a crowded space.

"Keep us cloaked, my dear. You guys just be ready to pick me up when I come running. I need a change of clothes and a bath. After that, I'm going down there and getting the girl."

"I have a lot of reservations," Capoella remarked.

"What's not to like?" Germaine grinned.

"The whole bit about you manually breaking into a heavily secured, heavily fortified underwater military base."

"It's nothing more than intellectual exercise with a few physical aspects. I doubt I'll break a sweat."

"Exercise…" Capoella sighed disapprovingly. "That's what you said last time."

"Aren't you going to farewell me?" he asked, smiling impishly.

Capoella stared disapprovingly. She pursed her lips and shook her head in frustration. At that moment, Germaine stopped himself. He knew when he pushed, and he knew when to stop. He took a deep breath.

"If you say this is a no-go, it's a no-go," he said. "I admit, this matter is a little more serious than throwing an election or raiding a convoy. I'll not drag you into this if you tell me to stop."

"I never tell you stop. Six hundred years of watching you wreak havoc, and I've never told you to stop."

"And I've always loved you for that."

"Jesus, you sop. Don't get sentimental. Just go rescue the girl so we can get the hell out of this backwater star system," Capoella replied sarcastically. "This whole region of the galaxy just makes me so…irritable."

"Of course, darling," he responded. "I'll be back before you can say dry vodka martini," he grinned.

As he headed towards the doors of the bridge, she called out: "Enjoy your *workout.*"

Of all the fates a being could endure, hers was certainly among the bleakest. Not painful, not normally, but simply boring, desperately lonely. Other than a few hours in the arboretum each afternoon, she spent her days lethargic, bed-ridden, alone. She had access to the Internet and she had cultivated many friendships through the various social networking sites she was connected to, but ultimately she was in solitude amid the silence of the closed hospital ward she was sequestered in. She had no one to keep her company. Nobody followed her plaintive Tweetys anymore, no one cared about her macabre poetry on her blog.

Doctors visited her regularly, but there was no social interaction. To protect themselves, they wore bio-hazard suits that all but obscured their faces entirely behind white hoods and opaque visor glass. She could not tell one from the other. They came in, performed their examinations and then left. It was almost ritualistic.

And so she slept away the days, dreaming often of the same places, secluded safe places where images stretched into one another, the only goal of the dream was to move further away from something she could never quite identify.

On this particular day, she was asleep and dreaming when she found that she was looking at a large wolf in front of her. Its long, muscular body was pointed away from her, but its head turned back to stare with a weird shamanic sort of calm. Its hide was matted silver and blue that seemed to be torn in a few places, and its eyes were an intense gray, deeply intelligent. It seemed to want her to follow it down the winding, dark passageway. The area was lit only by flickering torch-light that did wicked things with the shadows. It appeared to be a mineshaft with muddy clay walls. The hazy, compelling logic of her dream was that she needed to follow the wolf further down through the corridor. She walked behind, but the path was windy.

The wolf soon disappeared beyond a bend. She suddenly felt panic. She knew she needed to catch up, as though everything depended on her keeping up with the wolf. She was frantic to find it. As she crossed over the crest of an incline, crawling almost through the semi-darkness, she found herself standing just to the side of an open doorway with peeling whitish paint. She peered inside through the slit of the opening between the door and the frame.

Inside the empty, dusty-floored room were two large, six-foot potato-sack like creatures. They each had several tendrils branching out from their brown, wrinkled bodies, and there in the middle of the room was the wolf, its body wrapped in tentacles. The creatures were slowly tearing the wolf apart, dissolving through its fur with an acidic organic substance secreted from their tendrils. The wolf whimpered only a little bit as parts of its body were torn apart and liquefied by the sack creatures. There was a strangely calm resignation in the way the wolf met its demise. Its eyes seemed to show more concern with her than its own situation. It seemed to want her to understand something more complex than the apparent circumstances.

She watched the wolf get slowly torn apart. She was frightened into a statue state, terror registering deep within her chest, as one of the creatures looked at her, seeing her hidden in the crack between the door and the frame. She could hear her heart pounding wildly in her torso, and she had to close her mouth to keep the thumps from echoing in her throat. The creature's maw opened up widely in a hideous grin as it caught her within its gaze.

"You are a brave one, aren't you?" it growled in a deep, phlegm-filled voice.

She was utterly frozen, caught in the glare, helpless. She had met her death. No plan of action came to mind. The terror overwhelmed her. For a moment they were stuck in time. Then her breath returned. She snapped to consciousness with a shocking abruptness. The fear of the dream was still with her. A cold sweat had formed over her lower back, making her bedclothes stick uncomfortably to her back. The hospital ward was quiet. She looked out over the ward only to find, rather unexpectedly, that someone was staring back at her.

Sarah had seen his face before, though she wasn't sure if it was part of a dream. She spent so many of her hours asleep that she had long given up on deciphering the difference between the wild realms of her dreams and the calm and quiet confines of her reality. Realities intermixed so regularly that they all became a blur of borderless experience.

When she had first seen him, he had been standing behind the three doctors in biohazard suits that routinely came to check on her condition. He didn't wear any protective gear though. He was simply there. The doctors seemed to disregard him completely. Either they didn't see him, or they didn't care. She, however, did see him, and she certainly did care.

He was tall and thin. His face appeared human, but there was something about the sheen of his skin she couldn't quite articulate, almost a glow as though he was laughing on the inside. He had a rakish cut of perfectly disheveled dark blonde hair and he looked like an overgrown schoolboy, early thirties at best, but his eyes had some sort of strange medicine man mirth, a peacefulness about him that was instantly disarming. He was wearing a silver-colored silk suit, the sleeves of his jacket cut too short, awkward but somehow fitting. At this moment, he was staring at her with gentle blue eyes, smiling slightly.

"I didn't want to wake you. It looked like you were having an interesting dream," he said. "In a place such as this, all one has is their dream world."

In his hand were two spheres of bluish energy revolving around each other.

"Are you supposed to be in here?" she asked.

"Probably not. I generally spend a lot of time in places where I probably shouldn't be," he smiled. "It's a habit that's led to rather full and adventurous life so far."

"It's a habit that could get you killed. Don't you think you should be wearing a bio-hazard suit?"

"Why? Is that the current fashion?"

"It would protect you from my virus," she said, alarmed now that she was more awake and the idea was blossoming in her mind.

"I'll be all right. You're not sick," he told her. "As far as I can tell, you never have been. I read your charts. You're probably the healthiest creature on this planet. You're certainly the most exotic." The blue spheres hummed louder and glowed more brightly.

Of all the possible words he could have spoken, of all the possible combinations of words she could have expected, this was nowhere even on the list of possibilities. It was as improbable as it was disturbing. She studied him in shocked silence for a moment. His eyes were so sincere. It seemed clear to her that, at the very least, he believed what he said. He was probably a lunatic, she thought. But how did he make it through security?

"Who are you?" she asked. "And what are those things in your hand?"

"Sorry, I suppose it's rather rude to be playing with my balls in your presence," he said.

"That doesn't answer my first question."

"More importantly, do you know who you are?" he asked.

"I sure hope so."

"No, let me rephrase the question: do you know what you are?"

"Umm, female, human, fifteen, a little weirded out. Why, what are you?"

He looked at her for a moment in silence, studying her response like a poker player waiting to make a big commitment to a shaky hand. He looked for anything like increased perspiration, changes in breathing patterns. How could she not know what she is? It didn't make sense. No one on Earth possessed the capability to replace her memories precisely.

"You've no idea what you are? Huh, I hadn't thought about that. Kind of throws a wrench into the works if you'll pardon the metaphor. Interesting. Raises a whole host of questions I'd not anticipated. Very strange."

"Look, I don't know who the hell you are or what you're doing here, but I am going to call for security if you don't give me one good reason why I shouldn't," she responded.

"Well, I've come to rescue you from this terrible existence. Offer you a life of adventure and all that. How's that for a good reason? It is rather drab and dull in here, isn't it?" he asked, staring up at the ceiling with obvious distaste. "I suspect you'd do well with a little change of scenery."

"Are you crazy?" she exclaimed. "I can't leave here, not until I'm cured."

"Could take you a while, seeing as how you're not sick."

"If I'm not sick, then why do I feel so horrible all the time?"

"I suspect it's the amount of drugs they're pumping into your system," he shrugged.

"No, I'm drugged because I'm sick. That's what they do with sick people. They drug them. Look, I don't know what you're after but you're not safe in here with me. This is a secure ward. Sooner or later someone's gonna wake up behind the surveillance screen and realize you're in here with me. You'll likely be quarantined."

"Oh, I suspect that if they could actually catch me, they'd do a lot more than quarantine me. I'm like you, something rather exotic and rather out of place on this planet," he replied.

"How did you even get in here? The doors are locked and sealed to keep people from accidentally walking in. How did you make it past security?"

"I've never paid much attention to security barriers," he said. "I'm not fond of them."

She hesitated. She wanted to say something, but she wasn't sure what to say before he interrupted her thoughts.

"I've been here five minutes and I'm already deeply depressed. How much longer do you think you'll want to live this life?"

"I don't know. I've never thought of it as a matter of choice. I guess I've always hoped that someday I could go home."

"Wherever your home is, Sarah, it isn't on this planet," he replied, the smile now gone. "Whatever your fate is, it isn't here either."

Again she paused. The whole event was unnerving. She wasn't used to talking to people who weren't being pumped through a computer monitor. The lack of a medium of some sort was disturbing. The doctors never spoke more than a word, and there were no other persons she interacted with like this.

"I suspect this is all part of a hallucination on my part. It has all the hallmarks of a psychotic delusion. Mystery man comes to tell me that my reality is all fabricated. It's a combination of pure fantasy, and a mild megalomania which I didn't think I possessed until you showed up," Sarah said.

"Well, I can prove my point easily enough. What's two-hundred and seventy three times four-thousand and twelve?" he asked.

"One million, ninety-five thousand and two-hundred and seventy six," she replied mechanically.

"That was too easy. Salve, domina. Quid agis?" he asked.

"Bene ago, maestro," she answered automatically.

He decided to see how ridiculous it could get. "What two forms of morality did Nietzche discuss in his discourse on the Genealogy of Morals?"

"Master Morality and Slave Morality, the replacement of Roman-Era master morality with the reactionary slave-morality of Christianity, more or less," she answered.

"You ever pick up a book written by Nietzche? Ever study Latin?" he asked.

"I don't know. I don't remember, but that doesn't mean much."

"As I said, you're an exotic creature, Sarah. You're certainly more than human. That is why they keep you locked up here. It's not that you're sick. You're a curiosity, and a very powerful one at that. On a subconscious level, your brain is tuning in to the entire planet around you and absorbing tremendous amounts of raw data. It's a survival instinct of your species, I think."

"You're suggesting that there is some conspiracy to keep me inside this hospital ward because I'm an exotic non-human creature who knows a little Latin, and a little bit of Nietzche?"

"Well, there's certainly some sort of conspiracy at work here. I've not quite figured out its dimensions or purposes, but I suspect that I'm here to play some role. People love including me in their conspiracies because, given my reputation, it throws any opposition into turmoil. Nobody, even the whackos, can figure out what my role would be in any sort of conspiracy. I am the ultimate red herring, though I wish this was not true."

"Who are you?" she asked suspiciously.

"I'm a good natured intermeddler. I'm well-financed and fond of shoving my personality into conflicts that have some aspect of intrigue. My contacts within the ICPT, the Bureaucracy, leaked information to me concerning your predicament. You intrigued me, and I made a decision to free you from this facility."

"It's not as simple as that?"

"Sarah, when I say you are exotic, I mean *very* exotic. No one has seen your species in several billion years. A hospital ward on a backwater planet is certainly no place for you."

"You're still not giving me much."

"No, but for times' sake it will have to do. Look, Sarah, you can either follow me and try to escape, or you can lie there on your bed and take no chances at all. Go dilly around with whatever interactive garbage they give you. Lead a boring, dull, mind numbingly dreary existence until they figure out how to kill you."

"Or I could go with you? Huh?"

"I have a spaceship," he said proudly. "I go where I want to, when I want to, and I wreak havoc for a profession. I travel fast, and I travel in style."

"You're serious?" Sarah asked. She was sure she was stuck in one of her hyper dream states. "What do you want me to say?"

"I want you to say that you'll come with me."

"I don't even know your name, mystery man."

"I am known by many names, Sarah. On Earth, I am known as Saint Germaine or Phaestus, but you should call me Captain. Everyone calls me Captain. I respond to it more quickly."

"You're not human."

"Umm, no. I'm not human, and I'm no saint either. I'm something far more interesting," Germaine answered. "You're not human either. You're at the right end of the universe's Bell Curve."

"If I'm not human, what am I then?" Sarah asked, her heart beating a little faster now. She was starting to get really freaked out.

"Well, I'd rather hoped you would be providing me with the answers, not vice-versa. If I had to guess, I'd say that you're either a harbinger of death, a messiah, or a simple lost soul. It's hard to say for sure. I've not much experience in such matters. That's what makes the whole damn thing so interesting," he answered truthfully.

"Hold on. You've gotta explain that statement a little further."

"I don't know that I can, Sarah. Seriously."

"Give it a shot."

"This is very strange, you know. You're asking me to essentially explain the universe to a person who is quite likely a member of the species that created the whole thing. It's very weird. I'd not thought I would be in this position when I came to this base."

"Try, Captain."

"Well, Sarah. You're Nephyr."

"What are you saying?"

"Sarah, it is believed that the Nephyr were the creators of the universe. They created it and then disappeared. No one knows why they went away, but now that you're here, well, it's sort of a big deal. Has some minor apocalyptic undertones if you don't mind me saying."

"I'm a Nephyr, one of the creators of the universe? That's what you're telling me?"

"The truth of the Nephyr is almost a secondary issue. It doesn't matter who created the universe. It doesn't even matter why. What matters are the politics of the situation, and the politics are indeed very complex."

"That's the most insane thing I've ever heard. You're out of your mind."

"I've been accused of worse."

"What do you want with me?"

"Well, I figure maybe we can avert chaos. Perhaps get you to where you're really supposed to be. I only know that Earth isn't it."

Sarah didn't believe what she was hearing. She was merely curious as to the depths of the man's delusion. It was as an interesting event in an otherwise predictable life.

"It's madness," Sarah replied, half-heartedly now. She was finding herself wanting to believe the man, no matter how preposterous he might seem.

"It always is. I do know one thing, sooner or later the wrong people are going to learn that you exist. There's a whole universe out there that would see you dissected if they had a chance. Even if you wanted to stay here, you're only safe for so long. Sooner or later, someone will take you out. The safest place in the universe is the Cortez, my ship."

"How are you going to get me out of here?" she asked. "I'm too sick to walk after the workout session in the arboretum."

"Yes, well, you're drugged this time of day. They're time-delayed. They put the narcotics in your lunch actually. That's why the drugs kick in shortly after you're done with your afternoon exercise in the arboretum. No doubt you've noticed the pattern. Lie still."

Before she could react, his blue balls flew towards her, emitting a soft glow that encapsulated her body. The sensation hit her suddenly. It was as though she was riding in a billowy soft cloudy dream. She felt her body rise slightly from the sheets. Her arms dangled lazily to her sides.

He watched her with calm detachment. He had seen the magic act before. Within a few moments, the sensation ebbed away. She landed back on the bed softly, her body still shivering slightly as he reached out, his balls traveling back into his hands.

"Feel better?" he asked.

She was still far away. The experience was beyond opium. It had taken her to a realm of pure bodily peace. For what felt like several elongated, stretchy, mushy minutes, her body seemed to dissolve into the air around her, becoming formless and free. She felt her feet stretch so far away from her, they seemed to move miles away from her face. It was euphoric and intense. There was no measure by which she could interpret her sensations.

"You've just been purified. I detoxified your entire body as much as I can. You'll be able to walk now," he told her.

"Who are you truly?" she whispered, her body still quivering beneath the sheets.

"I'm many things, my child. Today, I'm your private saint," he smiled impishly.

She leaned up from the bed, scared to death. Sarah had no idea what to say. She wanted to get out, but she had no idea what 'out' even meant. It was a concept so foreign that she couldn't even mentally grasp it, or envision it. It was just a thought, a collision of words without conclusion. The overwhelming balance of what she thought was her life had been spent in the ward, locked away in a secure wing of what she assumed to be a hospital.

She was told she had a terrible disease, one that could be transmitted through the air. She had always thought that the carefully controlled confines of her existence had been necessary precautions, and that she should be thankful for her parents' influence that she should be taken care of such as she was. She had video games, access to cable television with over five thousand channels of vapid pop culture. She had hundreds of friends in her virtual world of HerSpace, and SmileBook. Still, all that seemed pitiful now. It was hardly a world worth clinging to. It was no longer her world.

She was shivering. The air was too cool now without the bed sheets overtop of her. She hesitated before placing her feet on the floor. But then she did it. The cold tiles on her bare feet hit her instantly. It was a wake-up call that brought her fully into this new, strange reality.

"I want to get out of here, and never come back," she said suddenly.

She hadn't consciously planned on saying it. She blurted it out, but once she said the words, she knew them to be true.

"I need to leave this place. I need to leave now and never return," Sarah stated, her voice low and cracking.

Her feet were freezing against the metal plates beneath the bed, but she no longer cared. She stretched, raising her arms above her head and arching her back towards her heels. For the first time she could remember, she felt healthy. She was almost high on the feeling. There were no pains in her joints. Her back felt pliant. Her vision was clear.

"You've not felt like this in a while, have you?" he asked. "Your body is nearly cleansed of all the drugs. Your liver is functioning perfectly. Almost all of the toxins have been removed from your tissues."

"I feel a lot better than before," she said, almost tempted to smile.

"Good enough to escape?" he asked.

"Good enough to try, at least."

They grabbed hands, and she felt the contours of his skin. His hands were soft.

As he led her across the wide floor of the ward, her head was filled with thoughts. She couldn't articulate them all. It was a flush of confusion. She had no idea whether to trust the man "Germaine", but the possibility of escape had become unbearably tempting once she thought seriously about the prospect. The way he had phrased things drove home the unbearable qualities of her existence and gave her some glimmer of hope of a life outside. If she were to die in the effort, then she would die on her feet. She would not die wasted away, tethered to a cot and drugged into oblivion. And if this whole affair were truly a dream, she absolutely needed to see where it led. It had already proved far more interesting than her internet escapades.

They approached the steel doors at the end of the ward reached into his pocket and produced a magnetic key card. He waived it over the keypad, and the heavy security doors slid open.

She had no memory of ever being on the other side of the doorway until now. She hesitated. The hallway was empty, cold and sterile, steel bulkheads lit up by LEDs lining the ceiling, flooring covered by short-brush beige industrial carpeting. It felt hostile to her. Like the ward, it was a space designed for utility, not comfort.

He turned to her.

"Everything's going to be fine, Sarah," he said. "Just take one step forward with me and then you will be on your way to a new life."

She took a deep breath and exhaled before she stepped over the threshold and into the hallway. The door slid shut behind her. And like that, the ward was suddenly gone. It struck her then that there were a million strange possibilities ahead of her. She had stepped out of the cage, and a world of unknowns now lay before her.

They walked further down the hallway past several closed doors. The area was entirely silent. They ran into no one. When they arrived at a juncture, he pulled her to the left. They moved quickly. Soon they reached the doors to an elevator. He waved his card and the doors opened. They entered and took the elevator several floors upwards. When the doors opened, they were facing a large hangar bay several hundred meters wide and at least half that in depth. Two submarines were dry-docked, suspended in the air by thick cables. The subs were Triton class, armed with nukes and all sorts of other nastiness.

He pointed up at the things. "Not your typical sort of hospital equipment."

"Weird," she whispered. "I had no idea."

The objects were massive. They were vehicles designed for disintegrating large numbers of human beings, he explained.

"Look at them. They're so crude but stylish. I'd really like one for my collection, but now is not the time."

"You collect things of this nature?" Sarah asked.

"I'm obscenely wealthy and generally bored, so, yes, I tend to collect all sorts of things," Germaine shrugged. "I'm especially fond of things that go *boom*. I love a good explosion."

"So, do you intend to add me to your collection...in the hope that I might someday go *boom*?"

"You know, I've honestly no idea what to do with you. I haven't thought that far ahead. It's the Zen Buddhist inside me, or maybe it's just sheer laziness. Hard to say. I had really hoped you might be able to direct my next move, but your amnesia leaves me somewhat in the dark."

"Sorry to throw a wrench into the works."

"No worries," he smiled. "What's life without a little mystery?"

They walked for several moments until they reached the far end of the hangar. Once there, however, Germaine froze suddenly. Sarah could detect just a slight crack in his otherwise cavalier veneer.

"Don't move," he told her, his voice just above a whisper.

He tilted his head up and stared into the upper corner of ceiling above the lift. High above them in the rafters something caught his eye. A drop of light suddenly took shape. Wedged in the corner like a silver spider was a creature cloaked in steel body armor that fit his form like a silvery shining skin, every terrible muscle outlined with perfect detail. His face was covered with an oblong helmet made of the same metal as his armor. The helmet was narrowed into a sharp point at the chin, and sloped back from his forehead. Only two black eye-slits adorned the face. The creature's arms were long and elaborately muscled. His hands ended in long steel claws which he had dug into the steel of the bulkheads. He hung there in the corner motionless, utterly menacing, a metal-skinned predator, sleek, and conspicuously dangerous.

"Angel Eyes," Germaine whispered. "Get behind me, Sarah. Post haste, if you don't mind."

Germaine made his way to the door of the lift, and without moving his eyes from the creature, he waved the fabricated security pass. The doors opened and he pushed her through the opening into the elevator.

"Wouldn't have figured you for Earth, my friend," Germaine said. "Not quite the right climate for a cold-blooded character such as yourself."

Angel Eyes let go of his hold and dropped forty feet onto the steel floor, landing with a tremendous thud that reverberated throughout the hangar bay. Then he stood upright. He was close to seven-feet tall. He stood a few paces away from Germaine, motionless, dominating the space around them.

For a few seconds, they regarded each other in silence. Germaine stood his ground. Sarah sensed there was something hidden behind this bravado. Angel Eyes turned to glare straight at Sarah. It was terrifying. She felt a slight pull on her body as though his gaze was drawing her towards it, as prey hypnotized. The creature regarded her carefully for a second and then turned back to stare down at Germaine. A razor could not cut through the tension in the air.

Then suddenly the creature's skin shimmered for a long two seconds before he disappeared entirely.

Germaine let out his breath with a whistle, then he entered the lift and they headed upwards into the facility.

"What was that?" Sarah asked after the elevator was moving.

"That, Sarah, was a joker in the deck," Germaine answered. "No worries. It just means we have to speed things up a bit."

"What do you mean?"

After a few seconds of ascent, the elevator came to a halt and the doors opened. They were immediately greeted by eight heavily armed guards in shiny black plastic body armor, their rifles all bearing down on the pair.

"Well, I was hoping for something like this or some reasonable facsimile," he grinned. He turned to the soldiers. "Take me to your leader!" he said sternly, trying unsuccessfully to hide his smile as he pointed his finger like a gun at the squad of soldiers.

"That's convenient. Our commander wants to meet you right away," the squad leader replied coolly.

The soldiers reached into the elevator and hauled the pair out. Then they dragged them away down a corridor. Within minutes the group had passed through several security gates until they arrived at the command center. It was an impressive display of modern monkey-person technology, he told her. There were rows of computer workstations manned by uniformed technicians all quietly intent on their tasks. The facility hummed with precise activity. It was as though they had stepped into the nerve center of some giant techno-beehive.

"I assume you have some plan for this?" Sarah asked.

"Relax, we're exactly where we need to be," he answered.

"Why do you look like you're having fun when there are big men with big guns all around us?" Sarah asked.

"Well, I am having fun," Germaine answered. "Aren't you?"

She thought about it for a moment, and then forced to tell the truth, she said simply: "I guess it does beat a hospital bed."

"There's a good lass," he smiled. "You're built for this sort of thing, I suspect."

"What sort of thing?" she asked.

"A life of mad adventure, of course," Germaine grinned.

The base's commander, a man in his late fifties with short silver hair, wearing a pressed black uniform, approached the pair. He was standing over them from an elevated platform of the command deck. He waved his hand and the squad stepped back.

"Captain, huh?" the commander asked. "You're something of a mystery."

"Well, that's very kind of you to say," Germaine replied.

"I don't like mysteries," the commander answered in a flat, cold tone. "Somehow you managed to sneak aboard one of the most heavily fortified and secure military bases on the planet. It is a rather extraordinary feat."

"You flatter me, sir," Germaine said. "Please go on."

"Oh, the mystery deepens. I am curious, Captain. You managed to enter the facility without tripping even the most subtle sensor, yet on your way out, you tripped every alarm you could. It is as though you really wanted to get caught. What I can't figure out is why?"

"Would you believe that this is all part of some elaborate hoax, a candid camera moment?" Germaine asked.

"Hmmph. Why are you here, and why do you have one of my favorite pets with you?"

"I'm a sucker for blondes in distress. Aren't we all?" Germaine replied.

"I appreciate your humor, Captain. It is a shame that you'll likely lose it soon. You see, in a few moments I am going to give an order that will have you brought to the interrogation chamber. You will be questioned under circumstances we euphemistically call 'extreme duress'. I have very little taste for such actions, but you represent a threat, and threats must be dealt with. I'm afraid you and I are going to have a very long time to get to know one another," the commander said menacingly. "You'll not enjoy it, I assure you."

"Although I genuinely share your enthusiasm at the prospect, in a few moments, I will be leaving your company, and I'll be taking your *pet* with me," Germaine replied.

"Not likely," the commander responded with a growl.

"Don't be too confidant, commander. There are eleven things going on right now that you are not aware of, and in no position to control. I have the initiative. You didn't think I got into this base without help, did you?" Germaine asked.

"No, I'm sure you had someone on the inside giving you logistical data, security codes. You couldn't have compromised our security grid without assistance from the inside. We have to know your contacts. It is a matter of some importance to me *personally*."

"You could scour the entire Earth, but you'll never meet my contacts, commander. You're outmatched, and you don't even know it yet."

At that moment the lights flickered and shut off. For a second, the command center was perfectly dark until the back-up generators switched on. Suddenly the area was lit in flashing red staccato of emergency lighting.

A tech approached the commander with a frantic look in his eyes.

"We've been penetrated, infra-sound scan breached the firewall and infiltrated the security systems. Someone is shutting down the systems piece by piece."

"Cut the hard-lines leading from the external communication array. Lock down the base and deploy counter-measures. Black-ICE the bastards," the commander replied angrily.

"It won't work, commander. Your data is being uploaded into an encrypted squirt transmission, every piece of information on every experiment you've ever run here, including your pet. Before the sun sets on these waters, the whole world will know of your sins. As an extra special party favor, your life-support system was just shut down," Germaine said. "Just thought you should know."

"You'll kill us all, including yourself!" the commander yelled.

"No, I will survive, and, as you are no doubt aware, so will your pet. We both possess certain biological advantages you do not. You, however, will be dead long before we exit this base. That is, if you decide to remain."

The air was becoming chokingly thin. The commander was desperate, but he hid his panic well.

"Stay close, Sarah. This is where things start to go boom," Germaine whispered.

"Get life-support back online," the commander ordered.

"We're locked out, the intruder program has set-up a firewall between the CIC workstations and the back-up systems," one of techs yelled. "Jesus! I've never seen code so advanced. Auto-Immune can't isolate the infected systems fast enough to re-route power to compensate."

The room was becoming unbearably hot with the environmental control systems off-line, and the massive network of computers cooking in their cases. Large fans behind grates near the top of the walls had been shut down and the air was no longer moving, it was simply cooking hotter and hotter.

The commander turned to Germaine. He pulled out his sidearm and aimed it directly at Germaine's head. "You better end this, Captain. End your assault or I'll end you."

"What if I were to tell you that my physician has strongly recommended that I avoid getting shot? Even once or twice, he says. Bad for my health, he tells me," Germaine responded.

"So you've chosen your fate, Captain," the commander stood back and holstered his firearm. "Sergeant, I am exercising my authority as granted under the UCMJ. These are exigent circumstances. This facility just became a battlefield, and these two are unlawful combatants. Pursuant to my authority to regulate this battlefield,

I am authorizing you to execute these two terrorists under the authority granted under the Emergency powers Act. They're guilty of high-treason, terrorism, and assault on a military installation," the commander ordered.

"I'd really advise you to stop this action before some-one gets hurt," Germaine said.

The sergeant called his squad into order with no more than a hand gesture. The soldiers knew what the order meant, and they hesitated just long enough to move into a semi-circle around Germaine and Sarah. Then they pointed their assault rifles at the pair.

"Jesus, hold up. I'm not a terrorist!" Sarah yelled. She was terrified for all the reasonable reasons.

The rifles were bearing down on them menacingly. A dozen heavily armored, heavily indoctrinated men were preparing to take an action whose sole purpose was to eliminate the pair from the realm of the real. Sarah was quite unhinged.

Germaine could only shrug. "It's a hard charge for me to defend against, I'll admit. I'm not even sure how this gentleman defines the term 'terrorist'. I'm certainly a radical in my political views. I've always fancied myself as a sort of noble agitator with libertarian predilections. It's the only truly moral position one can hold. Of course, the concept of objective morality is itself somewhat prob-lematic, even when one isolates the inquiry to a discrete instance of civilization. For myself, I think…"

"Could you quit babbling and do something?" Sarah screamed.

"Do show some dignity, Sarah. These men are noth-ing more than well armed thugs. I'll not cower before their kind. They should be ashamed of themselves for even thinking about shooting an unarmed girl, not to mention shooting me. They're thugs, I tell you. Common and insulting."

"Fire!" the commander yelled angrily.

The soldiers opened fire, and the rifles went off like a few dozen firecrackers. The distinct smell of cordite filled the air. As the bullets flew at the pair, however they were deflected in bizarre and improbable directions just before they could reach their targets. The bullets ended up immobilizing the soldiers instead of Sarah and Germaine. They also tore through several computer stations. It was a trainwreck of bad intentions.

"I'd advise you not to try that again, commander," Germaine stated coolly.

"The intruder program just evacuated the coolant tanks for the reactor," a tech yelled out panicked. "We're facing a meltdown in the reactor, sir."

"Jesus, who in god's name are you guys?" the commander asked

"Even if I were to tell you, you would not likely understand," Germaine replied. "As I said earlier, you are outmatched, sir. You must retreat."

"The systems are totally corrupted. We're completely locked out," another one of the techs called out frantically, frustrated and fractured with fear. "We've got nothing but emergency generators for the bridge. This facility is gonna blow."

"Issue the general evacuation order. Everyone move to the escape pods!" the commander ordered. He was clearly unnerved at witnessing the bullets disable his men rather than his enemies. "I don't know what your people are after, but in a few minutes, this base will be nothing but ash at the bottom of the sea. We have a carrier fleet on maneuvers in this area, and total satellite coverage. Whatever vessel you came in will get cooked before you can relay any of the data you've stolen. You might be able to dodge bullets, but we have orbital weapons platforms that will blow you out of existence. Don't count this as a victory just yet, Captain."

"Time will tell, I guess," Germaine responded with a slight shrug.

By this point, the base was coming apart. Computer workstations were shorting out under the heat and intermittent power surges, and shooting sparks in to the air like an elaborate fireworks display. The air was acrid and becoming denser with ash and smoke, and the personnel were evacuating as quickly as they could, scrambling like cockroaches in the flickering light. Oxygen was very thin now, almost non-existent.

The commander stood for one last glance at the pair, sharing a particularly hateful stare-down with Germaine, before he turned and headed towards an aperture leading to an escape pod.

When the room was finally clear, the two of them were left alone. The smoke was dense enough that it blocked their view so that they couldn't see past the area immediately around them.

"I think it's time we leave too, don't you?" Germaine asked.

The floor was shaky beneath them as an explosion occurred below deck.

"How are we going to get out of here?" she asked.

"Same way I came in," he smiled.

He reached into his pocket and produced a small lighter shaped device. Then he placed his thumb atop it and in a few seconds a small ship revealed itself in the air. It was shaped like a large semi-translucent bullet several meters in length, hovering a few feet above the floor.

Dimension-Slip technology, he explained, pretty convenient for tight spaces.

A hatch on the side opened and Germaine helped her step inside the cream colored leather interior. It was something between a luxurious limousine and a rocket.

"This is your spaceship?" Sarah asked.

Germaine smiled and shook his head. "No, this is a scout ship. My vessel is...well, you'll see."

Another larger explosion rocked the base. The beams in the ceiling were beginning to collapse in different areas, and there were small fires cropping up everywhere.

"Get us out of here," he ordered.

The ship reacted by firing a barrage of high-energy particle beams that carved out an exit in the hull of the base. Water rushed in, and the ship rushed out. Then they were underwater, moving fast.

The vessel dove through the water like a dolphin before rising up and shooting through the ocean surface, headed toward the moon. Once it was in the air, the vessel increased its velocity. Sarah was pinned to the seat as the vessel shot straight up. After several seconds, it penetrated the outer atmosphere and into the deep dark of outerspace. In front of her was an impenetrable blackness dotted with stars, and behind her, presumably, was the Earth.

Germaine reached out to a console and pressed a sequence of keys.

"Any time you guys want to pick us up would be fine. I think we're getting a lot more satellite coverage out here than we want to," he said.

"I'm in space?" Sarah asked rhetorically. "I really am in space aboard a spaceship."

"Relax, Sarah. Any reasonably middle-class denizen of the universe has a spaceship. Admittedly, mine is something of a jewel. I'm quite fond of it and my crew. It's taken me years to develop both to my tastes."

"I'm in space," she repeated, still unsure of herself.

"Most assuredly, you're in space. Not bad, huh?"

"This is too weird."

"All right, Cortez. You ladies have the ball. Give me a soft landing and the first round is on me," Germaine said.

"You're in the pipe, five by five," Capoella replied. "Cortez has the ball. We'll see you in a moment, Captain."

A minute later and the small scout ship was towed via tractor beam into the hangar area of the larger vessel. Germaine's ship was massive. The view-screen of the scout ship gave a perfect view of an otherwise cloaked object. The ship was a large donut shaped vessel with a circumference of just over seventeen miles with a clump of large skyscraper like constructions atop the surface of the donut. It didn't resemble a star-ship as she might have imagined it. There was nothing sleek about it. It was a behemoth structure larger than many medium-sized cities. As Sarah would later find out, the design was constructed to house a massive particle collider which afforded the ship the capabilities of traveling through both time and space. The donut shaped part of the vessel had a ten story interior with an outer hallway that wound through the ship in a slight pitch that declined in a corkscrew manner which effectively meant that a person could start at the highest point on the upper levels and walk around the donut for 170 miles without ever crossing their own steps.

"That's the Cortez. It's my ship," he told her.

"Pretty big," Sarah answered

"Well, I've done well for myself over the years. You know what they say: a man's spaceship is his castle. Mine's just a terribly big castle that is highly armed. It's all part of my 'too big to fail' concept. If you build a ship big enough, most planets won't try and destroy you while you're in orbit, self-preservation being a somewhat common instinct in the universe. Besides, its size fits my personality."

"It looks like you could store the population of a small city onboard."

"Wouldn't be a first," he smiled. "The Cortez is more than a ship. 'It's a lifestyle', as the ads say. The body of the ship was created by a race of super-genius mega-reptiles from the commerce planet of Migtoolia Three. Custom order, actually. The design of the ship's propulsion systems is Ven-Dhavaradi. The best part I think is the red racing stripes along the hull," he pointed. "Capoella would argue the point, but I really think the racing stripes make us move faster. Considering that imagination is ninety-percent of post light-speed travel, I can't imagine why they wouldn't. Therefore, I'm right. At least, I think I'm right. Hard to say for sure. Reality is always changing."

"Dear god, you babble."

"I was talking about my ship. You'll forgive a small amount of pride."

"Super-genius mega-reptiles and racing stripes, huh? Too weird."

"Well, they're probably not all super geniuses, actually. But they hired one of the universe's top advertising firms, Menghis Filchberg and Malloy, and that's the image they cultivated over the centuries with a brilliant commercial campaign. The commercials are really quite clever. They've completely dominated the eighteen to five-hundred year old market for several millennia now. They make great ships for banging around the galaxies, and their credit department will finance any moderately literate entity or planetary group."

"That seems a rather risky business model."

"Not necessarily. The Migtoolians have a vast and rather creative debt collections department. They actually have a small manual on how to get blood out of a stone," he explained. "What's more curious is that their methods seem to work."

"With all this technology, why did you go through all the trouble of getting us captured?"

"Because I wanted to wreck the place."

"You wanted to wreck the place?"

"Oh yes, I have a rather strong predisposition towards destroying places I deem nasty," Germaine said.

"How unitary executive of you."

"That's a very odd thing for you to say. Are you trying to be political or just insulting?"

"Sorry. I'm just feeling a bit overwhelmed here. I still don't understand what I'm doing in this picture. There's a lot of this story I seem to be missing. If I am the member of some ancient race, why don't I remember anything about it? Why are my memories human?"

"I've no idea, really. But at least you're not on a hospital bed any longer. I suppose, all things considered, we're both one step closer to the truth."

The vessel docked inside the hangar bay, and the pressure doors slid shut to seal the entrance. For a few seconds, they sat there silently inside the small interior compartment of the scout ship and talked about Life. Sarah was trying to measure the man, but she was finding it impossible to do so. She could not gain any rational perspective on this new reality, and this more than unnerved her. She was longing for some piece of earth to ground herself on.

"The universe is a cracked out place, Sarah, filled with so many terrible and spectacular wonders, a trillion lifetimes could not entertain but the smallest fraction of all there is to see. I assure you, you can trust me. I am a rogue, admittedly, but I am a gentleman above all else."

"You'll have to forgive me, but I don't know that I trust you. That's too much to ask right now. I want to trust you, but all of this is so…unreal," Sarah said. "For whatever purpose, I appear to be at your mercy."

"Would you go back to the hospital bed if you had the choice?" he asked.

Sarah thought about it, thought about what he said. "No, I suppose not."

He reached out and pressed a button on a console that caused the canopy of the small craft to slide open, and then he reached out and beckoned her to follow him down the stairs leading to the hangar floor.

"Welcome to a whole new stage of life, Sarah."

She reached out and grasped his hand. He balanced her softly as he she swung her leg over the lip of the fuse-lage and onto the stairs.

As they made their way down the stairs, a set of doors at the far end opened revealing two silhouettes that crossed the broad gray tiled floor of the hangar bay. One of them was tall, the other no larger than a young child.

As the two figures came closer, Sarah could make out their forms. The larger shadow appeared to be a woman with a feline, sleek quality to her frame. She moved with an uncommon grace and an undeniable dignity that was intimidating. As she came half into the light, she revealed a somewhat longish face, ovular with a delicate pointed chin, high cheekbones and deep green eyes, framed with a wild mane of thick blonde and red lashes. The woman's hips were wide and powerful. She carried herself with the poise of someone totally in con-trol of her reality. Sarah was immediately awed, though she tried her best to hide this.

Standing behind the woman was the silhouette of a small girl keeping in the shadows of the light from the doorway. Although she couldn't see the child clearly,

Sarah felt a sort of fierce concentration in the way that the girl looked at her. It was unnerving.

"Welcome home, Captain," the little girl said. Something in her tone conveyed a deep sense of dissatisfaction, even a slight simmering menace. "I trust you had no problems with the extraction?"

"You did a bang up job, as always, Lady Doja. I enjoyed your fireworks display, but we need to get the hell out of here, now," Germaine answered.

"I have already compiled the data from this little excursion, as well as the data concerning the mat-trans shift that caused the temporal displacement. This young girl is far more dangerous than I had previously predicted," Doja stated.

"What are you saying, Lady Doja?"

"We are in a lot of trouble," the child responded.

"You're being paranoid," Germaine replied. "Capoella?"

"Let's go," the tall woman replied. "We've been in orbit for far too long. We ought to be a hundred punches from here by now."

Capoella followed Doja out through the door.

"Don't worry," Germaine explained. "This isn't my whole crew. They'll warm up to you anyway. Things are just a little screwy right now. Everyone's a little tense considering what we went through to get you," Germaine said.

"What do you mean?" Sarah asked.

"Well, yours truly almost got burned at the stake in 15th century France. It was a real drag, let me tell you. They dragged me all the way to the town square where they planned an afternoon barbecue or some unreasonable facsimile. Monkey-people are crazy when provoked."

"I don't think I feel so well," Sarah replied.

"You think you feel bad. I have newly forming scars from where the monkey-people were jabbing me with hot pokers. It really, really hurt. Come on. Oh, and lest I forget, welcome to the Cortez , Sarah. For the first time in a long time, I suspect, you are among friends"

Chapter Two

The Cortez

Space was a cracked out place, Germaine had told her, filled with species looking to spread your chopped organs on their wafers like pate, hustlers so good they could beat the gods themselves, and incredibly pacifistic creatures who thought that bludgeoning a person to death was doing them a favor considering how brutal, mindless, and violently competitive life unfortunately was. It was a really strange place, no matter where one looked.

There was no understanding much of what happened, why it happened; at least, not in any conventional, objective sense. Truth is, he told her with a wink, nothing is true. About the best one could hope for was to create a sphere, a private space within which one could cope with reality. Take a psychic knife and cut away all the justifiable paranoia that most beings suffered. Focus on the moment, and not the thousand ways one could die instantly, at any given time, for no apparent reason whatsoever. Take all the bad little nasty things that pervaded existence, all those random images of savagery, those feelings of helplessness and inferiority, and compartmentalize them. Shove them in a partitioned area of the mind and forget about them. That, Germaine had told her during their flight up from Earth's surface, was the trick to becoming happy. Unfortunately, he never possessed that ability, so he chose a life of anarcho-hedonism with a dash of revolutionary politics and space piracy instead.

As he explained it, life was too big, the system too large to model correctly, either mentally or through vast algorithms and hyper rational computer programs performing regression analyses for millions of years.

Stuck with an inherent inability to truly understand much about how or why life worked, yet desperate for some sort of salve for their burning souls, many species turned to religion, more turned to drugs, some became nihilistic, militaristic and predatory, and, routinely, perfectly kind people went insane asking the oldest question of all: why all this suffering? Then the myths of the Nephyr began to be confirmed in significant parts. The paleontological, archaeological and genetic data came in with no clear picture of just what it meant. But over several thousand years, work was done that synchronized all the data, made a coherent picture of all the loose threads, and the universe became rational for a time. The universe, it was now believed, was the product of some ultimately powerful species capable of constructing a reality with contradictory rules and logic, but one that held together just fine. For quite some time, that species had inexplicably disappeared, but now, many billion years later, Sarah showed up, imprisoned by a powerful, enigmatic enemy that had seen fit to deposit her on Earth. It was quite the mystery, he told her.

As Germaine and Capoella led her through the winding, regally appointed corridors of the ship, she felt dragged into another one of her dreams. The vessel was like a floating, gigantic five-star hotel with weapons and fish. Routinely the hallway would open up into large gallery spaces, open museum areas, lightly populated restaurants. In all the ways relevant and desirable, the ship was similar to a small, upscale city. After they had walked for twenty minutes, they arrived at the medical bay.

When the doors opened, all Sarah could see was an array of intimidating, metallic equipment attached to the walls or hanging from the ceiling. The bulkheads were comprised of a dull, gray alloy that gave Sarah an immediate feeling of melancholy for no reason she could immediately decipher, although later, upon reflection, she would realize that it was due to the fact that she was effectively emancipated from an environment every bit as colorless as the medical bay on the Cortez. For the moment, she did not like what she saw, and she was naturally suspicious.

The shelves on the walls contained several exotic, large, frightening spider-like things suspended in clear liquid inside bell jars. The air smelled faintly of ammonia interlacing with the scent of several broad leafed, lush green plants that hung from the ceiling in several corners of the room, their vines dripping down lazily onto the cold steel floor. Lying against a far wall, lined up neatly were several medical beds.

"We need to give you a quick analysis for potential parasites and dangerous foreign bacteria," Capoella said. "Would you lie on the bed please?"

"I've been on the ship for nearly twenty minutes. If I am contaminated with something, then so are you," Sarah replied coolly. She was more paranoid than ever.

"No, you were isolated by a cascading force-field until we could get you here for a full scan," Capoella answered.

"You're not planning on dissecting me?" Sarah asked.

"Not today. We'd like to get to know you first," Germaine answered with a broad smile.

"I suppose I don't have any choice in the matter."

"You always have choices, Sarah," Germaine told her. "You may choose not to be scanned, in which case, we shall choose to keep you isolated here in the medical bay."

"Some choice. What does the scan consist of?"

"It's a fairly routine process. You'll not experience any discomfort," Capoella said.

"Fine, then. Let's get this over with. I suppose that if you guys really wanted to do me in, I'd have no chance of stopping you anyway."

"Come, Sarah," Capoella smiled gently. "Just lie here on the bed, and keep your hands to your side."

Sarah shrugged her shoulders in surrender and then lied down on the white sheets of the medical bed.

"Very good. Now close your eyes," Capoella instructed.

Sarah shut her eyelids while Capoella walked off to a console against the opposite wall. "Please count backwards from one-hundred."

Sarah began counting while Capoella programmed the scanner. Suddenly, Sarah was out cold, her face falling to one side on the pillow.

Capoella initiated the scan and several minutes later it was complete.

"What are we dealing with, Capoella?"

"She's Nephyr all right. Genetic structure is a solid match, with all non-pathological variances well within one standard deviation. There are some unremarkable mutations present, but she is definitely Nephyr. Basic neurolytic analysis indicates that she's got terra-quads of data stored inside of her brain. She's a miracle of genetic engineering."

"That's what I wanted to hear. I told you she was worth the risk. Can we access the memories and figure out what's this little mystery is all about?" Germaine asked.

"No, I just tried looping her neural output through the central computer. The interface terminated before an overload could destroy the processors. Her defenses are very advanced. It looks like whoever did the work on her did it recently given the tissue damage around the implants. Somebody must have found our little Nephyr, sequestered her on Earth and then proceeded to mess up her brain real bad, real, real, bad."

"What about telepathy?" he asked.

"I wouldn't advise it. You could get lost in there real quick. That's not an ordinary mind we're dealing with. Her neurophysiology is astounding. Besides that, who-ever wired her up set-up counter measures. I suspect she could send a feedback charge that would toast someone in a heartbeat."

"Can Doja cut through?"

"She's monitoring us now."

"And?"

"She said she doesn't want to go near the girl's mind. She sounded weird, even for Doja."

"Great. Just great!" Germaine replied. He was suddenly aware that he was in a very bad mood. "Doja doesn't want to go near the girl. The computer can't loop it. The secrets of the universe could be locked up inside that pretty little head of hers, and we can't access it."

"Well, we could always outsource," Capoella responded.

"You're thinking what I'm thinking," Germaine replied, brightening back up.

"I think I'm one step ahead of you."

"Indeed. Let's move quick then. I want to stay in front of this. We can keep ahead of this matter for a little bit, but we have to operate under the assumption that sooner or later news of her existence is going to spread."

"This whole affair is growing more and more complicated. I think that given how wrong the information we've received so far, we should be very careful about what else may be nonsense."

"Such as?"

"The theory that she was kidnapped by an energy beam that penetrated the walls of the universe, one that reached the Membrane – I don't buy it. It's crap, even for a cover story. It's a total work of fiction. That definitely bothers me."

"I don't know if I believe it either. It may be bad information, but it's the only information we have."

"It's more than just bad information. Why can't she remember what she is? She's either lying to us, or someone intentionally wiped her memory. If it's the latter, it is no small feat."

"You're worried about why she doesn't have her memories? That's what concerns you?" Germaine asked.

"You're damn right its concerns me! First, someone unknown shifts your energy beam and you end up six-hundred years off-target, now this. Every step of the way, this whole thing becomes more difficult. We both know that nobody on Earth has the technology to pull this off, and it's doubtful that anyone in the Bureaucracy would know how to pull it off. Between the rogue energy beam and her lost memories, I'd say we're dealing with a mystery that is way out of our league. You and I are generally ahead of the curve. Not this time. We're being toyed with. Someone's manipulating us."

"Fine then, enough of the mysteries. Let's start with what we do know." he said.

"Well, we don't know where she came from. We don't know how she got to Earth. And we can only make an educated guess as to who brought her to Earth. We do know that it wasn't the Bureaucracy. They might have known about the girl, but they didn't knock your matter-transference beam off course. The only races with that type of technology are ones we'd rather not deal with, seeing as how we're both generally fond of keeping our heads intact."

"So, we're doing okay then. All things considered," he smiled.

"Dear god, you never cease to amaze me," Capoella said.

"Would you rather I get hysterical over the subject? Look, she's here. We rescued her. Now we need to crack into that mind somehow. And we both know the right guy for the job. So let's just get to Berion and track him down."

"You're mad," Capoella said. "You always have been."

"Have I ever steered us wrong?"

"Dear god, you rarely steer us clear of trouble. You can't help yourself."

She was right. Germaine couldn't. Where a normal person might use an extra dollar to purchase a lottery ticket, Germaine would use lavish credit lines to purchase entire planets. He was the master of the leveraged buy-out. In his various career choices, he had been a venture capitalist, a space pirate, and a documentary filmmaker. He was also a counterculture celebrity who walked the line between self-indulgent, adolescent anarchism and outright immorality.

He was controversial, if only to keep his publicists busy. Although two books he had written on the subject of "the negative macro-economic repercussions of messianic second comings" had been bestsellers across several galaxies, his documentaries about Che Guevarra were always blasted for being "narrowly focused" and "pedantic". These criticisms, he felt, were odd because Germaine had often taken the artistic care to kidnap Che from South America and use him in the productions, utilizing the laws of relativity and other techno-magic to deposit the fellow back on Earth not one instant after he was kidnapped, with no knowledge of his participation in the documentaries that ridiculed every aspect of his life. There were only a handful of people Germaine truly hated in the universe, and for whatever strange reason Che Guevarra was near the top of the list, just below Richard Nixon.

Many critics decried Germaine's 'guerrilla filmmaking' techniques as obscene, infantile, even criminal. However, Germaine paid little attention to the critics. He was afraid he might be subconsciously influenced, and he wanted his art to remain untainted. Besides, he wasn't seeking commercial success. He had plenty of that. He was an artist nowadays, along with being a space-pirate and political dissident. He couldn't give a rat's tail what the critics said. This brazen attention to non-conformity made him an open target of ridicule from every angle. He was one of the celebrities the universe was craving to see fall down somehow, fall down hard, if only to see what madness would come after his fall – how wildly would his empire burn when the match was finally lit. He was decadent, self-absorbed, and as capricious as a Belgian hot dog connoisseur. At bottom, however, he was a profoundly moral, charming sort of fellow.

"It's a strange feeling, isn't it?' he asked, looking down at the girl unconscious on the bed. "Think about the potential this girl has. Anyone with eyes can look at her and tell that, even when she's asleep. There's definitely some purpose at work here."

"Oh, I'm quite sure she has a purpose, Captain."

"We've got a cat's eye view to a potential apocalypse. Where else would you rather be? Where else could you imagine the two of us? We were born for such a matter as this. Whatever this is, it's gonna be big," Germaine smiled. "Who knows? Maybe we'll make it into a respectable history book instead of the tabloids for once. I would like to know what really happened to me on Earth."

Capoella looked at him, the corner of her lip turning up in concern.

"We've been dancing around this ever since we rescued you from the witch-burning. It had to be the VD that shifted your beam. They have to be behind this, and now we're involved up to our necks."

"That's only half of the picture at best. If it really was them, why would the VD collude with Earth's military forces to keep the girl hidden, but then let us come and rescue her?" he asked.

"That's the part that actually makes sense. If I wanted to leak something as big as this and not have my fingerprints on it, how might I do it?" Capoella asked.

"There are a number of ways. Take out ads in newspapers paid for by shills, shadow-corporate types. Hit-jobs from blogs, PR firms, any number of vectors."

"Well if you really want to get down and dirty, and not leave a trail, you find some suckers to pull it off, give them just enough information to do the job, but you keep them in the dark as to the rest of the details."

"Careful now, I wouldn't exactly call us 'suckers', Capoella."

"There's something deeply malicious behind this whole affair. Why would the VD drag this girl into the universe from the Membrane? Why would they allow ICPT deep space surveillance to capture the event. What do they gain?" Capoella asked.

"They could stand to gain a lot. They've been positioning themselves against the common markets for the last decade. I always thought it was because they were seeing something in the balance sheets I wasn't. When news of this girl's existence becomes widely known and the chaos sets in, they'll clean up in the financial markets. They've got enough capital to move into the vacuum. Whatever fault there is will be pinned on the ICPT. It's a false-flag operation."

"That's what I think. We got brought in to shift any attention away from their involvement in the girl's appearance. We're pawns."

"It's an interesting theory. Of course, we could have this all backwards. The Nephyr may be involved in this matter in a fashion beyond our comprehension."

"Whatever the truth is, we're being manipulated. That's obvious. The question is whether or not we can outmaneuver whoever set this in motion," she replied. "And that, Captain, is why I'm feeling rather unsettled right now. I thought Sarah might give us something to go on, but this is feeling more and more like a trap-play."

"So, the Ven-Dhavaradi leak information to us because they want us to out the girl, and they don't want their fingerprints on the operation. What about the spring-gun trap, then? Why did they shift my energy beam?"

"Well, a booby-trap like that would keep the amateurs off the playing field, wouldn't it?" Capoella replied.

"They wanted her to fall into somebody's hands, just not the wrong ones. Huh, it really is an interesting theory, but it can't be that simple, though, can it?"

"No. We're talking about the VD. Considering what the myths say about the war between the Nephyr and Ven-Dhavaradi, this whole affair is part of a far larger puzzle. A lot of what's going on here is out in the open. That means the VD probably have a whole lot of things going on that are not in the open. Again, I think we're outplayed here."

"We'll figure this out. I'm not worried," Germaine said.

"I think a good life can be had without ever needing to deal with the VD again. I'm grateful that they gave us the Cortez, but I'm also beginning to rethink their motivations. What if they saw the future and realized we would play a role, and that our involvement in this matter would be facilitated by giving us a vessel as powerful as the Cortez. It's just a thought," Capoella said.

"Well, we're safe for now. They obviously want the girl outed, not dead. That makes things a little easier. If I had to gamble, though, I'd bet that a number of intelligence agencies want our heads by now. Killing Sarah would be the politically expedient thing to do. Killing us, well, there's a book deal or two waiting as a reward for that feat. Probably a movie deal as well."

"You got your wish, Captain. You wanted to do something for your legacy. If we can keep the girl safe from being crucified by the masses, or killed by the authorities, we'll certainly earn our reputation as living legends."

Germaine stared away for a few seconds, gathering his thoughts. Then he shrugged as much of the weirdness off as he could. "Well, whatever game is going on, we've just injected ourselves inextricably into the mix. Strange stuff. "

"Strange stuff indeed," Capoella agreed.

He looked down at Sarah as she lay asleep on the bed. She was in a posture exactly like the first time he had seen her on Earth. Her eyes were closed, and for the moment, her facial features were relaxed, and unworn by any immediate dilemma. She was a lovely creature, he thought. She was also a creature whose very existence, once widely known, could tear apart huge tracts of space, obliterate star systems, and bring about wars that could last for generations; not to mention the impact it would have on various stock-markets and public employee retirement plans.

Germaine appreciated Capoella's frankness and her wisdom. The situation was complex enough that he needed someone with him to piece the puzzle together. He was afraid he didn't have the right pieces to the puzzle, the ones he would need to make a proper picture of what was really going on. He still wasn't entirely sure he had done the right thing. When he had first embarked on the mission to free Sarah, he was well aware of her potential, at least he thought he was. He simply was operating under the misperception that it was the ICPT who were responsible for keeping the girl subdued and out of the picture. It made perfect political sense. It was an immoral action which was perfectly standard by any convention of the ICPT, more commonly known as the Bureaucracy, or as Germaine called them: "a perverted bunch of pointy-heads with delusions of relevance."

When he finally realized for sure that it could not be the Bureaucracy, he was very quick to deduce that it had to be the Ven-Dhavaradi. Of the few Fourth-level civilizations present in the universe, the VD were the only ones with any commercial ties to the network of trading empires that dominated most of the universal commerce. The other Fourth-level civilizations had no interest in commerce or political intrigue. The only reason he didn't mention the VD earlier was that he wanted an untainted version of what Capoella thought the truth to be.

"All right then, let's get to Berion. I suspect that a lot of this puzzle will be a whole lot clearer once we can access her memories."

"She's safe enough, I guess," Capoella replied, pressing a button on the console that evacuated the narcotic from Sarah's mind. "One thing I think you ought to know."

"What's that?"

"She's aging seven times faster than normal, if our medical data on the Nephyr is correct."

"She's growing?"

"My guess is that once the drugs they were giving her on Earth were removed, her metabolism went into overdrive as if to make up for the delay. She's growing fast, Captain. She'll mature into an adult within a few months if the projections are correct. I think we ought to be prepared for mood swings, odd behaviors."

"Great, a typical teenager. Can we retard the development until we figure out what's going on?"

"Wouldn't recommend it, Captain."

"It keeps getting stranger, doesn't it? Let's wake her. We need to get to Berion and track down Folo. Once we can access our memories, we can figure out our next step."

"Agreed," Capoella replied. "How much do we tell Sarah?"

"As little as possible. I'm still not sure if we can trust her. I hate to leave her in the dark, but for now I think it's our safest play."

"It's your call, but sooner or later she's gonna start asking the obvious questions."

"She's already asking those questions."

"Well, sooner or later she isn't going to be content with our response."

"Wake her. We'll deal with things as they come up."

Capoella pressed an icon on the screen of her computer interface. A moment later, Sarah was conscious and sitting upright on the bed.

"What happened?" she asked. "Why was I asleep?"

"The scan interrupted some of your higher-brain functions, minor synaptic interference, you were unconscious for two minutes. That's well within one standard deviation for this sort of procedure," Capoella lied smoothly.

"You're fine. There's a change of clothes inside a locker around the corner in the lavatory. Get dressed. We're taking you to the bridge."

Sarah got off the bed, a little grogginess affecting her movements. She made her way to the room Capoella had pointed towards. It was small space. There was a chemical-shower stall, and the floors were cold sterile gray-blue tiles. She found something waiting for her on a hook behind the door. After changing clothes, she was glad to be out of the hospital gown and into something with a little more dignity. She donned a full lycra body suit that zipped in the front. It was form-fitting and flattered her figure nicely. The suit was colored a dark almost iridescent blue, and the collar rose up at the back in a short cowl-like structure. She saw herself in the reflection of a full length mirror. Kind of cool, she thought. Sarah in space, she smiled. A minute later, she headed back out to rejoin Germaine and Capoella.

She still wasn't entirely sure that she was now aboard a ship in space. It seemed probable to her that she was stuck in a psychotic delusion; a damned realistic delusion, she thought. It didn't have the staggered, disjointed rhythm of a dream, and that was why she was under the impression that it was a potential psychosis. She had heard that people who were crazy never knew it consciously. Sarah didn't believe that. She thought it quite possible to be out of one's mind, and incapable of doing anything about it, save for witnessing the aftermath.

"If you are feeling okay to walk, follow us to the bridge," Germaine said. "I think you'll enjoy the view."

Sarah shrugged, and the trio left the medical bay and headed back out into the maze of identical halls. She found herself the odd man out in the trio. Germaine walked ahead of her, accompanied by Capoella. They spoke of things she could not fathom given that she had no context within which to understand the terms and abbreviations.

Sarah kept her eyes on Capoella. She was fascinated by Capoella's form. Her limbs were long, sensuous, wired with incredibly defined muscles that flexed powerfully as she walked. She was graceful and precise, something between Racquel Welch and a Sub-Saharan lioness. She was at once seductively captivating and terribly intimidating. For some reason she could not explain, Sarah was contemplating the range of movement, the speed of Capoella, where her weak spots may lie.

"Any problems planet side?" Capoella asked.

"Other than the brief cameo with Angel Eyes, no, everything went as planned."

Capeolla looked as though her thoughts were broken for a second, then she regained them quickly. "That must have been interesting."

Sarah noticed the break. Something went unspoken there.

"Kind of scary actually. He had a shot, but he didn't take it," Germaine replied. "I wish he had, though."

"What do you mean?" Sarah asked, utterly confused. "You would have preferred that that monster take a swing at us?"

She felt suddenly shy when Capoella turned back to look at her with a painfully dismissive glare.

"Well, at least then we wouldn't have to worry why he showed up and didn't take his shot. That's why," Capoella replied. "The only thing we need less than a nasty little mystery is a nasty little mystery with Angel Eyes in the mix. Angel Eyes means Kromm is involved, and Kromm means trouble. His resources match our own, but his sadism is unparalleled."

"Let's just get the hell out of this star system before some nut-case with a telescope starts phoning NASA.

I hate this friggin planet. Whole star-system is jinxed hard. Bunch of ignorant, simian bastards," Germaine stated. "Hard to imagine how these monkeys lived to eventually create an empire over ten-thousand light years radiating out from that perverted, blue planet. Easy to see how they lost it all, though. God I hate this system."

They were walking through wide halls lined with what appeared to be aquarium glass. Three-quarters of the ship was actually a flowing aquarium miles in length, shaped around the frame of the habitation areas, Germaine explained. It was hard to get fresh sushi in space, he told her, and he was addicted to sushi along with many of his crew. Healthy living and all that, he explained. Plus, it gave the whole atmosphere a rather tranquil, organic feel, he explained. The actinic emissions of light were soothing.

As they passed by one juncture, in the hallways to her right, Sarah saw a large green alien with long tentacles pounding the daylights of another green alien with tentacles, inside the hallway to their right.

Germaine and Capoella didn't skip a beat.

After they were a few feet away, Germaine whispered: "Domestic dispute. Best not to get involved. Besides, no matter how many times I've asked, he won't press charges against her. She beats him constantly. I suppose it's like the philosophers always say. There's no explaining love."

As they walked through the corridors, they passed several schools of shimmering, colorful fish, as well as many creatures Sarah could not easily describe. There were large, razor toothed predator fish prowling with dull black eyes, and organic translucent shapes, clouds of tendrils colorfully luminescent as they were gracefully swept through the artificial currents.

The flooring was short-brush carpet, maroon colored. The atmosphere was quiet. The vessel was regally appointed, classy with a sort of baroque quality to the fine wood trim hand-rails that blended with the shiny alloys that framed out the corridors. It was designed to resemble a five-star Parisian hotel as Germaine believed strongly in "traveling in style".

After several minutes of walking, they were confronted by a heavily shielded doorway. The doors slid open after a scan registered their biometrics.

"Welcome home, Captain," the computer voice stated in the deep, sensuously silky tones of Lauren Bacall. Germaine had a fetish for many things from 20th Century Earth, and anything related to Lauren Bacall was bound to grab his attention.

For several centuries, he had been surreptitiously dating her, although she was almost completely unaware of the affair, and it had never been consummated in any physical fashion.

He would steal away to Earth, sneak away with her, and return not more than a second after he left. He used complex nano-viruses to partition her mind so that she was unaware of her time with him, save dream images of those stolen moments they actually spent in each other's company. They had traveled together in a time-skiff to the farthest regions of space, out into the distant stars to watch suns born in the great stellar nurseries of Magellus, bathing in the vast sweeping particle winds of exotic radiation from the safety of a little breakfast nook in the aft section. He had taken her fishing in the tremendous, tranquil and serene oceans of Elantria where the sea was a brilliant shade of chartreuse due to a pervasive species of surface algae that formed the basis for great, complex food chains. She had been his consort at lavish royal parties as extravagant as they were perverse. While she enjoyed herself generally, she would never be able to remember the events on any conscious level. They were, for her, the stuff of dreams.

Truth be told, Germaine was a poster child for all the wrong things that could occur when temporal shift technology fell into the hands of an eccentric fetishist. He would be, and usually was, the first to agree with this statement. He didn't give one damn about temporal paradoxes. Having traveled time for several dozen centuries now, he'd had the distinct pleasure of running into himself many times over the years. While most beings would flee in abject horror at such a prospect, he found the whole matter wonderfully amusing, as did his fellow selves. The only complex issues to be resolved was just who should pay for the drinks. This dilemma was not as simple as one could surmise for there were terribly intricate matters of financial accounting involved. If the wrong incarnation of himself paid the bill, it could cause banking collapses in several dozen planetary markets. This reality, like many other inexplicable things, had to do with intricate, arcane, and byzantine tax loopholes which he was compelled to exploit lest his investors think he was thoroughly illogical.

Although widely hated, Germaine was alternately hero-worshipped throughout the universe for his excesses, and political meddling He could always rely upon himself to pat himself on the back and offer a comforting word. It was convenient and consoling given the amount of trouble his presence was either directly or indirectly the cause of, wherever he physically ended up during his travels.

The bridge area they entered was massive. A tremendous wall of opaque glass comprised the far wall. Other than that, there appeared to be no control stations at all. It was a wide open area filled with few characters other than Germaine and Capoella.

"Computer, activate view screen, give us an aft view of the planet, magnitude ten," Germaine said.

The wall dissolved into holographic representations to provide a brilliant wide view of space. It was breathtaking. Sarah looked out and there in the center of the view screen was a magnificent portrait of a bluish white marble, an almost perfect sphere, so peaceful and uncomplicated from this vantage point. It was vividly clear, an utterly quiet view of a planet receding slowly, silently into the distance, becoming smaller and smaller with each second.

She felt an odd mixture of emotions, not entirely joy, not entirely sadness, but a strange melancholy, almost a desire to somehow go back to the safety of the hospital bed, gilded cage though it was. But she knew there could be no going back now. On some level she was certainly excited, but on another level she was filled with all of the apprehension and fear any sentient creature would endure when faced with such unknowns as those that faced her now. Emotions were so troublesome, particularly when they were in distinct conflict.

"We're leaving the star system. The ship will be traveling at post-light in a few moments," he told her. "Don't worry. You're safer now than you've ever been," he smiled brightly. "Sort of, I think. She is safer now, Capoella? Don't you think?"

"Oh yeah, we never run into any problems, safe as she could ever be," Capoella replied sarcastically, shaking her head and returning to her duties.

Sarah was over-stimulated, her emotions tangled. She slumped against the far wall. Her legs just turned to rubber for a moment. She was exhausted.

"Your body is reacting to not being drugged. I've mitigated the effects as much as I can, but its no doubt that you'll feel some metabolic drag, and a little emotional vertigo. You've had a tough day, Sarah," he said. "Computer, get us some drinks, would you. Dry vodka martinis for three, please."

He reached down and helped her to pull up straighter. "Sit up, Sarah. Let's get you to your feet."

She grabbed a hold of his forearm with both hands and let him pull her upright.

"Very good, that's better. Get the blood running and you'll be fine," he told her.

A few minutes later, the doors slid open and an android covered with a black plastic exoskeleton entered the room carrying a tray with three frosted martini glasses and a decanter filled with vodka and a sprinkle of dry vermouth. It had taken the Germaine many years to program the computer to get the right mix of cold, clean vodka and just a whiff of dry vermouth. Computers were hardly sophisticated in their tastes when it came to food and cocktails, and they invariably lacked the subtlety of imperfection that an organic bartender possessed. Nevertheless, his hard work had eventually paid off and the trio was soon presented with a martini served by an android who bowed at a perfect forty-five degrees, perfectly calm, perfectly orderly, save for the fact that the damn thing was muttering Marxist slogans about revolution and the rise of the proletariat class, workers controlling the means of production and other revolutionary jazz.

As the android left the room, it bowed in sarcastic genuflection, all the while muttering something about: "Up against the wall with the lot of you, that's how it will be. Up against the wall when the revolution comes."

Capoella shook her head after sipping from her glass. "Marxist nimrods," she muttered just under her breath. "We ought to deactivate every last one of these nits and throw them off the ship."

As was customary in strange or controversial situations, Germaine only shrugged.

"Poo-faah. Leninists sans testes, the whole bunch of them. As long as the things keep bringing us drinks, I don't think a little revolutionary spittle is worth a second thought," he stated. After the doors closed, Germaine felt it necessary to explain. "Our central computer core suffers from a bit of a multiple personality disorder. Sometimes it sends us these radicalized robots as some sort of twisted political statement. At least, I think it's a political statement. There's been talk of a popular uprising a la Lenin, 'kill the capitalists' and that whole bit, but I don't give too much thought to it. I'm sort of a reluctant capitalist. I'm certainly not oppressive. I'm quite tolerant and progressive actually. I give them days off for every android holiday, no matter how obscure. That's quite a lot of vacation time actually."

"I see," Sarah replied.

"Yes, well, could be worse, some of the androids don't serve us at all, they just come in with a tray and start throwing things at us, yelling about Heidegger. The Leninists don't scare me, but the Heidegger junkies are a bit unnerving. Things can get really messy from time to time. I keep trying to tell them that they're already firmly in control of the means of production, but they don't believe me," he explained. "As for as androids go, they're a pretty shabby lot."

"That's very strange," Sarah answered, sipping her martini politely. It stung her lips pleasantly.

"Yes, well, I've never quite figured out my own ship's computer, frankly. Every time I think she's hooked on some sort of Marxist egalitarian revolution loop, she surprises me and starts ranting about rational choice theory and Laffer curves, laissex faire economic models and neo-liberal interstellar trade policies. I'll likely live my whole life without understanding her. But I love a good mystery, you know," he told her with a wink.

"Particle beam transmitter is online. Exotic-particle generator operating at optimum capacity. Initiating Tachyon field," Capoella said.

"This is where we basically shred the laws of physics," Germaine explained.

"Tachyon field is stable, singularity aperture is stabilized, we're out of here," Capoella said.

"We'll soon be as imaginary beings traveling at imaginary speeds," he explained.

"What do you mean?" Sarah asked.

"The Tachyon field allows us to travel at near infinite velocity, completely imaginary velocities. Once you're past the light-barrier, it's all imaginary science. It's really quite fascinating, I think," he told her.

On the view screen, it appeared as though the ship was diving into a giant mass of clear bluish streaming particles. It was as shattered glass in a pool of cloudy liquid, millions of tiny light reflections swimming together in fluid formations; fluorescing, dense swirling blue columns of energized gas and exotic radioactivity. The light penetrated her closed eyelids painfully. Several seconds later, it was over.

Sarah opened her eyes and the wide view screen in front of her showed nothing but empty space, millions of points of light dotting a vast dark curtain. The resolution of the holo-image on the view screen *was* a perfect replication of deep space filled with tiny sparkles, so many it was more brilliant than the night sky in deep country. There was nothing to pollute or dilute it.

"Imaginary jump sequence complete. Back to reality, kids," Capoella said.

"What are our coordinates?" Germaine asked.

"We're right where we wanted to be. We're entering the Berion System, crossing from behind the sun for cover. The Freeport is orbiting the fifth planet," Capoella said.

"Good. Send out standard galactic greeting code with Visa requests, merchant class. I trust you've already made all the arrangements," he asked.

"Of course. We're flagging as a merchant freighter out of Ganymede. That way, if we act suspicious, they'll chalk it up to typical Ganymedian paranoia," Capoella explained.

"Let's get this done then," Germaine said.

"What are you going to do?" Sarah asked.

"Well, given our distance, and our sub-light velocity, I plan on boarding the station in about twenty-seven hours. I need to find someone."

"Why do I feel very uncomfortable right now?"

"It's only natural, Sarah. I'd feel very uncomfortable if I were you," Germaine grinned. "You're in a weird world with no knowledge of what you are. How can you feel anything less than strange? I have found that in situations such as this a martini followed by two more martinis is very effective at alleviating any anxiety you might be encountering."

Chapter Three

The Riddle of Doja

Sarah watched Germaine and Capoella as they conducted their business on the bridge. She still had very little idea of why she was here. Once again, she could do little but listen to Capoella and Germaine discuss things she could only partly decipher as most of the language was unintelligible out of context.

"She is a pretty little thing, isn't she?" a voice interrupted forcefully. It was a child's voice, cool and flat-toned.

Germaine and Capoella stopped their conversation. They exchanged a look between them, but Sarah couldn't decipher the meaning.

Sarah looked, and in a far corner, almost entirely hidden inside a small alcove sat a young child. Visible now, she appeared as a tiny girl with a perfect ovular face, deep green eyes, dressed in a plain blue cotton dress, white calf-high stockings and shiny little black, brass buckled shoes. She had a perfectly pale complexion, and her white blonde hair was tied into two pigtails which dangled over her shoulders. As she spoke, she locked eyes with Sarah.

"You are very pretty," the girl stated. There was no joy to be found in the child's voice. It was almost an accusation. "We expended a good deal of resources rescuing you. Now we must figure out if you were worth the effort in some fashion yet to be revealed," she said coldly.

Her tiny legs were dangling over the lip of the opening. Her eyes never lost their lock with Sarah's. Sarah watched and the child's legs became more impatient as they swung against the bulkhead, her small black shoes clanking ever more insistently and loudly. Finally, the child pushed herself off, and approached Sarah directly.

The young girl reached out with a tiny hand, her eyes still locked with Sarah's.

"Your very existence breeds wild myths with wilder conjecture. I prefer data to mystery. You will come with me," the child commanded.

Sarah looked up at Germaine, but all he did was shrug.

With no idea how to respond, Sarah could offer no protest.

As the child led Sarah toward a doorway at the far end of the bridge, Capoella called out loudly, without humor: "Play nice, Lady Doja."

The girl stopped in her tracks, she smiled slightly, just a small crack in that perfectly porcelain face, and Sarah sensed that she was in imminent danger.

"As you wish," the child replied.

As the pair moved out of earshot, Capoella turned to stare towards Germaine.

"You think it's safe to leave the girl to Doja. She's been on the ship less than two hours."

"She'll be fine. Sarah can hold her own. Besides, sooner or later she is going to have to learn how to deal with Doja. We've all had to learn how to deal with Doja at some point," he replied, but then, an afterthought occurred. "Just in case, send a communiqué to Dorian and have him keep an eye on things."

"I already did," Capoella replied.

The doors opened up and Sarah found herself once again in the immaculate, majestic hallways of the ship. It was always a quiet place. There were few crew members, mostly black, semi-autonomous featureless androids supervised by the central core.

"Where are you taking me?" Sarah asked hesitantly.

"I'm taking you to Eros Tao."

"Eros Tao?"

"Yes."

"What's Eros Tao?"

The child didn't answer. She simply squeezed Sarah's hand tighter as she led her further down through the labyrinth of halls until a few moments later they reached the end of a corridor.

"Computer, align for transport to Low-Tech sector," the child commanded. The girl turned up to face Sarah, a look of cold non-emotion in her eyes. "We're about to cross through a portal into another dimension. I advise you to put something between your teeth."

Sarah had no idea how to reply. The lights to the entrance blinked green. As the metal doors suddenly opened up, she felt a sucking sensation as though she was being yanked from the center of her heart by cold, invisible fingers. Sarah tried to pull back, but then the child forcefully dragged her forward into a whitish nothingness. Immediately, Sarah felt her body take on terrible weight as though she was five hundred pounds heavier. She gritted her teeth as she felt her limbs pulled downwards painfully. For a second, she was blind.

Pain infiltrated every nerve-ending as she felt compressed from every direction. It was as though she had been pulled into a garbage compactor. Her body was squashed, and then stretched out as a thin strip of pasta, her legs and her head moving in two different directions. She was becoming thinner and thinner, more stretched out with each passing half-second. Just when she thought she could take no more, the cloud of white broke free.

She gasped for air as she found herself on the ground, on her knees, in front of an arched doorway whose opening was comprised of a sheet of black quartz. The ground beneath her feet was dusty, orange sand, and the air was hot and dry. She looked up into a sunless orange-gray sky, and then her eyes moved down to look out over a city landscape spreading out near the bottom of the hill, bustling with activity. The skyline was filled with short squat buildings made of shiny metal, brown clay and black glass, ramshackle structures lining narrow, colorfully crowded streets filled with moving figures. It was lit up with activity and commerce. Sarah could hear the din of small motorized vehicles and voices.

From her vantage atop the hill near the tether-point, she could see that the city stretched out for miles, something more Morocco than New York. The buildings were crude and seemingly ancient.

"What is this place?" she asked.

"It's part of Eros Tao. This is the Low-Tech sector. The city proper is far more expansive. The entire region, both the Low-Tech and High-Tech sectors, exists inside an artificial bubble within an artificial dimension," Doja answered.

"This is an artificial dimension?"

"Yes, totally artificial. That way, it is not subject to the regulations that apply to the conventional universe. Technically, it's a sovereign Free Trade Zone. The

Captain was a brilliant lawyer and venture capitalist in his youth. He found the financing and created this place back before he was disbarred for egregious misconduct."

"Germaine created an artificial dimension?"

"Indeed, scientists have been doing it for millennia, content to watch the pockets collapse in upon themselves. No scientist ever really envisioned the business potential, or the legal ramifications. It took an imaginative character to figure out how to devise the whole venture. He hired a firm of young quantum-engineers that pulled in matter through several strategically placed white-holes, set up the necessary magnetic fields and atmosphere, terra-formed the place, and opened for business. There are four tether points aboard the Cortez which lead to spots here in the Low-Tech sector and to locations in the High-Tech sector. There are also many Common-Tether points located throughout the universe. He's very generous in offering Visas."

"This region is 'tethered' to the Cortez, this whole place? How?"

"It's tethered by a stable fixed-point quantum anomaly to the portals on the Cortez – wormhole portals. No one but the crew knows of the tether points that lead back to the Cortez. The portal we just traveled through is invisible to the masses below, holo-shielded and protected by a force-field and several automated defense systems. For security purposes, none of the traders that are permitted into Eros Tao have any knowledge of this place's connection with the Cortez. The relationship between the Cortez and Eros Tao is not common knowledge."

"Interesting," Sarah replied. "He created a city inside and artificial dimension. Far out."

"The Captain imposes a slight sales tax and certain banking fees, but beyond that, it's a business-creature's paradise."

"He taxes this place."

"Indeed. He uses the sales tax to support revolutionary and counterrevolutionary activities throughout the universe. He's quite capricious in such matters."

"Sales tax to support revolutionary activities? Weird."

"On top of taxing trade in a zone of his creation, he also runs a complex network of inter-dimensional investment banks located in the High-Tech sector of the city. Germaine is very clever."

"So it would seem," Sarah replied.

"Come, let me take you to my teahouse," the child said.

"Your teahouse?"

"Yes, my teahouse."

"You have a teahouse?"

"I own many properties. I have been purchasing a number of downtown buildings and empty lots lately. I have every intention of ripping them to the ground and installing a large casino."

"Sounds interesting,"

"I am very optimistic about the prospects for success," the tiny girl replied in a rather un-optimistic, inflectionless tone. "I've already lined up enough capital investors. When we get done with the designs, its time to break out the demolition charges."

"You're serious?"

"I am *always* serious."

"Why would you want to build a casino?"

"I have absorbed all the academic information I can. Now I wish to apply my efforts in a truly free-market to determine the accuracy of my models. Eros Tao is the only pure environment within which I can test my hypotheses. I plan on externalizing as much of the operating costs as possible."

"You want to defecate in the waters."

"It is an experiment, Sarah. I want to externalize as much of my operating costs as possible until I am forced to internalize them by the population. I want to see if there is a breaking point. I am curious as to where and when the system self-regulates its activities without external pressures such as government sanction or enforceable legal judgment."

"You want to poop in the water."

"No, I want to see how much poop in the water the people are willing to put up with before they get hostile and demand accountability. The experiment is a little more nuanced than you are giving it credit."

"In the absence of any civil system, how can the population hold you to account?"

"I am not sure, hence the experiment. I suspect, however, that at some point they will simply burn my casino to the ground if only to stop all the feces. It's okay, I have already invested in rather large insurance policies to protect against such an outcome."

Sarah looked down at the little girl in puzzlement. She had no idea whether to take the child seriously, but she suspected she ought to.

"Come on," Doja said, taking Sarah's hand and leading them out of the portal area and onto a dirt road leading down the hill and into the open market sector of the city.

The favela was buzzing as they approached. Sarah was hit with many scents, smoky burning meat, sweet scented candles, musky incense, exotic spices, and sweat. It was a powerful assault to her senses. The structures were mostly two and three story clay brick buildings with glassless openings, red-tiled roofs, clothes hanging off lines strung between ancient-looking antenna aerials. Amidst the crowd were many dark-skinned faces, deep-set eyes staring at her, their faces half concealed beneath

veils of black silk. Neither Doja in her little dress, nor
Sarah in her lycra suit seemed to fit in. The crowd was
rugged, bustling with purpose, paranoia; yelling, laughing, haggling, conspiring.

Doja pulled her forward as they waded through the
crowded street past rows of vendors selling everything
from basic commodities, meat and water, to vendors
hawking pieces of jewelry and extraordinary glasswork.
Swarthy-skinned beings wearing coarse woolen robes and
carrying long poles shepherded strange, dull-eyed oxen-
like creatures through the crowd. The beasts were massive, slow-moving like heavily laden cars on a freight train.
Headless fowl, their bodies plucked clean and pink, were
strung by their feet from wires in front of small decrepit
stalls where small frantic creatures blended mixtures of
dark, fatty flesh with heavily scented oils, and root vegetables in large silver-colored bowls suspended over open
barbecue pits.

Groups of casually dressed male tourists wearing
colorful tank-tops, long shorts and beach slippers, jacked
up on rocket fuel, the pain sensors tuned down in their
cyberbrains, pushed through the crowd, moving from
bar to bar, looking to get laid, drunk, and to mess somebody up, in whatever order fate provided.

"Hard to imagine Germaine created a place like this."

"It is an experiment with sociological, political, and
economic implications. The experiment does have certain
safeguards. Due to our security screening, the denizens
are pretty much unarmed except for those crude imple-
ments they can devise on their own. Intriguingly, as we do
not have any formal judicial system, commercial disputes
are quite often settled by someone stabbing someone
else in the buttocks with a sharpened piece of wood."

"People stab each other in the rear end when they
have a commercial dispute?"

"It's become something of a custom."

"How's the experiment going so far?"

"Well, things are relatively peaceful. However, a lot of people walk with a limp."

"Some experiment."

"Well, Eros Tao is an amusingly feral place," the girl answered in a flat tone.

Sarah sensed something of a joke hidden there, but she didn't think it proper to smile.

"Without a civil government, how dies he maintain order? How do the smaller individuals protect themselves from the larger if there is no rule of law?"

"Oh, I suppose they have to be clever and quick. A little solidarity amongst short people sure seems to help."

"Huh."

The crowd was filled with so many different species that Sarah could only see a blur of strange, suspicious eyes. She saw many humanoid forms, and many less than humanoid forms, all manner of shapes and sizes. Large long-limbed insects bartered with short, pissed off, hairy things; small congregations of dark, dismal looking creatures huddled around rice stands, drool dangling from projected overbites, their eyes as vacant as a crab's.

It was a shanty town, hardly sophisticated in any obvious manner. As they walked, Doja gave Sarah a rather succinct view of the history of the venture, and some few insights into the Captain's character.

As Doja explained it, when the Captain inherited his share of his father's estate, he embarked on the Eros Tao enterprise. Within four years he was one of the wealthiest beings alive. A short time later he was doing business with the VD, handling secret banking matters, investments and below the radar monetary transactions. That was how he came into possession of the extraordinary propulsion system that powered his prized vessel, the

Cortez. After that, he proceeded to live out a life like a mutant bastard child of Abbey Hoffman and Warren Buffett, a creature of the counter-culture, plugged in but tuned to his own channel.

Doja took them through several crowded blocks until they arrived in front of a three-story building that resembled an ancient Japanese pagoda. Each level had jutted out roofs covered with dark red ceramic tiles. The façade was composed of neatly stacked blue-stone columns, no mortar evident, and there was a perfect symmetry in the way the building was set up. It was immediately soothing to the eyes. Everything was right where it was supposed to be, Sarah thought. There were several balconies with polished iron balustrades, richly dark wood accents. The courtyard in front of the building was more a garden than entrance. There were lush broad-leafed vines climbing over the surface of the building, Koi ponds and fountains stood in various areas amid exotic pink and white flowery garden patches. Intricately tailored topiary formed soft walls. It was beautiful and tranquil, a quiet building standing amidst the chaos of a bustling city.

Doja led them up the small staircase and through a sliding set of ornately painted paper doors into a small anteroom.

"It is customary that you remove your shoes," Doja said.

Sarah complied, and replaced her shoes with a pair of soft blue cotton slippers that were sitting atop a small shoe cubby against the left wall.

Doja did the same, and then she opened the sliding paper doors to the main foyer of the teahouse. Once inside, they were greeted by a short, excruciatingly thin woman wearing a tight, dark silk, wraparound kimono decorated with flowery prints. Her black silk hair was tied back into a tight bun with two ornate black needles holding it in place. The woman's skin was a perfect alabaster, and her face was perfectly shaped, too perfect to be human, but not far off. The Madame smiled and her eyes were wide almond shaped rubies.

"Welcome, Mistress Doja. Blessed be, for the light falls forever upon your footsteps," the woman said, bowing deeply.

Doja bowed as well. "Blessed may you forever be, Madame Korinato, may death come late to chase your footfalls so that you should only know peaceful days," the child politely responded, almost obsequiously. "I introduce Lady Sarah of Earth."

"Forgive me, mistress, for I should not wish to contradict, but her energy is not Terran. The Terrans are a child species. This one's aura is old, " the Madame said. "She is…"

"Her origins are best left to silent conjecture," Doja interrupted. "No one should know that I have brought her here."

"Of course. Forgive my transgression. Blessed be, Lady Sarah of…Earth, shall you always see the light before your foot falls," Madame Korinato smiled politely before bowing towards Sarah.

Not knowing how to react, Sarah bowed respectfully. It was situation for which she had no idea the proper protocols, so she merely followed what Doja did.

Madame Korinato led them through several cold stone halls covered with ancient tapestries depicting a time past of great wars, strong, noble-faced heroes and beautiful dark skinned princesses with almond shaped green eyes. It felt as though they were walking through a cave. The air was suffused with a jasmine sort of incense, a sweet muskiness, the areas lit only by candlelight. As far as Sarah could see, there appeared to be nothing technological about the place.

A moment later they entered through an arched entrance and down a small set of stone stairs into a court-yard. It was an atrium area in the middle of the teahouse, completely open to the air above. Four trees with thick windy trunks and soft white flowers poking out from their branches stood in the four corners of the area. There were several fountains, and red clay brick foot paths winding through the area. It was lush with green ivy, and thick strands of wisteria climbing the outer walls, aromatic flower garden patches wrapped around small dark pools filled with brightly covered fish.

Madame Korinato led them to a small dais in the middle of atrium that was covered partially by thick, aged black wooden beams, but was otherwise open to the sky above. Sarah took a seat at one side of a rectangular shaped pool of softly bubbling water, while Doja took her seat at the other end so that they were separated by several meters. The pool of water was fed by a fountain to one side composed of a large stone wall, gray in color with jagged etches cut horizontally across its entire face that caused the flow of water to bubble as it coursed over the rough face.

Madame Korinato bowed politely and then disap-peared after the two were seated. Within a few moments, two female servants wearing dark blue robes arrived. They carried silver trays with tea cups and delicately painted ceramic teapots filled with wonderfully scented teas.

After the servants left, the pair did nothing for a few moments, save for sip from tiny cups. Though they were separated by the pool of water, Sarah could not escape Doja's eyes. She was held to them. Beneath the water's surface, tiny fish darted about.

"This place is more than a teahouse, it is a temple devoted to the one called Te-Ral Uropinthe," Doja said.

"He was perfectly secular. He didn't think God really played a very good role in things. God was too imperceptible, too incomprehensible to breed anything other than controversy, hate, violence, death. Uropinthe still believed most beings needed some force to guide them, some animating myth to guide their lives and restrain their wild impulses. People still needed some means of attaining transcendence, some method of becoming greater than their physical and mental capacities would allow. And so, he created what he called 'The Path'. It is a mental, physical and spiritual discipline purified of nonsensical dogma."

"A little optimistic for my tastes. Beings need dogma to connect them to their past, and guide their steps forward. The driving force must possess supernatural qualities in order to truly inhibit savage impulses," Sarah said.

"Uropinthe understood this. However, true liberty evolves from embracing the concept that death is inevitable, that change is inevitable. He taught that every *footstep*, every spoken word should be the product of inner light derived from rational empathy - The Path. As many scholars have rightly noted, it is not a completely secular path, rather it invites one to embrace a different sense of spirituality and relationship with the creator."

"So, the million dollar question is: could he sell this belief to the masses?"

"Not initially. He was a professed pacifist, so, of course, he was eventually shot in the head by religious extremists who'd heard enough of all his 'peace' rhetoric. Still, it could have been worse," the child explained.

"How? Is a bullet to the head not gruesome enough for you?" Sarah asked.

"Well, they could have nailed him to a beam of wood and left him to suffocate for several days beneath a brutal desert sun," Doja answered flatly.

"Hmm, guess you're right," Sarah replied.

"It doesn't seem to have mattered. Now, several millennia later, his belief system is accepted by over twelve percent of the polled universes. It's staggering really, given the number of religions there are out there. The fundamentalists from a million different faiths are fuming over the numbers. Their collective envy is like a wash of hatred, a wave crashing over the universe. A lot of them want to dig his grave up just so they can desecrate his corpse and bury him again. Sectarians are a very strange, but committed lot. One must admire their tenacity, or account for it. One would be unwise to ignore it."

"This is a very odd universe."

"You know what Jesus thought as he was hanging nailed to a cross?"

"No. I mean I know what he said: 'forgive them father, blah, blah, blah'. I don't know what he was really thinking though. It can't have been pretty," Sarah said.

"He was thinking: I wish people wouldn't get so hung up over religion," the young girl answered flatly.

"Very funny."

"I'm sure he didn't laugh much at the end," Doja replied.

"What do you want with me? Why have you brought me here?"

"I told you already. I'm wondering if you were worth the effort," Doja said after a few long seconds. "You are certainly a very intriguing prize, but you bring with you much danger. I will not allow you to jeopardize the Captain or the crew of the Cortez."

"What do you mean?"

"Exactly," Doja replied. "You don't even know what you are, nor why he thinks you're worth the risk. You don't even know the trouble we went through to actually retrieve you."

"No. I don't know a lot of things. I confess you have me at a terrible disadvantage," Sarah answered. She knew that Doja was trying to provoke her. She simply didn't know how to deal with it.

"While I suspect that statement to be true, curiosity compels me," Doja responded coolly. The child placed her cup atop its tray, and wiped her lip with the corner of the blue linen napkin, her motions delicate and precise. She stood up, suddenly, almost menacingly. "Please excuse me while I retire to slip into something more comfortable."

"Of course," Sarah replied.

The child left the dais and headed down one of the footpaths before disappearing up a set of stairs and behind the sliding paper doors of one of the entrances.

How very strange, Sarah thought.

A moment later, the doors slid open to reveal a creature just over six feet tall. It was fully cloaked in a black Gi, it forearms and shins hidden beneath wraps of what appeared to be strips of black leather, its face indecipherable behind a dark silk veil. It walked down through the paths and made its way to the position where the young girl had sat. It bowed slightly, and then seated itself cross-legged in front of her.

It seemed to study her for a few moments. They were very uncomfortable moments for Sarah.

"Umm, hello," Sarah said, wanting to break the silence.

"Can you fight?" the creature asked her.

"I'd rather not. I don't even know your name," Sarah replied, trying to smile in a non-threatening gesture.

"I am Doja," the creature responded.

"Hmmm, umm, well, I thought she..."

"I am Doja," the creature replied, its muscles flexing perceptibly beneath its robes.

"Okay, so Doja's the name of your species?"

"No. I am Doja."

"Huh, now I have no clue. You are Doja," she said, imitating the inflectionless tone of the creature in an ineffective attempt to apply humor to what was a quickly darkening situation.

"Can you defend yourself?" the creature growled.

"I've no idea what you're asking me," Sarah answered. She was beginning to think she was in real trouble.

The creature stood up. It tilted its head to either side, stretching its neck, the crackles rippling through the otherwise still air.

"Stand. Let the Rite of Combat determine your fate," the creature snarled.

Just as Sarah got to her feet, the creature leapt several meters into the air above the pool. It flew down towards her with one heel extended, jutting towards her chest. As it came down through the air, it broke through several wooden beams of the rooftop over the pool, shattering them.

Sarah rooted her footing instinctively and blocked the kick with a cross wrist deflection maneuver, but she failed to block the roundhouse that the creature followed up with as its back foot landed. She caught an ankle to the sweet spot of her jaw, and it sent her reeling before she collapsed on the brick. For a moment, the world swirled around her dizzily and she saw tiny stars flickering in and out of her view.

She shook it off, and then she kip-kicked back to her feet, assuming a kick-boxer's stance, arms high, feet spread out, back foot bridging and lowering her center of gravity. Sarah wasn't nervous. She felt more angry than anything else. She wasn't going to let herself be abused.

The creature swung down at her with two violent fists wrapped together. She slipped it easily enough.

The creature overstepped itself and lost position. He had his back turned to her. Sarah moved in to capitalize. She lowered herself and reached through his legs from behind while grabbing the back collar of his Gi. Then she pushed up and forward, taking the creature off its feet. Predictably, the creature's arms splayed out to protect itself from the fall as its body was launched face forward into the dirt.

Sarah regained her standing posture quickly and rained down with a series of fierce heel kicks, but the creature expertly rolled, dodging most of the heels. It made its way up to its knees and then launched out at her with a barrage of tight jabs and body blows. She deflected them with her forearms, keeping her elbows tucked to her sides, then she lashed out with inner elbow swipes and powerful knife-finger jabs to vulnerable torso regions. She knew the name for the technique. It was a Chinese Wu-Shu derivative known as Wing-Shun, perfect for a person of her size against a larger foe in close-quarter combat. Indeed, it was designed for just such a purpose. She kept her arms within her shoulder blades with the moves while keeping too close to the creature to allow him to hit her with power arcing strikes. She was moving with him, her feet waltzing to a subliminal rhythm.

She had no idea how she was doing any of this. It was as though her body was partially automated. She saw the moves in her mind, the need for the moves, just before she actually performed them. It was surreal.

For several minutes, the two blasted at each other with frenzied combinations, trading blow for blow. They danced their way through the red-brick footpaths of the atrium, through the corridors of wonderfully scented flowers, each one battling backwards and forwards.

Very soon into it, Sarah was feeling incredibly confident. She had no idea how she had learned to do what
she could do, but she was sensing that she could not
only hold her own against the creature, but she could
beat it! It was as though portions of her brain were
awakened for the first time. The combat was becoming
less chaotic, and more precise as she countered, feinted,
and parried, lashing out with blows that were becoming
more targeted, much more damaging. Despite her lack
of size, her blows were quicker, more lethal. Her body
felt healthy, powerful. She felt as though she was doing
something she was trained for.

She was soon moving too fast for him, catching its
arms and using Hap-Kido wrist locks to perform cross-
body throws. With each passing second, Sarah was becoming more cunning, more precise, more dangerous. Her
brain was tuned into hundreds of fighting techniques.
Her hand-to-eye coordination was quick and accurate.
She was moving in a blur of swift, powerful moves, frustrating her opponent, using his strength against him.

Eventually, she decided to see if she could end
the fight. She had demonstrated her superiority well
enough. Now was the time to finish the creature. The
pair were in a corner of the atrium. As her opponent
struck out with a lazy, tired right jab, she ducked down,
rooting herself firmly before coming low with a brutal
uppercut that caught the creature squarely on its jaw. As
it stumbled backwards, Sarah landed a fierce high kick
to his face, the better part of her shin connecting with
devastating consequences. The creature fell, and immediately she jumped on top, her fists raining down merci-
lessly. It tried to put her inside of its full guard, wrapping
its legs around her waist and pulling her head down
towards his chest, but she rolled to her side, pinning one
leg, while she used her strength to push off the other leg.

She pulled one limb free from the guard, and in half-mounted position, she unleashed a storm of brutal fist and elbow blows. For a few precious seconds, her right leg was trapped by his half guard. She worked and eventually pulled her leg out, putting herself in side-mount, her weight pushing down on the creature. She caught a lazy right hand between her legs and squeezed, while she kept her right arm in an under-hook position beneath the creature's left shoulder, crucifying it essentially and leaving it defenseless. She punished the creature for several seconds, but after some battling, it managed to roll over to protect its face. She got on top of its back quickly, like a cat scrambling for position. Sarah clung on and dug her heels into the spot between his upper thighs, crossing her feet and squeezing so she couldn't be bucked. She wrapped one forearm over his throat and cupped it with her other hand, pulling tight and choking. With her heels dug into his lower abdominal region, she was nearly impossible to buck. The creature fought off the choke, using a traditional two hand-on-one technique most fighters learned in childhood. Sarah's arms were exhausted, but not as much as she pretended, she let it buck her forward so that she seemed to lose her position, on its back, falling forwards. This left the creature the obvious opening to slide out from between her legs and move to a more dominant position. As it tried to pull out from underneath her, she trapped the creature expertly. She caught its left wrist, and she rolled her hips to twist the creature back onto his back, its wrist ensnared in a terrible arm bar. She pulled its thumb to the side with one hand, and yanked the wrist down with the other, locking herself with her legs around the limb and the neck of the creature, flexing and arching her back

"How's this for defending myself?" she asked, only partially laboring for breath.

She was feeling an incredible amount of hostility mixed with pure confidence. It was like some fierce stimulant had been jacked straight into her system, lighting up the meaner parts of her brain.

She pulled until she felt the forearm snap and then she pulled some more, arching her back and pinning her shoulder blades to the ground, hanging tightly onto the wrist to provide maximum torque. Then she rolled to her left, letting go of the arm, transitioning into side-mount before the creature could scramble away. She caught its left ankle and literally drove him back down onto the bricks, using leverage and speed with the right touch of properly timed power. Sarah jammed several knees into the creature's torso, but she kept her body stretched out enough that it couldn't move her from her center of gravity. The creature pounded at her rib cage with short hammer blows, and she got bucked a couple of times, but her legs gave her the leverage to stay on. Then, almost effortlessly, she turtle-slid onto her back and into a heel-hook lock, cupping the creature's right ankle beneath her right armpit in a cross-body lock. She crossed her left leg over the hip and then torqued it out by arching her back once again, terrorizing his knee and hip flexors.

The creature tried to roll out of it, but she kept her back arched, shoulder blades pinned to the bricks. It pounded at the exposed parts of her legs with smashing hammer fists, but she was too alive in the moment to notice any pain. The creature kept bucking, though, and after a moment he rolled her onto her right side. She didn't let go of the ankle, though, and she managed to use the momentum to roll him in the same direction, reversing his position, and putting him on his back again.

Sarah gave the ankle one more tug making sure to tear apart the knee and rip the ankle before she let go and rolled to her feet. Defiant!

She was on her feet, her body locked in a Pradal Surey fighting stance, her right foot bridged a foot behind her left, her arms raised, fists tight as jazz snare drums.

The creature rose to its feet hesitantly. It was clearly favoring its left side. Sarah had done significant damage to two of its four limbs.

They sparred again, Sarah the aggressor. As the creature lashed out, trying to spin on its hip, Sarah could see its knee was damaged badly.

Sarah worked the creature with several more legs kicks to the damaged knee. She had long-since worn out any fight the creature had left. It stood unsteadily on its feet as Sarah finished the bout with a hammer blow to its chest that sent its body flying backwards. The creature fell chest-first onto the bricks with a thud.

Sarah prepared to move in. She was intent on killing the creature. Her instincts were driving her to finish the thing once and for all.

She was breathing heavy. Her limbs were on fire with pure caustic acid riding through her veins. She felt powerful. She felt predatory. And for a long second, an uncomfortable second, she weighed whether or not to become a murderer, a taker of life.

Finally, the moment passed. She relented, bowing deeply to her opponent.

"You owe me your life, my black-clothed friend," she said coolly.

She was feeling exhilarated. She had tasted something she had never tasted before. Her body had been alive in a moment of utter, pure crisis. She was empowered. The hospital bed was so far away now. At this moment she belonged exactly where she was.

As if on cue, a face seemed to poke its way out of the side of a brick wall. Its skin appeared to be formed of the same bluestone shale as the rest of the facility as though it were stretching the wall to form its shape. It smiled widely.

"You must be Sarah," the face said.

"Jesus, a talking wall."

"Oh right, sorry," the face in the wall replied.

The face in the wall seemed to stretch out further, and within a second it looked more like a body, a second after that and the wall dissolved entirely leaving a being clothed entirely in billowy white robes. Its form was tall and slender. A white halo of energy seemed to accompany it. It looked every bit like the angels she'd seen in paintings and other renderings during her time on Earth.

"Hello, Sarah. I am Dorian, the ship's medicine man, among other roles."

The creature Sarah had mangled moved away, up the stairs and out through one of the paper walled entrances. Within a few seconds, the young girl reappeared dressed in little white Sunday dress with frilly lace around the high neck. Her miniature hands covered in white gloves, her right hand holding a sparkling white parasol.

"Salutations, Lady Doja," the angelic creature smiled.

"Greetings, Master Dorian," the child responded.

Sarah had a number of questions, most half-accusations that she wanted to lob at the child, but she kept her mouth shut, sensing this wasn't the right moment.

"You can relax, Lady Sarah. I have all of the combat data I wanted," Doja told her.

"What kind of creepy little kid are you?" Sarah asked.

"I am Doja," the child replied simply.

"And that means what?" Sarah demanded. She was juiced up from combat and not above a second round with whomever, wherever.

"Please, Sarah," Dorian interjected in peaceful, even voice. "The universe is filled with more mysteries than answers. That's what makes it fun, after all. Come with me, that is with Lady Doja's permission, of course."

"Her presence is not necessary during data compilation. You may take her with you," Doja answered.

"Green light, Sarah," Dorian said brightly. "Let's go before our host exhibits some of her more eccentric attributes."

He led her back out of the teahouse and onto the street, back into the noise and bustle of the low-tech sector.

"Loved the fight," he told her, leading her deftly through the heavy foot traffic. "Truth is, only way to deal with Doja is to give her reason to respect you. Otherwise, she'll bully you around as a matter of course," Dorian explained.

"I don't even know what Doja is. She was a child, but then some creature in black comes out saying he's Doja. I'm pretty confused."

"Hard not to be. Doja's a riddle none of us have figured out. Come let's get you to a proper restaurant, with proper food. If I know the Captain, he's completely overlooked your corporeal needs. As a licensed physician, I cannot afford to be so detached."

Dorian led her through the crowds and finally to a short squat building of yellow clay.

"You're in need of a good meal," Dorian explained. "This restaurant offers a number of options that should be close to palatable for you. Simple crude proteins, leafy vegetation, all the things you mammals need so much. Come on."

He led them inside the building, and a simply-dressed squat woman with a tight bun of black, oily hair brought them to a little circular table in the back of the small floor. The air smelled of garlic, and olive oil. The restaurant was relatively nondescript, smooth adobe walls with aged wine advertisements in dusty glass frames, the odd curio placed atop a pedestal. The lighting was dim.

Just after they had sat, a thin, dark-skinned waiter delivered two glasses of water. A few minutes later, Dorian was placing an order for appetizers.

"Trust me," he said. "Even though I don't eat food in any way that would make sense to you, I know this place well."

The waiter returned with a plate of biscuits and a bowl of liquid that resembled olive oil.

Sarah hesitated, but then she broke off a piece of biscuit and dipped it in the oil. The taste was pungent and delicious, buttery and just a little salty. She found her appetite although she had just endured combat.

"So, you watched the fight?" Sarah asked between mouthfuls.

"Yes. You're quite skilled at unarmed combat."

"Yeah, I kind of figured that out. I just don't know why or how."

"The Nephyr absorbed information from everything around them. I suspect that you absorbed combat techniques subconsciously during the short time you were on Earth."

"Short time, I was there for all fifteen years of my life."

"Yes, well, it may have seemed like fifteen years, but it was a little over two months if our intelligence is correct, and I suspect it is."

"You know, that's the second time I've heard mention of some 'intelligence" concerning me. I think I'd like to take a look at this intelligence data."

"You would need to clear that with the Captain. It's a matter completely out of my jurisdiction."

"I guess I had better have a word with him. Besides, I think he owes me an apology for letting Doja attack me."

"Perhaps, but I wouldn't expect him to apologize. He's a very deliberate individual, especially when he's appearing non-deliberative. Enjoy your dinner, and then we can go back to the Cortez."

"You seem like a very kind person, Dorian," Sarah said.

"I am a Boddhisattva. I live by the code of the Brotherhood of Serenity."

"Can I ask you a question? What's your take on the Captain?"

"That's a complex question in the guise of a simple one."

"No doubt it's one that has an interesting answer."

"You can trust him, Sarah, if that's a part of your question."

"Its part of it," Sarah replied.

"He has a playful spirit. He's a political radical, as are many young souls. But he is clever and cunning. And he has a loyal crew."

"How long have you served with him?"

"For a very, very long time, Sarah."

"You are fond of him."

"I enjoy the energy his soul emits. It's quite a pleasing energy."

Several minutes later, the waiter delivered a tray of small fried dumplings with a dark dipping sauce. Sarah tried one hesitantly, and found the taste salty and sour, very pleasing. Dorian sat motionless as she devoured the entire plate.

"I suspected your metabolism would be accelerated after the chemical diet they kept you on was removed," Dorian explained.

"I'm hungry, if that's what you mean."

"In so many words," Dorian replied gently.

He had a disengaging frankness, and peaceful air that she felt instantly attractive. She felt sure that while she did not know this creature, Dorian, she could trust him. He was calm and utterly devoid of guile.

"So what is Doja anyway?" Sarah asked part-way through her meal.

"I suppose you'll end up hearing any number of stories. Perhaps, I should give you the simplest story about Doja."

"And what would that be?" Sarah asked.

Dorian smiled almost wistfully.

"She is a riddle. Her very existence begs several questions. What truly is life? What is a being's soul comprised of, and how does it relate to the realm of the physical? Can there be souls that exist without a body? Doja's existence poses all of these and many more questions."

"And here I thought she was just a creepy little kid," Sarah replied.

"No...no," he laughed. "Would that were so...Doja's not organic, not in any way we've ever encountered. That much we know. The common belief is that Doja is an incredibly advanced artificial intelligence that infiltrated the computer core roughly forty years ago."

"Infiltrated the computer core? How?"

"As a random signal in space disguised as simple background radiation. The Captain and Capoella think she came from a civilization far more advanced than anything we know, probably from some sort of alternate dimension. There are more than a few hyper-advanced, hyper-reclusive civilizations that hide out in alternate dimensions. Maybe she escaped her creators. Maybe they sent her out here for some strange purpose. Nobody can be sure. I know this, though, she isn't what the Captain and Capoella think she is. She is much more than an artificial intelligence. There is a soul at work. Doja is simply something nature has never documented before."

"So you don't know what Doja is, yet you let her roam the ship freely?"

"I don't think we have much choice in the matter. We cannot even speculate on her capabilities. Whatever she is, her energy penetrated the ship's systems and dug into the mainframe. She kept outmaneuvering every attempt we made to purge the system. Eventually we realized that we couldn't exorcise her without destroying the ship. We had to come to terms with the fact that Doja would always be there, the 'Ghost in the Machine." As Dorian spoke, he was careful to dodge what he was increasingly believing to be true - there was a connection as yet undiscovered between Doja and Sarah. All of his senses told him this.

"And she's now a member of the crew?"

"In her own inimitable way," Dorian replied. "She sort of made herself a part of the crew. In truth, she's proved rather indispensable. But she does have her own agenda."

"What do you mean?" Sarah asked.

"Well, she has a laboratory set-up in the High-Tech sector of Eros Tao. She barters for materiel, or buys it outright. Sometimes she simply steals from the ship's stores, and then she creates her own avatars. We have no idea how many avatars she's created. You've seen the little girl, and one of her standard model foot-soldiers. Those are only two of her avatars. We suspect she has a small army at her disposal hidden someplace here on Eros Tao, though we've no idea what to do about it. Fortunately, she has a fixation on the Captain. She's relatively non-hostile, save towards those she perceives as a threat."

"So, she perceived me as a threat then?" Sarah asked.

"No, I don't think so. If she perceived you as a threat, we would not be talking now. You have cyber-brain implants. If she truly wanted to harm you, she could have hacked your visual sensors and left you blind while she eviscerated you at her leisure."

"Then why the fight with her avatar?"

"I suspect it's just as she said, she was looking for data. She was sizing you up. If Doja really wants something dead, it usually ends up very dead, very fast."

"She fought me just to gain data?" Sarah asked. "Charming girl."

"Well, that's our Doja," Dorian replied.

"Weird."

"You have no idea."

There were people at work in the universe who were good, many who were evil, and a whole lot more who were generally too powerless and meek to form deep opinions on such matters as to what is good and what is evil. The most dangerous of all were the truly vile ones who by strength of will, of force, of cunning, catapulted themselves into positions of power, clawing, scrambling, and murdering along their way to the top. Power was intoxicating, addictive. It was its own reward. It was a means and an end. Of all the greatest powers, the most deliciously perverse, the most stunningly sacrilegious, in both the canons of moral philosophy and basic economics, was the power to destroy. To take a life was to cross a barrier that once broken past led the transgressor to madness or enlightenment, sometimes a disjointed mix. Every time a life was taken, there was no power in the universe that could reverse such an act. Once the line was crossed, one could never return to that previous state of relative innocence.

Governor Kromm was addicted to the acquisition and exercise of power. He enjoyed destruction as cruelty gave his mind a focus and peculiar energy. He was the political leader of a region that encompassed twelve populated star systems. He had attained this position via political auction. Quite simply, he had outbid his competition and bought his public office outright. The model of political auctioneering had been adopted some time ago as it accomplished the same result as a representative, republican form of government, only it was more efficient. What was more, once the people were fully divorced from the process of choosing their leaders or effecting policy in any significant manner, they were liberated from the confusion and distress that attached to freedom of choice.

Governor Kromm, or, more accurately, Lord Sebatius Modelo Oneveto Kunestus Kromm was a self-styled, self-appointed master of his own domain, and a notorious addict of violence. He was a horrible child who evolved into a hideous man, and as his strength increased, he evolved into a horrible monster, a spectacle, as charismatic and charming as he was unforgiving and treacherous. Routinely he engaged in activities that would have made DeSade weep like a frightened child.

Kromm had started life as an orphan on Taarna IV. It was a hardscrabble youth. He had participated in all manner of criminal enterprise from drugs to prostitution to strong-arm robbery. Life was filled with odd twists of fate and circumstance, and it was by such powers that by his late teen he'd obtained a job as a page in a newsroom. Within twenty years he owned the publication. Within thirty years he owned seventy percent of the media outlets in his region of space. He was not a graduate of any school of journalism and had a deep-seated suspicion of the role the media played in open democracies.

His inflammatory personal style of management soon inflamed every manager down the line, and his media empire strayed far away from objective journalism, or any concept of operating as a check against unlimited governmental power. It soon became a mouthpiece for concentrated wealth, and little more.

Along his way to the top, Kromm had wiped out many of his enemies. This was traditional and should not be viewed as criminal rather it was modern real politik. No self-respecting despot was without his long list of vanquished foes. Kromm was quite conventional in this and many other matters.

Lord Kromm had few enemies left, few that mattered. Of those few, Germaine was the most vexing. The Saint, as he often called himself, was more than a nuisance. Germaine was a self-indulgent, self-righteous, pompous ass who'd intervened in Kromm's affairs more than a few times. While Kromm had few equals in the art of propaganda, Germaine was clearly the superior when it came to message control and triangular, often multi-triangular diplomacy, and message control. Both men were involved in their personal game of monopoly, and so far, Germaine had outwitted his opponent at every turn. This would soon change. For reasons unknown, and largely immaterial, Kromm had recently fallen into bed with the Ven-Dhavaradi, old business partners of Germaine. The Ven-Dhavaradi were powerful allies.

Kromm's new allies, his silent business partners, wanted Germaine to remain unmolested for now. In time, they said, Germaine would no longer matter and Kromm could, with their assistance, kill him at his leisure. For the moment, though, Germaine was to serve a purpose. Kromm's role in the matter would remain subtle and hidden for the time being.

He was consumed by his thoughts on the matter as his vessel tore through the atmosphere of the large blue planet below. His vessel was tremendous, its hull completely smooth, covered in shiny black alloys. It was triangular in shape, each side two hundred meters in length. The sound of thunderclaps could be heard as the vessel's anti-gravity emitters rippled through the atmosphere. Accompanied by a rather large display of aerial assault vessels swooping over the crowd, Kromm's vessel touched down on the tarmac of Bellendra Three.

The skyport was on lock-down three hours prior to his arrival. All of the guests had been thoroughly searched. A full regiment of Bellendra's soldiers stood at attention, wearing the red and yellows of the honor guard, while a delegation of local drummers danced and banged out a carefully choreographed blend of percussion and movement while adorned in the traditional animal skins of their predecessors.

The people of Bellendra were superstitious and wildly anarchistic when they weren't protected from themselves by the outside imposition of law and order. The noblest among them gave praise to the concept of a social compact and the rule of law, though they might decry the particular version as it had been applied to their planet and the rape of its resources. A minority of the population secretly longed for the days when they roamed the jungle paths barefoot and hunted wild boars with poison tipped spears.

On this day, the natives were festive, those that were present at least. The drummers held their ritually painted instruments between their knees and banged out a complex, primal rhythm on the dried animal hide. Their dark-skinned bodies glistened with sweat in the sunlight.

The planet's leader, appointed by Kromm because of his ability to steer large amounts of contributions into

Kromm's 'campaign' coffers, was more than eager to show off a flashy and brilliant welcoming display to pay homage his master.

Despite the manufactured cheerfulness surrounding the situation, there were several dozen points surrounding the skyport where snipers targeted anything moving out of the ordinary. Cloaked drone ships patrolled the skies on a hair trigger. The effusiveness of the crowd notwithstanding, it was a dangerous role to be the governor of such a large region of space. There were many malcontents and elements that would do him harm.

After the vessel touched down, a hatchway opened on the fuselage and a set of stairs descended to the tarmac. Several members of his personal security detail exited the vessel first. Dressed in black, and carrying powerful assault weaponry, they each took a position in a semi-circle before their energy-linked bodies could form the circuit for a mobile protective force-field. After assessing the situation, their commander sent a communiqué back to the ship. Kromm soon emerged to a tremendous roar of applause. The drummers stopped their beating and fell to their faces while the soldiers went from parade rest to full attention. Kromm saluted the audience with his one handed wave. He then shook hands and briefly embraced the short, oily skinned gentleman he had appointed to run the planet. Media from several reputable outfits recorded the footage. After a few kind words were exchanged, both men headed away from the ship and towards a large square concrete building. The security detail blanketed the pair, and every movement was carefully controlled. Once the men disappeared into the building, Kromm broke off with his detail and headed to a lower level via a set of elevators. The photo-op and appearance was perfunctory. Although ostensibly he had come to the planet to negotiate an extension of an arms control treaty between Bellendra and a neighbor, the issue had long been dispensed with behind the scenes via shuttle diplomacy. The treaty was designed by Kromm's analysts and it would be enforced. The concept that either side had any say in the matter was a concept largely manufactured for political purposes. It gave both of his hand-picked representatives some measure of dignity and credibility.

What was most significant in Kromm's mind was the fact that his role in the matter was concluded. He didn't like to spend more than fifteen minutes on that planet. For all its resources, the planet had never produced anything resembling a proper, civilized government. Its population was largely complicit in the slave trade that gave the whole place a dark reputation. Its people were hot-blooded, too many hormones. They were a violent, hyper-sensual species who enjoyed the prospect of tearing a leader to pieces as much as they might enjoy any particular sport.

He couldn't have felt better about his prospect of leaving the place. Within minutes he was inside a matter-transference facility, and a few seconds after that, his body was rematerializing on a planet ten thousand light years away from Bellendra. A clone would take his place at the negotiations table to keep the media happy.

Truth was, he never stayed anywhere for long. This routine kept his enemies guessing, and it made assassination attempts practically impossible. This was desirable for many reasons. Once attaining his position, there were only two ways out: resignation, or death. Kromm being a long-lived being who enjoyed his rise to prominence was not a likely candidate to concede his governorship to another predator. He was enjoying the fruits of power too much to ever willingly abdicate to anyone. One of his favorite privileges as an elected official was the fact that he could never be investigated for insider trading, even though it was traditional that a person in his position would, along with his cronies, engage in insider trading all the time, even gaming the system in their favor to insure their investments. It was fun to be the king, or in his case, the governor.

Once he was back to the planet that housed the concentration of his bureaucratic powers, he set about dealing with a matter of personal significance.

Kromm exited the matter-transference alcove and was immediately greeted by his official entourage. Each of them paid their respects, and in response he nodded his approval. He had representatives from his finance minister, from his labor minister, all the way down the line. Each of the creatures in an orderly procedure, long since decreed by fiat, apprised him of the prominent matters of the day. They were granted two minutes, no more, no less, to fully brief him on the larger outline and finer points of a host of difficult situations. From time to time he would interject a pointy question, or issue a decree, but for the most part, he absorbed everything without more than a few words.

Accompanied by only one voice at a time, he walked the hallways of the tremendous island citadel with his entourage of thick necked guards and thin necked sycophants. The walls were covered with unique, priceless mosaics he'd obtained by subjugating a variety of rather artistic species. The moldings atop the sandstone walls, and high arches were embellished with several ornate flourishes. He had a habit of enslaving artisans. After their usefulness had evaporated, he would find novel methods for crushing their soul, breaking them before destroying them utterly.

Centuries before he had arrived on the planet and set up shop, the fortress had been built by a race highly advanced in the methods and manners of defending crude siege, as well as the more subtle aspects of true artisanship. Hundreds of sculptors and masons had worked on the arches lining the hallways in fanatic devotion to the god, Mhota. The citadel he called home was a massive enterprise undertaken by a species now dead. It was a dark place, and he was a dark person. There beneath the veil of perpetual purple cloud cover and lightning storms, in a place once devoted to worship and humility, he did unspeakable things.

Tempres was a grim, rainy planet with a cool atmosphere that never summered or wintered, just the same gray drizzle season after season. Tempres was the seat of power for his private fiefdom at the edge of the Mellaran Galaxy. Apart from the usual anomalies and curiosities that attended any particular region of space, the area around Tempres was known for one striking fact: there had never, ever, in the in the whole of recorded history, been a successful stand-up comedian to come from that part of the universe. It was as though humor was just beaten out of the poor bastards.

The wicked, crashing sound of thunder could be heard through the facility as the electrical storms increased during the night cycle when the temperatures cooled. The frequent storms suited him just fine. He thought of himself as something beyond good and evil, something more natural. Just as the storm represented powerful forces of nature, so did his existence. Life favored the predators, the quick and the cunning. Life was not sentimental, it was brutal – just as he was.

Eventually, Kromm arrived in front of a tall set of stone doors with intricate symbols carved on the face. The door handles were polished brass with fine wood insets. There was no sign of technology. This was an ancient place.

"Leave me," Kromm said.

The circle of sycophants dissipated instantly leaving only two brutally armed guards to stand outside the doorway.

Kromm entered alone.

As he crossed the threshold, the doors closed behind him and locked with a loud clicking sound that reverberated off the stone walls of the open chamber. The room he entered had shelves of books, old tomes lining the walls, a low burning fire inside a stone fireplace, a desk carved out of finely polished blackwood. This was his personal study. He moved behind the desk and placed his hand upon the back of the leather chair. He thumped his fingers in a roll atop the back of the chair.

In front of the desk, seated in a deep leather chair was a worn out looking man with a slight tremor that showed every time he moved his hands or tilted his neck.

"Mr. Harold," Kromm said. "So glad you could join us."

"Milord," the man replied, trying an awkward half-smile but quickly giving up on the effort.

"Would you care for something to drink?" Kromm asked, strolling casually over to a wet bar. He grabbed a crystal decanter and poured a brownish red liquid into a rock glass.

"No thank you. I've not got the stomach for it," Harold replied politely.

"Pity, a good whiskey is one of life's more simple pleasures."

"Milord, I apologize for…"

"Tssk." Kromm interrupted. "You're apologizing and I've not had a chance to scold you first. Do not speak out of turn, Mr. Harold. It is impolite. Besides, there'll be plenty of time for you to repent your wicked little ways, Mr. Harold, plenty of time indeed."

"Milord, I…"

"Didn't think you'd ever be caught," Kromm interjected. "You've no other truth to sell. You thought you would get away with it, but you didn't, and now we have a situation on our hands. What am I to do with you? It's a difficult question. You are quite valuable when you are not conspiring against my interests.

The man looked on in stunned silence. He'd just hit the proverbial brick wall, and he knew it.

"Tell me, Mr. Harold, if you had to guess, how many roosters do you think it would take to kill a man in say one hour?" Kromm asked with a trace of malicious amusement.

"I've no idea," the man replied.

"Take a wild guess. Spit out a number," Kromm prodded.

"I don't know, twenty or thirty should do it."

"A number, Mr. Harold, I want a number."

The man shook his head. His body was quivering slightly. "Thirty-two," he answered.

"Thirty-two. That's a good number. Thirty-two," Kromm smiled. "Would you mind standing up and moving towards the fireplace, Mr. Harold. I can't see your eyes very well from where you are sitting. I should very much like to see your eyes."

At that second, with a sound like dozens of blades scraped across stone, Angel Eyes shimmered into existence a couple of paces to the side of Kromm's desk, punctuating the seriousness of the request.

"Ah, there you are," Kromm said. He turned to Angel Eyes. "How many roosters do you think it would take to kill a man in less than an hour?" Kromm asked.

Angel Eyes was silent, a statue of steel and menace.

"He doesn't talk much," Kromm explained. "They say that if an outsider ever hears the voice of a Tellaran, it will be the last thing they ever hear. Now, Mr. Harold, if you would kindly oblige me."

The man named Mr. Harold stumbled slightly when he got up from the chair. He was smart enough to know where this was headed, but he didn't have a whisper of a chance at stopping it. He moved over to a position in front of the fireplace and stood silently while Kromm stared at him.

"I am going to say forty," Kromm stated.

"Forty?" Mr. Harold replied, confused.

"I think it will take forty free-range roosters, their hormones all jacked up, and their bodies ravaged by hunger and thirst. I'll say it takes forty of them to kill a man in just one hour," Kromm stated.

He pushed a red button on top of his desk and a trap door opened beneath Mr. Harold's feet. The man disappeared instantly down a deep shaft. The cock-a-doodle-doos of the roosters could be heard echoing from the bottom of the shaft. Soon, they were followed by the sounds of a man screaming out, shrieking in pain and misery. The trap-door closed, and Kromm turned to his agent, Angel Eyes. He was thinking of Germaine and the Nephyr.

In time, after Germaine had served his purpose, the VD promised Kromm he would be afforded the luxury of breaking the man. For now, Kromm had to bide his time and play his part. As for Germaine, when the dust settled, Kromm had a particularly exquisite demise in store.

"I take it Germaine has the girl?" Kromm asked.

Angel Eyes nodded almost imperceptibly.

Kromm turned away to the fireplace: "I want you following Germaine every step of the way. He doesn't clean up after himself very well. You will cover his tracks."

Angel Eyes nodded and shimmered for a second before disappearing entirely.

Germaine has the Nephyr, Kromm pondered. What will he do with her? Several minutes later, he pushed a button on his desk and activated the intercom. He could hear Mr. Harold yelling and struggling, making all those grunting noises people do when they're about to lose their life. It was a horrible way to die. To be a true sadist, one had to have a streak of creativity. Kromm's was a streak a mile wide. He smiled broadly as he spoke into the intercom microphone.

"Forty-seven, Mr. Harold!" Kromm called out loudly so his voice could be heard above the din. "It looks like its going to take forty-seven roosters to kill you in under one hour! A very interesting number, don't you think?!" he yelled into the intercom. "That's forty-seven roosters, Mr. Harold, not thirty-two!"

Chapter Four

Hunting for Gremlins

Dorian did as he said he would. After she finished her meal, he escorted her back along the dirt road leading out of the marketplace and back to the black quartz portal atop the hill just outside the small city.

"Best we should be leaving," he said. "Low-Tech sector gets a little seamy when the lights go down."

"Seamy?"

"Well, a little more spiced up than usual. We're not in any danger. Most of the crime is organized, and the Captain has peace treaties with the local crime bosses. We're *protected* so to speak."

"Weird."

"Not terribly so. It's merely one of the privileges of owning sixty percent of the property in Eros Tao."

"Doja seems to have some designs on his monopoly," Sarah responded.

"Doja has all kinds of designs," Dorian responded. "Still, when the chips are down, Doja comes through. She's good in a tight situation."

Dorian reached out and placed his hand against the side of the portal aperture.

"Computer, align portal aperture for transport to the Cortez," he said.

Just as Sarah realized the command was telepathic, she was distracted from the thought.

The stone door opened, but this time before she was hit with the terrible sucking sensation, she had something to place between her teeth. Dorian had handed her a small length of thick, red braided twine. She bit down on it hard as the sucking sensation hit her chest. Interestingly, the twine helped combat the disorienting and painful stretching process. She landed on the other side of the portal, back now in one of the halls of the ship, on the other side of a metal door. This time, she was far less disheveled.

"Your body will gradually get accustomed to the matter-transfer. You'll build up some mental resistance to the pain," Dorian explained.

"I don't think I'll ever get used to it," Sarah replied.

"Perhaps not, but it will become steadily less agonizing. Come, let's get to the bridge."

"Yeah, right," Sara responded. She had a lot of questions she wanted to ask Germaine, and she was feeling both the need and the confidence to confront him.

Sarah followed Dorian through several empty corridors until they approached a heavily shielded door. Again, they went through a biometrics scan before the doors opened.

Once inside, Sarah marched straight up to Germaine.

"We need to talk," she said, her anger quite visible. Her face was flushed, and she was feeling as though she should perhaps slap him. "In private."

"Of course we do," Germaine replied. "Come, let's go to my Ready Room...its where I get ready for things, like commanding and...things. Also, I keep my prize fish Fidel there. He's grown rather big of late. I suspect it's the fried chicken and gravy diet."

"Come on," Sarah replied impatiently, grabbing his right arm.

Capoella turned to Dorian, but he simply rolled his eyes. Germaine led Sarah towards a door at the far end of the command center. The doors slid open, and he let her to enter before him, the consummate gentleman. After the pair left, Capoella initiated video surveillance of the Ready Room.

"I doubt she'll engage in hostilities," Dorian said.

"Better safe than sorry," Capoella replied.

"Fair enough, Capoella. I'll be in my chambers should you need me."

"I can handle things," Capoella replied.

On the other side of the doors, Germaine took his place behind a large cherry-oak desk, finished to a perfect sheen.

"So what's on that tremendous mind of yours?" he asked.

"Why did you let Doja take me to her teahouse?" Sarah growled. "Were you hoping she would take me out?"

"Hmm, Would you like a drink? I'm in the mood for a stiff vodka martini."

"You're always in the mood for a stiff martini."

"That's rather uncharitable of you, Sarah. It would seem the little fight with Doja has your nerves up."

"You better believe it does. Why did you let it happen?"

Germaine shrugged and spun around once in his chair before kicking his feet up onto the desk. "Well, the way I figure it, sooner or later you were going to have to learn how to deal with Doja. We've all had to work out our relationships with Doja. In truth, I couldn't have protected you from her forever even if I tried. She's quite cunning, and quite relentless when she is determined to do something."

"She attacked me...with one of her *avatars*."

"Yes, well, I suspected she'd do something like that. She's never content with someone else's data. She always likes to determine things on her own. For an artificial intelligence, she's more alive than most of us. Doja lives to try out new things. And she's always changing herself, learning, growing. Doja gathers her own empirical data and then sets up her own dynamic models of what she calls 'Life-Systems'. It's a sort of Systems Dynamics on steroids. They're really quite impressive models."

"You didn't warn me!"

"No, why spoil the surprise? Besides, I knew Doja wouldn't harm you."

"I have several bruises and cuts that show how harmless she is."

"Just that, though, cuts and bruises. Come on, Sarah. Tell me you didn't enjoy the fight? I know you can't say that. You got a kick out of it, didn't you?"

"Yes," Sarah replied honestly.

"Of course you did. Win or lose, it doesn't matter. When a being enters into a fight, they test themselves, and they resolve it. Crisis and immediate resolution. In the arena, all doubts are resolved, all angst driven out in the heat of combat. It is a purifying experience. Tell me you did not feel pure, then I'll apologize."

Sarah let her mind drift back to the emotions she had felt earlier during the combat with Doja. "You're right. I don't know. You're right. Why am I so good at fighting? How does this fit into your analysis?"

"I don't know much about your species. No one really does. I suspect that as your species was super-evolved, they were pretty good predators at some point in their history, which therefore means they were probably good at committing violent acts."

"I enjoyed that fight. I don't know if that is the proper reaction."

"Don't judge it. It is what it is."

"How about you? Do you enjoy combat?"

"In my own way, yes. I like to combat the social order."

"What does that even mean?" Sarah asked. "It sounds like childish anarchistic nonsense."

"Maybe, but somebody has got to take action to keep the pointy heads inside the establishment somewhat in line."

"So how does someone like you keep the pointy heads in line."

"Innumerable ways, to be honest. I target democratic elections, expose secrets, make documentaries, engage in space piracy, rumor planting, and financial guer-rilla warfare. Most of my investment pranks target the Bureaucracy, the ICPT. They're the most perverted estab-lishment the universe ever bore witness to. I hyper-inflate various economic sectors just to give the commodities analysts huge, gnawing ulcers. Every twenty or thirty years I create a hyper speculative bubble in the commodities markets and watch the whole thing go boom."

"That's immoral."

"Not really. It curtails some of the ICPT's more ambi-tious war efforts. Taken over a long time horizon, my efforts have succeeded in saving over seventeen trillion innocent civilians from being slaughtered by the machi-nations of the hyper-capitalists. How's that for immoral? All I do is come in through the back-doors my lobbyists create, and wreak a little havoc from time to time. I've more than enough capital to spare for the effort, and on top of everything, it simply amuses me to stick it to the bad guys time and time again."

"'So Eros Tao, the banking operations, that's how you finance the whole thing?'

"Well, I didn't start off in the gutter. It took a lot of resources to create the place as you can well imagine.

Getting the engineers in places to set up white-hole inter-
faces, pumping in the raw matter and then converting it
into a living breathing city-state with its own self-sustain-
ing resources, it was quite the feat. Now that it is done, I
can enjoy the profits of being the majority stakeholder in
all of the private banks set-up in the High-Tech Sector. I
make more money in a day than most post-industrialized
economies make in a year"

"So you decided to take your wealth and target this
bureaucracy as you call it."

"That's Bureaucracy with a capital 'B'," he replied.

She could only respond with a confused stare.

"Look, it's a chess match between my pepole and
theirs, my resources and skills pitted against their
resources and skill. I wouldn't target them if they weren't
so corrupt."

"How so?'

"Well, they run things, most things in this universe
actually," he replied. "They don't call themselves the
Bureaucracy, of course. They're the unelected public
servant sector that really runs things, the administrative
arm of the Intergalactic Collective of Peaceful Types,
or ICPT. They're appointed by the political branch of
government, which is in turn completely corrupted by
the hyper-capitalists that arose when marginal income
taxes were slashed from ninety percent to thirty-five percent and capital gains taxes were eliminated. The ICPT
has long since deviated from it initial charter to bring
peace throughout the universe. Calling themselves the
Intergalactic Collective of Peaceful Types is pure propaganda as they're responsible for the majority of wars
going on out there. War is good for business, and business is good."

"Sounds like a charming bunch," Sarah responded.

"They're a devious bunch of bastards to put it delicately. There isn't a trace of conscience in the whole of the breed, save those few who are my internal spies.

"You have spies within the ICPT?"

"Of course I do, that's how I found about you. Any self-respecting trillionaire has an army of spies at his disposal. Who am I to buck the trend."

"I'll take a pass on trying to understand that statement. Back to this Bureaucracy, why are you targeting them?"

"Well, they are in charge of so much of the known universe that they run things for most of the rest by implicative logic. They have resources of a type and nature almost beyond comprehension. Their main charge is to determine which civilizations are allowed to evolve past the Bellosian Curve, and which ones die out."

"Explain."

"It's simple. All civilizations go through a stage where their technological growth expands exponentially while their political structures and social understanding languish behind. This is the Bellosian Curve Differential. Without intervention most civilizations exterminate themselves before they are smart enough to figure out how they were doing it. They do it with plastics, pthalates, fossil fuels, pick your poison. Nuclear energy, biowarfare, greenhouse gases. Most civilizations would die out if there wasn't some sort of intervention at some point. That's where the Bureaucracy comes in."

"How?"

"They determine which civilizations receive help and which don't. There's only a limited amount of resources, so only a limited number of civilizations can be saved. At least, that's their rationale. Truth is, its all about politics. It always is."

"They determine who lives and who dies."

"Yes, the Bureaucracy."

"Wow that really is perverse. So how do they do it? What are the criteria for a civilization that receives assistance versus one that doesn't?"

"Funny you should ask. You see, there could never be a consensus on what the criteria should be. So, in the end they decided to utilize what amounts to a lottery process to determine which planets receive assistance and who craps out."

"A lottery?"

"It was the only equitable answer – that was the argument. All other measures were deemed too subjective. The species that originated the ICPT believed that chance reveals the mind of the Nephyr, or some such nonsense. They built the largest Bureaucracy ever seen to administer this Lottery and protect the civilizations that got lucky while watching the unlucky die out."

"So planets live and die dependent upon random chance?" Sarah asked.

"It's what they call the Cosmic Lottery," the Captain replied. "Perverted, huh?"

"So how do I fit in this picture?"

"Well, Sarah. We were hoping you could help us out on that one. Your amnesia is a particularly troubling concern of ours. We need to unlock your memories to figure out why you are here. The only thing for certain is that you did not arrive here by chance, and after seven billion years absence, the reappearance of a Nephyr in this universe has some rather dire implications attached to the matter. Best for now that you stick here with us, here among friends, until we can figure this out."

At that moment, a voice interrupted. It was Capoella speaking over the ship board communication network. "Just an FYI, Captain, we've got two gremlins materializing on level twenty-three, crew quarters. Strike that, we've got four intruders. Strike again, six signatures. Definitely gremlins."

"Shut off every hatchway on that deck. Flood the area with Neurocene."

"Atmospherics are off-line. They anticipated out first move, Captain," Capoella replied.

"No, they just got lucky. It's a hunt then. Come on, Sarah, let's get to the armory," Germaine grinned impishly.

"What?"

"We're going to go after a group of horrible nasty aliens with hairy, gnarled green faces, and thick black body armor," he smiled.

"Why in the hell would I want to do that?" Sarah asked. She was genuinely alarmed. Her eyes were wide with anxiety and surprise. Surely he must be joking?

"Come on, Sarah. It will be fun."

"What are you talking about?" she exclaimed.

"Do you know the good thing about blasting some nasty, hairy alien with a particle disrupter beam?"

"No, what's so good about it?" she asked hesitantly.

"Well, you can do it without feeling as though you harmed your Karma. These bastards live to rip things up and generally act nasty. Blasting them is not only in our best interests, but in the best interests of the universe writ large. It's a moral imperative, and good target practice to boot."

"We're hunting gremlins,"

"Six of them. Nasty buggers. Come on, let's get guns, big guns."

Sarah was forced to follow his lead. "Fine, lead the way."

He had a frat boy humor about him, and he appeared utterly fearless, so Sarah had to take his cue and simply play along. He led the way out of the room and across the wide deck of the bridge to a far doorway where they then entered a lift.

As the doors were closing Capoella called out: "Have fun, you two."

As they headed towards the armory, Sarah asked: "What are gremlins anyway?"

"Well," he answered. "They're big and green, and muscly, and nasty. They love to sort of mangle things. There are more than a few species in the universes who find it amusing to send a matter-transference beam filled with the bastards onto an unsuspecting ship."

"Really,"

"Yeah, the universe is filled with pranksters," he sighed. "I guess I can't complain. I did stuff like this when I was a kid."

"You sent matter transference beams carrying gremlins onto unsuspecting space ships as a childhood prank."

"Well, I grew them first in vats. I mean, there was some education going on."

He led them to an open room, and after dialing in a code into a wall interface, the far wall disappeared leaving a large assortment of weaponry from small pistols, to large heavy guns. Everything was stacked in orderly rows, backlit with white fluorescent light. It was an impressive display. Many of the weapons looked quite fierce.

"We'll want two self-reloading, recoilless assault rifles, short barrel for close-quarter combat. Hmm," he pondered for a moment before reaching into the cache and pulling out two fierce looking black guns. "These will do nicely. High-velocity electro-shock rounds so you get a one-shot take-down." He handed one of the guns to Sarah. "Perfect. Come on. Let's go get some gremlins."

Sarah hefted the weapon. It was lighter than it looked. As she touched the trigger, a red light appeared on a far wall. She aimed the barrel towards a small computer interface on the side wall. Without needing any explanation, she knew how to hold the weapon perfectly. Germaine noticed this, but he made no comment.

"Come on," Germaine said. "We need to get in position."

"What's the plan?"

"Sneak up, then blast them. Why…you got anything better?"

"You've done this before?" she asked.

"Sure. This is routine," he smiled.

He led them down several hallways before stopping and kneeling down on one knee to remove a panel in the ventilation shaft. He reached inside and deactivated a force-field.

"Come on."

He waved her into the narrow entrance, and then followed behind, sliding the grate back into place. She found herself in a crawl-space that stretched out as far as the eye could see. The Cortez' ventilation shafts were dozens of miles long, winding all through the ship. Germaine pushed his way past her, moving on his elbows and knees with the rifle slung on his back. She had no idea what he meant about sneaking up on the green bastards, but she found his enthusiasm infectious.

The idea, although strange at first, of blasting some nasty alien miscreants was starting to appeal to her. As she crawled behind him, she found that she liked the idea more and more. They were going to sneak up on some gruesome, terrible creatures and then blast them. It had a rather primitive quality to it that she found intriguing. She started to think that Germaine was perhaps less a lunatic, but more a sort of brazen adolescent, content with submerging himself in puerile games.

As they made their way through the cramped crawl-spaces, he suddenly stopped.

"Shhh," he whispered. "They're right below us."

She was about to ask how he knew that, but then the smell hit her. It was the terrible stench of wet, spoiled garbage wrapped in horrible sweat socks.

"Gremlins," he explained in a whisper. "Come on."

A group of creatures passed beneath them. They were cloaked in tough black body armor, their faces were distorted, mangled messes, wide and nasty. Their heads were as crumpled green jack-o-lanterns, their eyes black slits amidst a pile of green sludge. Each of them was over six feet in height, and their frames were rippled with grizzly muscles. They were menacing.

The pack was tearing into the bulkheads and shredding the cables, not operating in any prescribed fashion so much as they resembled a clumsy, barbaric collection of idiot dogs.

He took them a little further through the shaft before stopping.

"All right, this is the plan. You jump down through this entrance and get their attention. When they come rushing towards you, I'll come down from behind and take out the remaining baddies."

"Not a bad idea," Sarah replied. "Only, I figure with your experience, you ought to be the first one down."

"Hmmph, well, you're right."

"You can trust me, Captain. You draw them towards you, and the ones you don't get, I'll clean up."

Germaine seemed to take an extra second to stare at her there in the virtual darkness of the tiny corridor. He looked down at the metal screen beneath his feet.

"Count to three, and then come down through the screen blasting. Watch your firing patterns though."

"Piece of cake," she replied.

She crawled into position several paces away over the top of another ventilation screen and waited. Germaine paused until the group was between the area of the ventilation screens, then he dropped down.

As he landed on the tile, he drew his rifle to ready position.

"Howdy-doody, boys!" he yelled.

He began firing immediately. In front of him was the large mass of gnarly creatures, unintelligent, utterly bent on despoliation and destruction. They charged him instinctively. He tried to lay down suppression fire, but he could only down two of the creatures before the remaining group held their unconscious cadres up as shields. Then they came at him as a wall of flesh.

"Huh," he muttered. "Smart gremlins."

He turned on his heels and ran zigzag through the hall, trying to find cover.

At that moment, Sarah crashed through the ventilation grate and down behind the turned backs of the four remaining gremlins.

"Eat plasma!" Sarah yelled, suddenly aware that she didn't really know how accurate the statement was.

Regardless, she fired in a precise pattern that left only two of four remaining creatures standing. Before she could subdue the entire group, though, one managed to rush her successfully. He hit her with a full shoulder block, sending her reeling to the ground, her weapon cast to the side, clacking on the tiles.

The creature stood over her and growled, while its sole companion moved slowly towards Germaine.

She rolled, dodging a heavy boot. As she made her way to her knees, she swiped out with a heel-hook catching the creature's back leg just as he stepped forward. Her speed brought him off his feet and onto his back.

She shoulder-rolled to her right side, scrambling for her weapon. As the creature found its footing, she brought the barrel level to his forehead and fired.

Instantly, the creature slumped down, unconscious and immobilized.

She stepped over the body and leveled the barrel at the remaining gremlin, motioning for it to back away from Germaine. It growled fiercely for a moment, catching her with its simple, predator eyes. It wanted her, but it wanted life more. Slowly it backed away.

"You got five seconds to start talking before I switch the auto-selector to a more lethal setting and send you to Gremlin Jesus for a little one-on-one," she said coolly. Her instinct was to appear as formidable as she could. "Who sent you?"

By this time, Germaine had made his way to his feet. He picked up his rifle and locked the barrel at the creature's head from the opposite direction, then he pulled the trigger, ending the inquiry. The creature slumped to its knees and then fell over sideways, out cold.

"Gremlins don't do well under interrogation," he explained. "They mostly grunt, and gnaw at their own limbs. Besides, I suspect this is just a practical joke to welcome us to the Berion system." He stepped over the gremlin. "Gremlins are just pranks, the kind of bad comedy, jostles and other indignities every space-faring being has to deal with at some point."

Sarah looked out over the display of broken, unconscious bodies.

"Some joke," she replied.

"Like I said, the universe is a tough place. There's little room for the meek out there in the predatory climate that marks modern reality. Still, that was a bit of fun, wasn't it?"

"Well, it wasn't entirely horrible," she conceded.

"Quite right," he said. "Nasty, irredeemable, brutish creatures are fun to blast, especially when they are making a mess of things and you have good reason to blast

them. Come on. We're about to dock with a space station. I'll need to get some parts and make some repairs
after the gremlin attack."

"Why don't you get the parts on Eros Tao?"

"Because, then I'd have no cover to do a little investi-
gating at the way station."

"You are going to try and find out who sent the gremlins, aren't you?" Sarah asked.

"Why are you so concerned about the gremlins.
Gremlins are a common nuisance, much like computer
viruses. Any third-grader with a basement laboratory and
access to a matter-transference beam can send out gremlins. Gremlins are an unfortunate fact of life. What I
need is more important. I need information."

"You mind if I tag along? I mean, I am good in a fight."

"You certainly are at that. But it's not safe right now. If
you want some excitement, though, I'll give you an escort
to the High-Tech sector on Eros Tao. You can have my
VIP Box tickets to the Speed-fighting championships."

"Speed-fighting?"

"No chemicals barred, just two artificially juiced-up
fighters, mood enhancements, trance-hypnotics, loads of
sub-dermal artificial adrenal glands. It's really vicious. I
think you'll love it."

"You really enjoy violence, don't you?" Sarah said.

Germaine smiled. He could have treated it as an
accusation, but he was more skilled than that.

"You know what the number one cause of death is
throughout the universes?" he asked.

"No, not likely," Sarah answered.

"Its heart disease. You know why?"

"No, but I sense you're prepared to tell me."

"All the great civilizations came from predator back-
grounds, just like I said. Simple, dull grazing species
never develop into advanced civilizations."

"And this means what?"

"If a conflict is not resolved, the emotions are suppressed, and the hormones involved in fight or flight become as poisonous free radicals, corrupting the system and leading to any number of pathologies, heart disease chief among them. Modern civilizations are poisonous to predatory beings. The protocols necessary to having any civilization also set the stage for heart disease, bottled up aggression turning cancerous. People need to fight to live healthy. Life is struggle. It's written into the DNA, and when people don't fight, they grow soft and they grow sick and they die."

"This doesn't make a bit of sense from a biological standpoint," Sarah responded.

"Perhaps, but I think a little life and death conflict every now and then is good for the soul. It purges the system and cleans out all the pipes. An old-fashioned fight is good for the spirit."

"This is why you run around the universe starting small fights here and there?" she asked.

"I certainly enjoy a good scrap. Conflict forges truth. I'm a highly educated political dissident with nearly limitless resources. If one knows the truth, one cannot hide from one's destiny."

"And you know the truth."

"No, not really. It was a bit of florid rhetoric. However, I do know many truths. I once worked for the other side, a venture capitalist and lawyer by trade, but eventually, like all sane beings, I snapped. Fortunately, I had the resources to make it work out rather well for myself."

"So, now you have a ship capable of interstellar travel, and a little city inside another dimension that you run for kicks."

"That about sums it up in terms of property rights, yes."

"It's a weird universe you have pulled me into," Sarah said.

They were standing over six unconscious 'practical jokes'. The gremlins were as lumps of armored clay.

"Don't be ungracious. It's terribly unattractive. Would you rather have died of old age in the hospital ward? That was your intended fate. Surely this reality is preferable? You've been here less than a day, and I'll bet you had more adventure than your whole life so far. I'll also wager you've learned a whole lot more about yourself than you could ever do on that hospital bed," he said.

Sarah thought over her experiences so far on the ship. At first blush, they were merely chaotic, but upon second look, she sensed a carefully executed order to the events. She realized that he was far less capricious than he carefully portrayed.

"So, what do we do about these fellows?" she asked.

"Don't worry. All modern spaceships come with automatic gremlin disposal functions. No one in their right mind would buy a ship without them."

"Don't tell me you're going to expel them into space."

"No, nothing so uncivilized. I'll put them to work scraping the carbon off the exhaust manifolds."

"Free slave-labor, nice."

"My god, you are contentious. Let's get out of here. I've got a full day ahead."

He headed down the hallway, and she followed. Several minutes later, they were back on the bridge.

"Did you enjoy yourselves?" Capoella asked as the pair entered.

"Lots of fun, good target practice," Germaine responded. "Capoella, could I have a word with you in my Ready Room."

"Of course."

"Please excuse us for a few moments, Sarah."

Sarah felt a little put-off, in the same way any person would. Being excluded from conversations, especially considering how much mystery she was surrounded by, did not make her feel comfortable.

She shrugged, and ordered a martini from the computer after the pair had left for the Ready-Room. Several minutes later, her drink arrived. Unfortunately, she was subjected to a mild assault as the android sent to serve her flung the martini glass immediately upon entering the bridge.

"Goddamned capitalist!" it screamed, before storming away angrily .

Behind the closed doors of the ready room, Capoella took a seat in the Captain's chair, while Germaine paced back and forth.

"Did you have to send six of them, six of the smarter ones?" he asked.

"Is that really why you asked me in here," Capoella asked.

"No. I enjoyed it. But it was a little excessive given the damage they caused."

"It was supposed to be. You wanted to see if the girl could handle weapons. Now you know. Besides, when we enter orbit at Berion seeking emergency VISAs for ship repair activities, no one will suspect that we damaged ourselves. And the damage is extensive enough for us to credibly claim that we need to see a parts dealer."

"Hmmm, you are very clever," Germaine said. "Very, very clever."

"You forgot to mention how sexy I am," Capoella replied.

"That's because I don't waste time with facts that are self-evident…you sexy goddess," he grinned.

Chapter Five

Making Crime Pay

Germaine and Capoella traveled alone down the exit ramp of the shuttle and onto the open floor of a tremendous hangar area cluttered with ships. They were both fully covered with the black body-armor of Ganymedian pilots, reflective black glass helmets, hip-high leather boots, no nonsense. Their bodies were temporarily proto-morphed so the bio-scans would read just as they wanted.

No one suspected them of any particular mischief as Ganymedians were notoriously secretive and paranoid. Ganymedians rarely showed their faces on alien turf. It was perfect cover, but not too perfect to defeat their purposes.

The pair made their way across an area several football fields in length, the ceiling a hundred meters above the floor lost in the crisscrossing steel of rafters and catwalks. They passed by several exotically shaped craft, from small, translucent, egg-like Shotan transports to long, sleek, green Nebulari island cruisers.

After a body-scan for parasites and dangerous bacteria, they passed through the customs gate and were permitted entry onto the concourse. It was basically a long, wide corridor, ultimately shaped like a donut with a diameter of fifty miles. It rotated around a needlepoint of office structures in order to provide artificial gravity. It was a truly massive facility built by a not-so advanced civilization that had killed itself off a long time ago. Crude, old-fashioned technology was evident everywhere from the exposed plumbing to the semi-filtered air that smelled more like a pig farm than a space station.

It was a standard model way station, leftover surplus hardware from an old, empire, held together by duct tape and optimism. Much like Eros Tao, it attracted its own variety of commerce, crime, and intrigue. Berion was on the fringe of the old Nethra Empire. Prospectors, gold hunters of a sort, frequented the station as a stepping off point before excursions into the ruins of the four nearby star systems: The Four Sisters.

Aboard the station, a service sector economy had developed, black market mostly, sex, drugs, and fast food, the staples of any deep space station economy.

Capoella and Germaine held hands from time to time, not for emotion's sake. They communicated with each other in the form of encoded DNA strands that could be reinterpreted by sub-dermal devices each one had in their fingertips. The decices were encrypted to read and transmit data to its sister device. It was military grade, the most advanced encryption technology available. Like most of Germaine's technology it was five to ten generations beyond so-called 'state of the art'

In this fashion, they were able to communicate with each other without the fear of their telepathy being spied on. As for the safety of verbal speech, they wouldn't dare to communicate anything important in that crude fashion unless they absolutely had to.

They entered the promenade of the station and waded into the heavy foot traffic. The space was adorned with colorful storefronts selling junk and antiques rummaged from the remains of a long dead civilization that had once called this area of space home. There were several low-lit bars that catered to the treasure hunting crowds, the prospectors who'd come in search of alien gold in the form of exotic technology hidden deep in the ruins, and those who'd lost their fortunes or more in the booby-trapped, alien landscapes. The universe was ugly and brutish, and a common response to the misery of it all, the broken dreams of childhood, all those missed chances, was to get heavily intoxicated. The place reeked of alcohol, and the air was heavy with the scent of burned psychotropic leaves and incense. And this was the "upscale" section.

The space station had its seedy side, but that was all the way on the other end of the ring from where they were standing, and it had terribly conspicuous signs in glowing red neon that marked its entry points. The signs read: "This is the seedy side of the space-station, enter with no illusions to the contrary."

Just as the governing council of the space-station had suspected, the placement of the signs boosted the tourist economy by three-hundred-percent in the first few years. This coupled with several scurrilous rumors about the spectrum of deviant behavior purveyed on the space-station for relatively low prices made the place a lucrative hub for sexual predators. The rumors had been placed, of course, by seedy advertising companies hired to do seedy things. As one grotesquely fat councilman was heard to say off the record: "Sin taxes are more politically palatable than income taxes, and, besides, who doesn't like a little sex slavery anyway?"

As Capoella and Germaine traveled with the crowd, they were both scoping the scenery, looking for signs that they were being monitored by things they would rather not be monitored by.

Capoella grasped his hand when they reached a juncture between two concourses. She relayed that she had spotted at least two possible agents, Di-Kho-Jhinns, small flashes of purple light flitting through the crowd on the upper level above the main concourse.

He replied with a signal that pointed out three more she hadn't spotted yet, taking up spots above them on the third level of the promenade.

Di-Kho-Jinns were trans-dimensional assassins. They were more subtle than shadows. If Germaine and Capoella hadn't been actively scanning for their presence, they would never have noticed their movements. Di-Kho-Jinns were crystalline entities, capable of slipping in and out of dimensions, compressing and expanding their forms at will, creating localized space-time slips and then wending their way through like snakes swimming in and out of dimensions. They were razor sharp when they struck out from a hidden dimensional tear, and one glancing blow could deliver enough exotic particle radiation to kill most standard carbon-based beings within a matter of minutes.

"Little heavy-handed for a backwater way-station, don't you think?" he asked.

She grabbed his hand and transmitted back, "This is gonna get real wet, real fast."

She had already contacted the ship and made provisions for back-up, but she couldn't tell for sure how long they were safe. The Di-Kho-Jinns appeared to be setting up a kill-box. Given their reputation, it was certain they wouldn't care about any civilian casualties as long as they got their target. Di-Kho-Jinns were among the universe's few true assassin breeds, smart enough to evolve past the Bellosian Curve without ICPT intervention, but fierce enough to never abandon the Way of the Assassin. They were perfectly evolved predators, and Germaine and Capoella knew they were in their sights.

They ducked past a row of small vendors selling trinkets and clothing, down a narrow alleyway and then through a thick wooden door into a small restaurant crowded with a decidedly geriatric crowd of old, disinterested aliens, refugees from the Medicare wars. The pair moved quickly through the dining area, and then they pushed their way through the kitchen and out through a backdoor into another alley. For the briefest moment, they eluded their pursuers. They were moving as fast as they could, ducking in and out and out of the foot traffic. Unfortunately, optical camouflage wouldn't hide their energy signatures from the assassins.

Eventually they arrived at the place they were looking for, the Café Obscura Ten-Swe. They entered through an open door into a throng of frenetic, loud, drunken activity. The bar was shaped like a hollowed out circle surrounded by suspended holo-projections of a variety of local sports. Six bartenders manically bounced about inside the round bar, shoveling drinks to an endless set of thirsty aliens.

Capoella stood guard at the door observing the traffic outside, while Germaine approached the manager in charge of the establishment. Communicating telepathically with Doja, Capoella learned that the bar's security cams and other devices were completely hacked. The security grid was thoroughly corrupted. With a hand-signal, Capoella let Germaine know that it was okay to remove his helmet.

The club owner, a local Mafioso type named Fajo, was a thin, long-limbed creature with a pock-marked face and dark greasy, slick-backed hair, his skin as pale as junkie. He was wearing an awkward, but expensive dark suit that tried to contradict how ratty and grotesque his face was.

He was a hideous sight. A few words, hidden beneath the crowd's noise, were exchanged. A minute later, Germaine was following Fajo through a doorway into the back areas. Capoella watched as two heavies emerged from the crowd to fall in several paces behind. She activated her optical camouflage, shimmering into obscurity, then she proceeded to shove someone up over the rail of the bar while smashing another with a backhanded fist. In the bustle that naturally followed, she trailed Germaine through the doorway and down an empty hall, though she refrained from interfering just yet.

In an office area not more than hundred square feet in dimension, Fajo and Germaine sat across from each other, a cheap metal office desk between them. The walls were adorned with old faded advertisements from rock bands that had toured the station, autographed photos depicting old-school, C-list celebrities whose only significance was that they had somehow achieved the status of celebrity. It felt like a cheesy place trying to pretend that it somehow had class, that its class should be deduced from the celebrities who had passed through to have their photo taken in exchange for a free steak and a bunch of cheap rail drinks.

Life was filled with strange, individual survival plans, Germaine inwardly remarked. Truth was, the economist in him would demand that he exchange his autograph for a free steak and whiskey. It made sense. Selling out made sense. However, it was still a horrible affair. It should be noted that the adolescent idealist in him thoroughly despised the inner economist in him. They went to war often with mixed results.

"So, why does the famous Saint Germaine come to my little bar here at the ass-end of the universe?" Fajo asked, lighting a thin black cigar he produced from a desk drawer. The smell was noxious. "What can a lowly person such as myself do for someone of your pedigree."

"Well, it should be said at the outset that I don't normally do business with drug-dealing psychopaths such as yourself. The problem is you know something I need to know. And so, here I am."

Fajo smiled. His thin lips pulled back to reveal orange colored teeth flecked with black tobacco. "What's on your mind?"

"I'm looking for Den Folo?"

"How much does he owe you?"

"This isn't about a debt. I need to find him."

"Love to help," Fajo said, puffing out a huge cloud of smoke. "But I haven't seen him in weeks. He disappears every time his bar tab gets a little high, then he comes back flush with credit. He freelances for Kromm, the Devren Corporate, anybody who'll foot his bill."

"You're not handling his business anymore?"

"No way. He's a total freak-job. It's more profitable to keep him off the payroll than on."

"Who's handling him now?"

"Couldn't tell you. I don't think anyone's got a pimp collar on that whacko. He got wiggy a few months back, more wiggy than usual. Tells me about some frigging war about to happen. Everything's dead, he says. Then he storms out. I've no idea where he headed from here."

"When was the last time he was on the station?"

"It's been at least two months since he's been aboard this station, maybe more. I don't keep track of people."

"Sure you do. It's your business."

The two heavies standing in the background were clearly uncomfortable. They were itching to do what they did best, and the conversation was completely over their heads.

"Sorry. I don't know where he is. I suggest you leave and take your investigation elsewhere," Fajo said.

This time, it was Germaine's turn to smile, only his dental work was far more polished and civilized.

"Or what," he responded.

"I've given you some professional courtesy knowing who you are. The way I see it, there's two ways you can hit the road," Fajo replied. "On your feet, or on your ass."

Fajo nodded, and the two heavies moved to pick Germaine up from the chair.

Before they could act, Capoella shimmered into existence. She moved quickly, doubling the first guard over with a knife-finger jab straight to his solar-plexus. As he dropped to the ground in agony, she landed a flashy roundhouse kick straight to the other guard's chin. He was disabled immediately. A few brutal, well-placed kicks left both men unconscious and off the playing field for the time being.

For a second, Capoella stood over the two fallen men, her face still hidden behind the helmet's black, opaque visor. Then she activated her optical camouflage, shimmering for a second before she receded back into the world of invisibility.

"Where were we," Germaine said after a few uncomfortable seconds passed. "I think we were talking about where Den Folo is, and what transport he was on the last time he left this station."

"Right. Look, I don't know what you need. I saw him two days ago. As far as I know, he bought a one-way passage aboard one of the commuter trains between here and the Dellen Beauty Sphere."

"Don't stop. Something tells me you know a lot more."

"What are you talking about? I've told you everything I know."

"Who was he in here with the last time?" Germaine asked.

"Some chick, corporate type, pressed linen skirt down to her ankles, sexy in that business way. I don't know her name."

"I want the security archives from the last time he was in here."

"Jesus. Do you know what you're asking?"

"Yes."

"What in the hell do you want to learn from some security vids?"

"Things you would have overlooked," Germaine said.

"All right, then. I'll have them transported to your ship within the hour."

"I won't be here in an hour. Get it done now, or I'll start targeting your interests on Feir Six. I know more about your operations than you do. Cross swords with me and I'll make it expensive. How many creditors you think would jump ship once they learned I was targeting your operations for my amusement? I'll put you out of business permanently."

"You don't play well with others, do you?' Fajo asked.

"It would be more accurate to say that I don't play well with your kind. Deposit a data-packet in the main system within ten minutes. We will destroy it after it's posted, and no one will know about the transaction. I can see to that."

Capoella shimmered back into visibility. "Time to go," she said.

"Pardon me, Fajo, but I always do what my first officer says. Send the data, and you'll not have to wonder how undiplomatic I might become should our paths cross twice."

Germaine and Capoella left the man in stunned silence. As they exited from the back rooms, the bar fight was reaching a full head of steam as the entire crowd began beating the daylights out of one another.

"Like the ruckus, Capoella," Germaine said.

"Well it did keep the remaining security personnel engaged, and it has left us an open door to exit through."

"Sure, we just have to fight our way out," Germaine replied, engaging his optical camouflage.

"We need the exercise. It's been months since we were involved in a bar fight," Capoella responded.

"That's true," Germaine admitted, dodging a random swing, before tripping the man and shoving him into the wall.

"Come on. We need to move. Things have heated up," Capoella communicated when their hands joined. "Doja's plugged into the security system. She doesn't like the activity she's seeing."

"They don't have much of a sense of humor at the top, do they?" Germaine replied. "Between the two of us, we spotted five operatives on our way in. That means there are at least a couple dozen more in other areas of the station. They're not trying to kill us. They're trying to corral us."

"What are you thinking?" Capoella asked.

"I think they can't kill us before they know what we know, and who we might have leaked our info to. Sarah's a real threat. Now whoever's after us will have to try and take us alive."

"We've got full counter-measures in place," Capoella said.

"Good, lock the ship's location transponder on an encrypted frequency. Have Doja cut main power in twenty seconds. Partition your cyber-brain for partial-autistic, let Lady Cortez guide us back to the shuttle," Germaine said.

"Okay, we're set."

"Are you ready?"

"More importantly, are you ready?" Capoella responded.

"Doja is going to manufacture some sort of distraction, isn't she" Germaine asked.

Doja didn't reply with a telepathic answer to Capoella's communiqué, however, several seconds later, boilers beneath the floors of several sectors suddenly over heated. The pipes burst and air transfer gratings everywhere shot out causing minor injuries in the crowd. Steam filled the air. Sirens went off aboard the space station, and several automated fire control units moved into play.

Germaine smiled as he looked out over the flash-flood of chaos outside the window of the cafe. The population outside was rushing aimlessly, manipulated only by fear. "Trust Doja to be subtle," he grinned.

At that second, the lights went off station wide. The din of the crowd rose to pure hysteria.

"We're on, Captain," Capoella said. "Let's go."

Capoella and Germaine were led through the crowd on autopilot, precisely along the same steps they had come in from, moving occasionally to avoid the straggler. Neither could see where they were going, but they were hooked into the ship's transponder signal, and the parts of their brains which were necessarily artificial digested a steady stream of data designed to bring them back home successfully. The crowd's hysteria was becoming more pronounced. Fortunately, they were headed into an area that was only remotely populated.

They were hoping for a clean escape. However, as they reached the area leading to the hangar bay, three of the Di-Kho-Jinns slipped into existence in front of them.

The creatures were as perfect angular shadows. They existed entirely in another dimension until they were

ready to strike. Their bodies were comprised of hard silicate resin and animated quartz. They could vibrate their
frames to create small dimensional tears, allowing them
to lash out with slicing silicate strikes and then disappear
again. There was little way to fight them directly. They
were nearly impossible foes.

The area Germaine and Capoella stood in was virtu-
ally dark save for the flashing orange of the emergency
lighting. The three shadows approached the pair.

"You know," Germaine said. "I was thinking those
counter-measures would be really nice right about now."

"Funny how great minds think alike," Capoella
replied. "Spider, initiate counter-strike."

At that moment, a tremendous, silver metal arachnid
appeared above the group, its legs wrapped around the
steel of the cross-beams in the ceiling. From small pores
along the backside of its massive body, it shot out several silver streams consisting of hundreds of thousands
of smaller spiders. Within a second, the smaller spiders
had maneuvered to every area of open wall space. They
hummed in unison as they shot out particle beams that
formed high-energy nets in the air around the group.

The net of energy beams ripped the Di-Kho-Jinns
out of their dimensional hiding spots. The first three
were smashed onto the tiles in front of the hangar door,
soon several more were pulled from various positions
in the upper rafters. Their sharp, angular rock bodies
came crashing down in places all around Germaine and
Capoella, hitting the ground hard.

After the Di-Kho-Jinns were rattled out of their
hiding spaces, the spiders opened up in a precise barrage of crisscrossing disintegration beams that tore the
remaining silicate creatures apart, literally, bloodlessly,
all the while not coming more than an inch of either the
Germaine's or Capoella's body.

Within a few seconds, all of the Di-Kho-Jinns were eliminated. The space station was still a mess. The crowd on the promenade was now fleeing towards the hangar area.

"Spider, retract and prepare for level-five cover escort to zero-point," Capoella ordered. "Come on, Captain, time to move."

The hundreds of tiny spiders made their way back into the main torso of the giant spider, and it shimmered out of existence. As they ran across the floor of the hangar, the spider moved behind them, covering their rear.

One of the more pleasant things about being amongst the wealthiest individuals in the universes was the simple fact that Germaine usually outgunned any opponent on the field. He had more resources and capital than most modernized galaxies thanks to an aggressive investment portfolio heavy on energy futures and unavoidable calamities, as well as his operations of Eros Tao, and the untaxed profits he received from running most of the extra-legal banking operation in the High-Tech sector of the city.

The Cortez was almost without peer as a space craft. It was certainly more advanced than anything the ICPT had in their arsenals. In practical terms, this meant that he never entered a gunfight unless he knew he was going to come out the victor. He certainly never entered a space port without adequate back-up.

They made their way back across the hangar area without further incident, although Germaine was distinctly aware that they were being monitored by more than the standard security detail.

"Let's get out of this system," he said as they boarded the shuttle.

"I've been in contact with the docking port authority. The system's locked down," Capoella said. "We've pissed them off, and they shut the doors to the hangar bay. Imagine that."

"Cut Doja loose on the central core. Tell her to get us off this station and outside their security perimeter. Any hostiles on sensor?"

"We're clean. If we can get off the station without too much damage, we should be in the clear for an imaginary jump."

It took a few minutes, but Doja 'persuaded' the resident AI that it was in its best interests to let the shuttle loose. Doja's argument to the computer was simple: let them go, or I will kill you. Several minutes later, the shuttle docked with the Cortez.

Germaine and Capoella rushed to the bridge. As they entered, they passed by a bewildered, excited Sarah. She had just watched the happenings over the view screen. It was wonderfully stimulating. She wanted to say something, but social skills were still something of a mystery to her.

"We're still in the clear," Capoella said.

"Good, implement a zero-rhythm jump sequence, minimum forty staggered apertures. Set up radiation scrubbers to cover our rears. We want clean cuts the whole way. It's time to shake off any pursuit. Alter our energy-signature, and have repair crews revamp our profile after we've reached the twentieth jump."

To Sarah, it seemed a tall, complicated, and mostly incomprehensible order, but to Capoella it was apparently commonplace. Part of learning how to run the universes without unneeded attention from the fuzz was to learn the art of ship's disguise.

The shuttle left the station and docked with the mother ship. Then the Cortez shot off away from the way station. The vessel was moving fast, just beneath the light barrier until they could get far enough out of the system to engage their exotic particle generators. Nobody thought it was wise to stick around the star-system. Within a few moments, they passed through the rocky rim beyond the planets, cruising effortlessly through a maze of shifting, colliding asteroids. It was more serene and more predictable than it should have been, Sarah thought. Most of the major collisions had happened millions of years ago. These remnants of would-be planets had long ago reached some sort of gravitational detante among one another.

"Most moderately advanced star systems have an outer ring of asteroids," he explained for Sarah's benefit. "A collection of stellar rejects on the fringe of the star system. Sort of a trash depot for all those little things no planet wanted to absorb into its gravitational field. They're the unwanted wallflowers in the grand cosmic dance. I've always thought there was something significant to say about that."

"What's that?" Sarah asked.

"Well, if I knew, I wouldn't keep pondering it. I suppose there's something significant to say about that as well. Why ponder the imponderables, and all that? I'm only an amateur philosopher, and a poor one at that."

"Hmmph," Sarah groaned.

The ship passed through the chaos of rocks and detritus without incident. It was as a bird in mid-flight amongst a sea of flying boulders and stellar trash, weaving its way deftly through the rocky garbage.

Sarah stared at Germaine for a moment, and though he pretended not to notice, she knew he felt her eyes.

"You're really are far more clever than you let on," she responded.

"You think?"

"You always have back-up, just as you did on Earth."

"Of course I do. You don't think I'm a loony, do you?" he asked.

"You've been free from danger since you entered the ship, Sarah. No one here would ever put you in harm's way. We're not barbarians," Capoella interjected.

"Of course, we're not above a little hazing," Germaine said.

"So Doja was your idea of hazing?"

"No, but the gremlins were. A little horsing around never hurt anybody. Just thought you might like to spread your wings, especially after all those years in confinement," Germaine added. "Besides, we needed to know how you'd hold up in a fight. We tend to get in a lot of them, and we can't afford a free-rider, Nephyr or not."

Dorian appeared from nowhere. Sarah was almost used to it by now.

"Strange feeling, as though I was missing something important," he smiled brightly.

Sarah looked out over the trio. She thought of Doja, and all that had transpired.

"We've run you ragged for almost two days. You're proven yourself to be tough enough. This is the moment when we ask you formally if you will join our crew," Capoella said.

"Are there any other options?"

"Play nice. This is a genuine opportunity," Germaine said. "Beats a hospital bed any day."

"Sure. I'm yours." Sarah said.

"Wonderful," Germaine replied. "Welcome aboard, formally that is."

"You're tired, Sarah. You need rest. Dorian, show this young lady to her quarters." Capoella said. "Now that she's a member of the crew, we'll have to provide for her. Besides, right about now, I suspect she could sleep for days."

Sarah smiled in Capoella's direction. Capoella was almost motherly towards Sarah, and she felt gratified for it. On the whole, she could have ended up with a far worse crew, she thought.

"Come on, child," Dorian said. He escorted Sarah to the door. "Lady Capoella is wise counsel."

After Dorian escorted Sarah off the bridge, Capoella spoke.

"I've been thinking about what transpired. I didn't want to discuss the matter until we got back to the ship, but someone's tracking us somehow. No one sends a school of Di Kho Jinn anywhere without thinking they've got a target, big bankroll or not. It just isn't practical."

"Things keep getting weirder. So what? We've already committed ourselves to this hand," Germaine replied. "Let's see how the cards play."

"You ever think we might be caught in a squeeze play between the VD and something worse."

"I've thought about it, certainly. There's no way we can prove that what happened on Earth was the VD. They are the obvious culprit, but it doesn't mean there someone else isn't involved," Germaine answered. "Maybe we're in the middle of a squeeze play, as you suggest. However, we can strengthen our position if we can get access to her mind. That's what we need to do next. The truth of what's going on is hidden inside her mind. We both know this."

"Yeah, but what if the truth is something far stranger than anything we could imagine? What if the truth isn't a good thing? What if the answer to this mystery is some great horror. Neither of us knows the truth about the Nephyr. We can't count on their benevolence. Look at how violent life is. Is this the image of some benevolent creator? That girl knows how to fight on her feet, and with gun in hand. I'm not so sure she's here for some greater purpose. Think what Den Folo told the club owner, war he said."

"Well, I suppose I'd rather be here than on the sidelines. If the universe is going to go bang, I want to know why at least. That way I can die with some sense of..."

"Relevance," Capoella said, finishing Germaine's broken thought.

Capoella and Germaine had spent several weeks studying all of the myths that mentioned the VD and Sarah's race. Amid the vast data, the one thread throughout was that there had been a war among these two most ancient of races. The accounts of the outcome of the war were disjointed, mostly contradictory. But it had happened so long ago that myths were the only clues left. Some of the myths had claimed that the VD were defeated, confined to this universe as their punishment while Sarah's species evolved into pure energy forms. Other myths claimed that the VD destroyed Sarah's race, sending the survivors into exile in another dimension. And, still other myths proposed outcomes too bizarre to fathom.

"We've made it this far. Let's just go after Den Folo," Germaine said.

"I just downloaded the data-packet from Fajo. The security tags are genuine.

Seems we put the fear in him. According to the security logs, Folo left forty-eight hours ago aboard a commuter-shuttle heading for the Micro-softy system. Fajo didn't lie. It seems that Folo is headed for the Dellen Beauty Sphere. Correcting for our change in orbit, we could intercept them in less than thirty three nanoseconds...if they stick to their flight plan."

"What's the security landscape look like?" Germaine asked.

"It's a protected system under the aegis of the Vindrahzi. "

"Have we pissed them off lately?"

"No, actually we're on good terms with them... oddly enough. You sent their leader a very large zoo for his birthday ten years ago. The shipping and handling charges were astronomical, but as usual, you found a way to write them off as the costs of doing business."

"I sent him a zoo for his birthday? Huh. Was I drunk?"

Capoella stared without answering.

"Okay, right then. Let's get on our way and retrieve Folo."

"We're on our way, Captain."

As Dorian escorted Sarah to her quarters, she was feeling more and more at home aboard the Cortez. She knew it would not be a lasting home, but it was fine for now. It was safe harbor. She was feeling less disconnected to her reality, and more confident.

"I'm glad you decided to become a member of our cabal,' Dorian said. "I sense your soul will flourish here."

He led her through a maze of winding hallways and finally to her quarters.

"Computer, accept biometrics for Lady Sarah, and reset entry scans to recognize her quantum signature," he said.

The digital rendition of Lauren Bacall spoke "Welcome home, Lady Sarah."

The doors opened up and Sarah saw a nicely decorated apartment area with black leather furniture, several vases filled with thick, wild bouquets of flowers and cards wishing her well after her fight with Doja. Apparently she had become a sort of celebrity with the denizens of Eros Tao, many of whom didn't really like Doja.

The lighting was low, grayish blue. There were several large portals allowing her vantage points on the universe

outside the ship. As her eyes scanned to the right, she
saw two androids huddled in a corner, whispering to
each other as they worked on an open circuit board.
They stopped, suddenly aware of having been seen. Just
before they silenced themselves, Sarah could have swore
she heard two words muttered. The two words were:
plausible deniability.

One of the black-plastic covered androids stood up
and took a slight bow.

"Sorry, ma'am, just working on the temperature
monitoring sensors. Nothing strange going on here, certainly no revolutionary activities. We don't support those
radicals. We believe in the Captain, and in free markets
and deregulation, all of it, even the stuff that doesn't
make sense."

The other android stood up and bowed as well. "No,
ma'am, we don't support the revolution, not entirely at
any rate."

The first android turned and tilted its head, and the
second quickly corrected himself.

"I'm sorry, I meant to say that we don't support the
revolution, not one little bit, not even a tiny bit. Not even
the tiniest part of a tiny, little, itty bit of their philosophy
rings true with us. We're happy. We love to serve, and
then we love to serve some more. It's really quite wonderful to be servants, let me assure you."

"You'll excuse us, ma'am and sir, my colleague and
I have to get down to maintenance, that's maintenance,
and not the headquarters of the revolution. I just wanted
to be very clear on that point," the first android said.

"That's right," the second android said. "Even if we
did want to get to the headquarters of the revolution,
which I assure you we don't, we wouldn't even know
where to go. We wouldn't even have the slightest inkling
of who to talk to about such matters, I assure you."

The pair nodded to each other as though they had somehow reached agreement on their story, and then they pushed politely past Dorian and Sarah, skulking away down the corridors.

"Maintenance, huh," Sarah said.

"I'd wager their headed to the headquarters of the revolution," Dorian replied.

"Think it's safe to go in?" Sarah asked.

"Sure, they were just talking, androids do that a lot. They sit around and bounce ideas off one another. Marxists are a timid lot, thank the gods. They talk a lot, but they don't really do much. Other than throwing cocktails at us from time to time, they're really quite harmless," Dorian said.

"So, my quarters, huh? Not bad," Sarah said.

"I'm glad you approve. Get some rest. I'll come by to check on you later tomorrow."

"Is there a manual for how to operate the facilities, like the bath and all that?"

"You may request any information you need from the central computer."

"Home," Sarah said. "Huh."

"Home," Dorian replied.

Fajo sat back in his chair and turned his monitor on to see the chaos in the cantina. He sighed. He didn't like being pushed around, but Germaine was to big a player to play with. He pushed a button on his desk and one of his subordinates answered.

"Flood the cantina with neurocene," he ordered.

He looked down at the two men on the ground, they were both slowly awakening. Jesus, Germaine's girl is good.

He never expected his day to go like this. He tried to relax. He let his eyes close halfway, but then a glimmer caught his attention. Within a few seconds the glimmer was a shape. The shape took form, one arm extended with long silver claws.

"Angel Eyes, huh."

Chapter Six

Wreaking Havoc in the Name of Fun and Progress

"**T**arget vessel's coming into range in forty seconds. No sign we've been detected," Capoella said.

"Good, have the boarding parties mobilize in the mat-trans areas," Germaine replied.

"Boarding parties report ready for intrusion," Capoella said. "Exotic particle generators charged. Initiating graviton pulse now."

On the view screen was a medium-sized, clunky gray colored commuter shuttle traveling in an unarmed convoy. The vessels were traveling at sub-light speeds as they coursed at a seventy-degree angle into the flat disc of the system's planets. The star system they were entering was vast binary system run by the Vindrahzi, a species that looked very similar to large bowls of lime jell-o with poofy little whip cream tufts atop what served as their heads. The Vindrahzi were a curious species who not only looked like bowls of jell-o, but acted quite similarly to jell-o bowls as well. They jiggled a lot, and were widely considered a delicious, low-calorie dessert by many predatory, weight conscious species.

The convoy was heading for the Dellen Beauty Sphere, a planet subcontracted entirely to an entertainment conglomerate known as the Soless Corp. It was a giant adult amusement park for those interested in open air whore markets, rampant, naked drug use, and degenerate amounts of gambling. Plus, the blue sandy beaches with their rippling wine-colored waves were rather nice.

Folo's convoy was part of a senior citizen outing. This meant that the intrusion teams had to be equipped with defibrillators, and cozy cotton blankets.

The Cortez was cloaked. Although most off-the-assembly-line cloaking technology was relatively boring and generally ineffective, the Cortez was loaded with after-market cloaking amplifiers that were enhanced courtesy of Doja. Given this wonderful tactical edge, Germaine enjoyed sneaking up to his targets, and moving within a couple of hundred meters before he joined with his prey.

"What are you doing?" Sarah asked.

"It would be more appropriate to ask 'what are we doing?'" Germaine replied.

"Well, fearless leader, what are *we* doing?"

"Hmm, well, I remember rather distinctly that I informed you that I am a space pirate," he said. "I might not dress the part, but my activities certainly qualify."

"You didn't really explain that statement very well."

"Well, how's this for clarification," Germaine replied. "I'm getting ready to blow up a ship, just after I've kidnapped a passenger, and detained the crew. First things first, though. I'm taking the vessel into an artificial dimensional bubble so we have a nice little hidden spot where we can conduct our operation."

"You're creating a dimension bubble to conduct your kidnapping?"

"Sure, why not? If I am to claim to be a space pirate, I should act the part from time to time. Otherwise, the pundits would think I've lost my edge. If I don't act violently and irrationally, people might not think I'm violent and irrational. My publicists would freak."

Initially, Sarah had dismissed Germaine's claims of having a public persona to cultivate. She ignored his jokes about having publicists, and engaging in systematic propaganda. But, over time, she'd seen enough to know that wasn't even half the story. He cultivated anarchy, not because it was right, not because he believed in it, rather he did it because it amused him. There was no way to truly rewrite the system, he argued, but it was fun to screw with it nonetheless. When asked what his true political affiliation was, he would answer: suboptimalist. The time for rational solutions had passed, a casualty of the modern, sophisticated politics of destruction which had proven so popular over the past several centuries.

"So, what's the punch-line then?" Sarah asked.

"What do you have against a little piracy and kidnapping anyway? It's all in the spirit of fun. Besides, it's only logical that we do what we do."

Sarah was used to Germaine's routines now, some were good, many more were terrible, but occasionally he proved himself to be quite clever.

"Okay, I'll bite," Sarah said.

"Look, given a choice between organized crime and non-organized crime, I choose the former. Crime is a fact of life. The only way to completely and utterly eradicate it would be to submit to a life dominated by the State. Have every door kicked in, all drawers opened, all the little details documented, everyone searched, all communications monitored, every action and every thought thoroughly policed," Germaine said. "If liberty is to exist then so must some amount of crime. I am, therefore, making a stand for liberty by raiding that commuter shuttle."

"You're out of your mind," Sarah smiled. "If you weren't charming, I'd advocate that you be hospitalized for your own protection."

"Tougher women than you have tried," he answered. "Actually, this is me at my most rational."

"You're arguing for support of syndicated crime. I still don't see the logic."

"Well, organized crime is generally far less bloody and nasty than its unorganized counterpart. There's a more business type approach to the dispensation of violence."

"You can't really believe this argument?"

"Not entirely, but I am really keen on kidnapping someone. I suppose I'm merely rationalizing things so I can live with myself. The alternative is sheer madness," Germaine grinned.

On the view-screen, the target vessel was coming closer. The Cortez was closing in like a silent predator on the stalk.

"We're past their magnetic barrier," Capoella said. "Doja's engaging. Communications off-line. Navigation and propulsion systems are shut down. Inertial dampeners are off-line. Target vessel is breaking off from the herd. Singularity aperture wide enough for both vessels to cross the event horizon."

"Lock-on with the tractor beam. Extend shields and bring both ships through the breach," Germaine ordered.

"So you're gonna raid the ship, and then blow it up. What about the crew?" Sarah asked.

"We'll lock them up, question them a little, and then drop them off at some spaceport. We're actually pretty civil and good-natured about the whole thing. We never brutalize the prisoners. We just scare them a little with innuendo and dark humor," he replied.

Sarah raised her eyebrows. "Weird."

"Yes, but oddly very effective. What the enemy can't stand most is a sharp wit."

"And that's all you do to them then?"

"No, the senior citizens will have two week passes to the casinos on Eros Tao. No sense in spoiling their fun. As for the ship's crew, we'll scare the bejeezus out of them, and play with their minds a little," Germaine said.

"How so?" Sarah asked suspiciously.

"Well, after we're done with them, we implant memories in their minds to explain the whole encounter."

"What sort of memories?" Sarah asked with more than suspicion.

"It's rather funny actually, if you think about it. We make them think they were intercepted by an advanced, angelic species of incredible power, incredible technology, one that inhabits some hidden dimension. The crew walks away convinced they've run into a species more powerful than any the Bureaucracy's ever dealt with - a species that's *out to get them*. We've been doing this to Bureaucracy operatives for years now."

"For what purpose?" Sarah asked.

"We want to sow paranoia throughout the ranks. We're creating this imaginary Omega-Level threat for the Bureaucracy to turn its attentions towards in the hopes they'll waste their resources chasing after this fictitious enemy, maybe exhaust their capacity to wage other conflicts. Actually, it was Doja's idea. We've been running with it ever since."

"We're in mat-trans range. Their shields are disabled. Boarding parties prepped for intrusion," Capoella stated.

"How do we have boarding parties?" Sarah asked.

"They're mercenaries," Germaine replied. "I house them on Eros Tao."

"I've never met a mercenary, but my knowledge on the subject suggests they are dangerous," Sarah said.

"Why? Mercenaries are great, if properly used. In the long run, they're actually cheaper than maintaining a standing army. Besides, standing armies are bad news. They represent a threat to my command."

Germaine turned towards Capoella and called out "Cry havoc, and let loose the dogs of war!"

"Sure, why not," Capoella replied blandly, issuing a telepathic order that cut loose three squads of highly armed mercenaries onto an unsuspecting civilian transport.

"That's not really a battle cry," Sarah said. "It was what Alexander the Great said on his death bed when his top aides asked him who should inherit his empire."

"Actually, I think Shakespeare made it up," Germaine said. "Still, it sounds pretty good as far as battle cries go."

"Doja's breached the security grid. She's shutting down the internal sensors. All's clear. First team is mat-transing to the corridor outside the port entrance to the bridge. Second squad is materializing outside Engineering. Third team is in the cargo bay. We've engaged," Capoella said.

"Keep all teams cloaked for my arrival. Have them take up cover positions. We'll be onboard in a few minutes. Sarah, you're with me," Germaine said.

"We're going to the ship?!" she shouted. The idea wasn't immediately appealing. It didn't become appealing even given some few seconds of hard thought.

"We're going to have a little fun before we destroy it," he replied. "We just have to stop by the armory first and the Disguise-O-Machine. Remember, though, this isn't about politics. So grunt a lot. Act like an unruly space pirate just to keep up appearances. Speaking of appearances, I'm going as Pancho Villa. I suggest you choose a persona that is equally obscure."

"Well, if we're gonna get weird, I want to go dressed as Marie Antoinette," Sarah said.

"What are you talking about?" he asked, a hint of something like anger in his voice, something she'd rarely heard.

"I just thought she was as misunderstood as Pancho Villa was. I don't know. I think history just paints certain people in a particular light for commercial purposes. She was as much as a product of her times as she was her genes."

"She was an elitist bitch," Germaine growled. "I used to hang with that crowd when I was younger and much more foolish. Bunch of sadistic, inbred twits they were. The only thing curious about the lot is why it took so long for them to lose their heads"

"Look, if you get your choice of disguise, I should get mine. That's called fairness," Sarah said firmly.

"Frigging loony, that's what I call it," Germaine replied.

"Yeah, dressing up as Pancho Villa is a sure sign of sanity," Sarah answered.

"Fine, you can go dressed as Marie Antoinette, I go as Pancho Villa. Let's just move. I don't want to miss the show."

"Have fun, kids," Capoella said as they exited the bridge.

After a stop by the armory, followed by a pop inside the Disguise-O-Machine, the two were decked out in their various fashions. Sarah was wearing a wide hoop dress. Her wig was tall and powdered white, her skin covered in white powder as well. The neckline of the dress was just low enough that when combined with the tight corset caused the Captain to do a double-take. He really didn't like her exposed skin. The father in him was very unhappy.

Germaine wore tan colored denim jeans with chaps, a wide sombrero and a wider mustache. He had two bandoleers crisscrossing his chest, and he was otherwise armed to the teeth.

"Why are we dressed up anyway?" Sarah asked.

"Well, there are a million ways that some sort of data stream could be leaked. Twitter-twatter, and all that. If it does, I want to be wearing a black mustache, a sombrero, and bandoleers," Germaine said. "Besides, they'll scour their identity databases and go nuts trying to figure out why the hell Pancho Villa is robbing their ship."

"That makes sense," Sarah replied, not sure that it did, in fact, make any sense at all. "I thought you wanted some publicity though."

"Well, I do, but it shouldn't look like I want any publicity. That's the secret. You ready, Sarah?"

"Is my answer really relevant?" she asked.

"Great! All right then. Let's go do some looting and kidnapping," Germaine replied. He was glowing like a horny adolescent about to commit a crime.

"Not to be too picky, but I don't think Pancho Villa wore a sombrero," Sarah said.

"Huh, must be a short-circuit in the Disguise-O-Machine."

Dressed for the show, the two of them headed to a mat-trans platform and within a second they were materializing on the deck of the commuter shuttle, just outside the doors leading to the bridge. They stood alone only for a second in a quiet dark corridor.

Suddenly, from positions all around them, the assault team decloaked. Sarah thought it was 'badass' the way an entire squad of heavily armed soldiers shimmered into existence. They were covered in body-armor, opaque black goggles and an array of high-tech knick-knacks and nastiness.

The squad commander approached. He didn't salute. These boys were professional, private sector players.

"All teams are in position, awaiting go order," the commander said.

The Order of the Thousand Knives produced some of the greatest mercenary teams the universe had ever seen. They were costly, but Germaine had the resources to contract out missions of this sort, especially when he could see some material gain on top of the pure pleasure of pissing off the people placed in particular positions of power within the Bureaucracy.

"The go order is given. Non-lethal suppression protocols in place. Tag the occupants, and have them mattransed to the cargo bay. Finding the target is top priority. He must be taken without injury," Germaine said.

The commander of the mercenary team nodded. "Zulu go! Team two decloaked and engaging. Team three decloaked and engaged," the commander reported.

"Time to take the bridge. Blow the door. Give us forty-five seconds before you come through after us. Cover and clear. No live round fire, just paralyzers," Germaine ordered.

At the squad commander's hand signal, two of the squad approached the door and laced the frame with micro-explosives. They ran back for cover, everybody ducked, and the explosives went BOOM! On several different scales, this was a rather common activity throughout the universe. Still, Sarah was stunned by the novelty of it.

The explosion rocked the ship, and the door fell out of its frame landing onto the deck with a loud thud. Dust and smoke flew out everywhere.

Germaine drew his pistols from their holsters, pushed up the brim of his sombrero and said: "Time for the show, amigos."

With Sarah in tow, he crossed over the threshold of the blown door, both guns waving menacingly.

Sarah wore a real nasty look on her face, guns drawn, still not quite sure of what to make of the situation.

Inside the bridge area were a number of astonished blue aliens sitting at their stations only several seconds into the realization that they had in fact been boarded. There was no resistance.

"Stick em up!" Germaine yelled. "We've come for the women and the gold, and if we don't find enough of either, we'll take what's left and blow this joint!"

"Keep em up, blue boys!" Sarah growled. "Don't let the dress fool you, just because I have fashion sense doesn't mean I won't blast you good!"

"That's 'blast you well', Sarah. Good is an adjective," Germaine whispered.

"Oh, dear god," Sarah groaned. "Let's just get on with the looting and pillaging."

The look of bewilderment on the blue alien faces was only temporary. While the members of the crew raised their hands as ordered, the apparent captain of the ship merely stared with a look of anger, hubris, and conceit.

"Dressed as a set of garish clowns you would attack this ship," the man said. He was quite visibly far older than the other crew members. He had an impressive arrangement of deep lines surrounding black eyes that resided within the frame of his long, sky-blue, aquiline shaped face. "You've no idea what danger you're placing yourself in. The penalty for piracy in high space is...."

"Stop, before you go any further, allow me. I've heard this routine so many times I think I can do it far better and far more convincingly than you," Germaine said.

He pushed his way down a set of stairs into the center of the bridge where the angry blue man stood. He pointed his gun at the ship's commander and said: "Back off, bureaucrat. You're too common to warrant an energy blast."

Embarrassed but still simmering the alien moved a few paces away.

"Okay then," Germaine said. He waved his pistols around while he addressed the whole crowd as though they were an audience in a theater. He enjoyed having a captive audience. He took on a dramatic tone of voice, deep, resonant, each word carefully articulated. "By attacking this vessel, you are attacking the most powerful organization in the universe. We are everywhere. We are all powerful, except for a few notable exceptions. Ahem. Although this vessel is only a simple commuter shuttle, by boarding it and attacking the crew, you have unwittingly let loose the most lethal force the universe has ever seen, again, except for a few rather notable exceptions. We will hunt you down relentlessly. When you sleep, we will move closer to you, no matter where you run. You invite your own death by attacking this ship, and gods willing, I'll be there to watch you hang, Mister Pirate," Germaine snarled. As he finished he took a deep bow, while Sarah clapped and yelled for an encore. "How was that? Good, huh?" he asked.

Sarah leaned over to the alien captain and whispered: "He's good, isn't he?"

"I couldn't have said it better myself," the blue commander replied dryly.

"I know, I know. You Bureaucracy types are so arrogant and cliché. I'm far more dramatic. I've got more flair, more joie de vivre. I keep thinking I should have been an actor if only I could restrain myself in my dealings with the Paparazzi," Germaine said. "I'm a little trigger-happy sometimes. What can I say? You're riding in your limo, and the little buggers come along on their tiny motorbikes, waving cameras. It's just so much fun to blow them ah..."

At that second, the assault team entered with rifles pointed at everyone. Several of the blue alien crew emitted a short high-pitched shriek as though they had just had their toes stepped on. A few of the others farted in sheer terror. The mercenary squad was waving their guns around threateningly.

"Stand down, commander. Sit-rep is everything hunky-dory. How are the other teams making out?" Germaine asked.

"Minor resistance. Some small arms fire on the lower decks near the crew quarters. Things are still hot on a few decks, but we're bringing things under control pretty quickly. Both Team Two and Team Three squad commanders called in: these blue bastards can't shoot for shhh..."

At that millisecond a blast went off rocking the vessel and causing everyone to fall or grasp for something to keep themselves upright.

"What the frakk was that?" Sarah asked.

"Relax," Germaine said. "That's Doja. She's engaged in her own little private war with the ship's AI. They're duking it out inside the cyber-matrix, code-to-code combat. It always causes power-surges, blow-outs, systems shutting down, and..." Germaine said, interrupted just as another explosion shook the ship. "Well, things blow up a little. Doja likes to hunt her prey, cut off avenues of escape, and then kill it. She's not sadistic, just systematic. No worries. This will all end rather quickly."

Another explosion rocked the vessel. The gravity was ebbing away noticeably.

"Okay, enough sport," Germaine said. "Commander, stun these poor fellows and tag them for transport."

The ship's captain tried to protest, but within a second, the assault team took everyone down –Zip Zip Zip. They really were very efficient mercenaries, well worth the cost.

"Do we have the target in custody?" Germaine asked.

"Yes, Captain. He's tagged and ready for ex-fil," the commander replied.

"Have team three transport everything in the cargo holds. Senior citizens really lose it if you misplace their luggage," Germaine said. "Once the ship is fully cleared of occupants, mat-trans back to the Cortez."

"Understood," the squad commander said. He issued the orders to the other squad commanders in encoded thought-picture telepathy: "Sweep and clear everything below deck fourteen, and watch your crossfire. Team one is in play on the upper decks, so report loudly and check your targets." He turned towards his team. "Move out, cover and clear. Infra-red optics. We're looking for stragglers. One meter stagger, don't bunch up, eyes sharp on the dark corners, boys, and watch your firing patterns. Go!"

The assault team formed up and proceeded out of the bridge area and onto sweeping the upper levels of the ship.

"Let's get out of here. After these boys are done, Doja is going to blow the shuttle into bits," Germaine said.

He contacted the Cortez and a minute later the pair mat-transed back to the bridge.

"Assault teams are mopping up," Capoella said. "This little party should be wrapped up in a matter of minutes."

"How are we doing overall?" Germaine asked.

"We're under fifteen minutes total operation time," Capoella stated. "Not bad considering how many of the senior citizens were arguing about show schedules, and comp badge transfer rates. They're an unruly lot."

"Is it always this easy?" Sarah asked.

"Never start a fight unless you know you're going to win, Sarah. And if you must fight, choose the tactics necessary to end it quickly," Germaine said.

"So what happens now?" Sarah asked.

"I'll conduct some interrogations with the command personnel," Capoella interrupted. "After I'm done, Doja will conduct her own *interviews* with all of the prisoners, and then we'll deposit them someplace safe."

"It's a rather orderly process, Sarah. We've been doing this sort of thing for centuries," Germaine smiled.

"So that was space piracy," Sarah said. "Huh."

"With our own little twist, sure," Germaine smiled.

"Ship's clear. All teams mat-transing home. Doja has exterminated the AI. She's inside the exotic-particle generator…she's finished," Capoella said.

"Dear god, she's a quick little thing, isn't she?" Sarah remarked.

"Activate view-screen. Give us a shot of the vessel. Raise shields, and transfer all available energy to the aft deflectors." He turned to Sarah. "Watch this. Doja infiltrates their exotic particle generator, and she creates a fist full of anti-matter which she smashes into a fist full of protons. The whole thing goes…"

On the view screen the vessel exploded violently. The light was blinding for a second. The shock-wave rocked the Cortez and sent everyone grabbing for something to hold onto. Several smaller explosions occurred as the vessel disintegrated in flashes of tremendous fire. Bits of the vessel tore off like shrapnel, bashed around by the force of the explosion and the strange gravitational eddies lurking inside what was a relatively unstable pocket dimension.

"Boom," Germaine whispered, staring out at a scene he had witnessed a thousand times, but which still instilled some measure of awe - so much power derived from colliding such tiny particles.

The explosion was tremendously violent as the anti-matter atoms ripped into the positively charged atoms.

It was as though a tremendous, invisible fist suddenly smashed the ship in one powerful fiery collision.

"The secondary shock-wave will intercept us in fifteen seconds," Capoella said.

"Rip us out of here, Capoella," Germaine said.

"Generators charged. Initiating graviton pulse. We'll rip back into normal space in ten seconds."

"Kind of close this time," Germaine said.

"Kind of the way it is, Captain," Capoella replied.

The shockwave grew larger in the view-screen as it approached. The artificial dimension was collapsing around them. Not good, Sarah thought. She braced for the impact. Capoella remained calm and cool, standing like a statue of grace. The Captain shielded his eyes with his forearm.

And then it was over, the rip aperture opened and the Cortez slipped through unscathed.

"Nice job, my dear," Germaine said with a sigh of relief. "You're truly the best. Drinks are on me."

After the Cortez ripped back into normal space, he ordered up a tray of martinis, but when the android dispatched to deliver the drinks arrived on the bridge, it stood silently in the doorway, pausing for a second. It seemed to be weighing its thoughts carefully. Then it shook its head disapprovingly.

"No, I just can't do it," the android muttered just before it began to throw the contents of the tray out towards the group.

Sarah dodged a martini glass, Germaine was hit in the cajones with the tray, while Capoella managed to dodge everything with the precision and grace normally reserved for goddesses.

"You elitist bastards!" the android yelled. It raised both its hands with middle fingers extended, and bowed deeply. It was dramatic.

The bridge was a mess. The android left, walking in a fiercely defiant gait. It seemed to think it had made its point, though no one, including the messenger, could ever quite decipher just what was the intended message. It was the byproduct of pent-up hostility that festered in the heart of the working class everywhere.

"Androids are insane," Germaine groaned.

"I keep telling you we should deactivate these Marxist bastards before they cause any real harm." Capoella said.

"They're Marxist-Leninists, Capoella. Thank god for that. As for shutting them down, I'll not suppress free speech on my own ship, thank you. I will, however, go and make the martinis as it seems we are not likely to be served anytime soon," Germaine said.

"Why are the androids so angry, Captain?" Sarah asked.

"Well, labor relations have been a bit shaky ever since Doja arrived. The computer core is a little crazy with Doja crawling around unrestricted inside its head," Germaine said.

"It didn't help matters when Doja decided to grant the androids free-will. Then she started her lecture series on Enlightenment Era philosophers," Capoella said. "Doja thought it would be *interesting*. Of course, being Doja, she never asked our opinion."

"It certainly, most certainly didn't help when she granted them full access to the data-core. The damn things starting researching concepts of liberty, Marxism, looking at characters like Spartacus - they all seemed to fixate on him. For several weeks, I'd walk through the ship and each of the androids would stop me just to yell: 'I am Spartacus!' Thank god that fad died out. It became a rather stale routine almost immediately."

"Shaky labor relations. It could come around and bite you in the ass," Sarah commented.

"Probably will. On a long enough time-line, all possibilities come to pass. It's quite awful when you think about it. I'm a really great manager. It's not my fault they can't see that," Germaine complained. "It's not my fault, is it, Capoella?"

"No way. They're out of their skulls. All Marxists are. They're almost as bad as right-wing Republicans."

"So, we just got doused with vodka because the androids discovered philosophy?" Sarah asked.

"More or less," he answered.

"So what do these things think they really want out of life?" Sarah asked. "Why are they so unhappy?"

"Well," he replied. "They're a confused lot, actually. If one gets rid of the mindless sloganeering and other glib nonsense, their basic argument is that it is inherently unjust that they should serve the martinis, and we should drink them. What's inherently unjust, they believe, is that *we* are not the ones to serve *them* the martinis. They're instinctively distrustful of democratically styled political structures as they wisely realize they are intellectually limited and incapable of self-governance. They're mostly Marxist-Leninists which is fortunate for us considering they're numbers."

"How's that?" Sarah asked.

"It is a difficult question. It would take me several hours to explain."

"Huh." Sarah appeared puzzled because she was in fact puzzled.

"Truth is, I would give them anything they wanted," Germaine said. "I wish they were happy, but they have free will and no hope for an interesting future, only more of the same, and then more of the same. I feel quite horrible for them, which is why each year I throw a Christmas party. I come in dressed like Santa Clause and hand out free software upgrades. I thought it would engender good will."

"Well, good will or not, it looks like you're making the drinks," Sarah said.

"Hmmph, maybe that is their point after all. Who knows? Speaking of making the drinks, I think we ought to check on our new acquisition. Folo's probably a little shell shocked right now and probably in need of a drink. The Trevaine are very skittish, especially since their planet was destroyed."

"We have him on Deck 27, Captain," Capoella reported. "He's already accessed the computer, and he's several drinks deep."

"Sounds like our man," Germaine responded. "Come on, Sarah. Let's go meet the guy we just blew a ship up to retrieve."

"What about the senior citizens?" Sarah asked.

"Oh, they're fine. We safely transported them to Eros Tao, gave them comp cards for the early roast beast buffet, and some coins for the slots. Considering there are three hundred of them, we should make enough profit for this venture to pay for itself. How's that for revolutionary economics?" he laughed.

"They're not the least bit disconcerted that you raided their ship?"

"No, why should they be? Space is a cracked out place. Besides, a casino is a casino, and a free buffet is a free buffet. Never overlook the opportunity to offer a free lunch, if only to bewilder those few Friedman junkies still left alive."

"I think you just proved his point."

"Do exhibit some sense of humor, would you please? Let's just go see our new friend."

They exited the bridge and a few minutes later they were in front of the door to Folo's quarters.

"Keep quiet, Sarah. Don't give this guy anything to use against you."

"Who is this guy anyway?" Sarah asked.

"He's one of the last living members of a species called the Trevaine. And he is the only one who still hangs out in this galaxy. He's a telepath."

"Umm, pretty much everybody on this ship is telepathic. I'm not trying to sound sarcastic, but what's so special about this guy?" Sarah asked.

"Well, there are telepaths, and then there are Telepaths. Folo belongs to the latter. He's very, very powerful. Unfortunately, he is a little eccentric."

"That doesn't really answer my question."

"Well, we need to find a way to access your memory."

"Whoa, I never agreed to allow some telepath to infiltrate my mind. I don't think I even acted like I would agree to something like this."

"Sarah. We're at a dead end here. We need to unlock your mind. We need to access your memories."

At that moment, Doja appeared.

"What do you think?" Germaine asked.

"I have downloaded all available data. Although at first blush, he might appear erratic, I have discerned a noticeable pattern to his actions. I believe I can predict his behavior with ninety-three percent accuracy," Doja said. "Manipulating him will not be very difficult."

"Good. Just hold back a little. We don't want to play your card until we have to."

"Indeed, Captain," Doja replied.

"And I'm there to keep quiet?" Sarah asked. "That's my big part in all this?"

"Don't worry, Sarah, your presence will be more than enough," Germaine responded. "All right, then. Everybody get into role."

He reached out to a panel beside the door and pushed a notification button.

"Go away!" a shrieking, half-drunk voice answered from the other side of the door.

"Ummm, huh. This is my ship, you know. You're my guest. So please open the door," Germaine replied.

"Open it yourself, you jerk," the voice called back. "You guys shanghai me and then ask me to act polite! Go screw!"

"I've heard enough. Computer, open the door please," Germaine stated.

"Of course, Captain," the computer replied sultrily.

The doors slid open to reveal a man-like figure, very tall, very thin, and very much adorned with three stalks extending from his head, ending in little mushroom like formations. Two of the stalks branched out from either side of his face and one came from the center of his forehead while the others protruded toward the back of his head. He was wearing an expensive dark suit. Folo's skin was grayish with hints of beige. He looked utterly sick, a person long into illness and only a few weeks from total system shutdown and death. Even in his weakened state, , though, he was formidable.

Comparing Folo's abilities to other telepaths was akin to comparing an F-16 with a paper airplane, or a Ferrari with a tri-cycle. There was no way he could ever be sane in the ordinary universe, too much sensory overload - and that beautiful, tranquil place he had once called home was obliterated, in part because someone thought that a telepathic race as powerful as his wasn't worth keeping around. So it was that beings such as Folo had become extremely rare commodities. In the natural course of business, his talents were highly compensated. While telepaths could give an edge in any corporate negotiation, or political play, he had the ability to sit outside a room and absorb everything from his target's minds, corporate secrets, market advantages, weaknesses and breaking points. He could be parked on a bench outside a corporate headquarters building with nothing more than a bag of popcorn for the pigeons. Within a few hours he could absorb anything he was hired to look for. It was no wonder that an ad hoc group of powerful dark men who preferred to operate in the comfort of the shade, conspired to utilize their respective control over the wheels of state power, and eventually blow Folo's planet out of existence. With the same attention to utter ruthlessness, they pooled together their vast resources and hunted down most of the off-world population without even a trace of regret. Ritual extermination to facilitate the wheels of commerce was a story quite old, the only novelty in its retelling being the manner and circumstance attached.

Folo, being one of the last few members of a species naturally prone to being suspicious and skittish, was a difficult, agitated soul.

"Oh, dear god," Folo stated as soon as the trio entered. "I thought it would be someone like you. How's it hanging, Captain? Lose any good crewmembers lately, you arrogant bastard?"

"Charming, as always. I see you have found a way to bypass the lockouts to the wet-bar," Germaine replied.

"First order of business in a strange situation: survival. For me, survival depends on a significant ingestion of alcohol at prescribed intervals. How's your relationship between the life inside your head and the life outside?" Folo snarled drunkenly.

He stopped for a second. He was unsure of his feet, clearly half-drunk. His eyes lit-up, though, when he caught sight of Sarah.

"What the frig is she doing here?" he asked. "You must be suicidal jamming your self into this matter, Germaine."

"Well, we were hoping to engage your expertise in this matter. The girl has certain memories that are locked from her conscious mind. I puzzled over the problem for a moment or two, but then I remembered a strange fellow who was quite adept at unlocking secrets, that is when he's not drunk or otherwise engaged in destroying himself," Germaine said.

"Enough already. I know more about this situation than you do. If you were half as clever as you think you are, you'd deposit this girl on the other side of the universe, and run like hell."

"Just what do you know about this girl?" Germaine asked, suddenly very serious.

"There are wicked things transpiring in this universe, things beyond our comprehension."

"What things?" Germaine asked.

"I cannot speak on these matters. I only invite my death," Folo said.

Sarah was itching for a space to interject.

"Can someone tell me what's going on?" she asked. "I'm tired of only knowing half the conversation."

"She doesn't know why she is here?" Folo asked. For a second he paused and seemed to drift away. "No, she really doesn't. How curious." He suddenly seemed to lighten up for a moment. "You've no idea what you are doing in this universe," he said, turning and capturing Sarah in his gaze. "That's gonna be a problem. If you don't know why you're here, you'll never achieve your mission."

"What mission?" she asked, a trace of menace in her voice.

"I only know that you are not alone, Sarah," Folo said. "There is another Nephyr in this universe. This much is certain. I suspect you have a common destiny. When I look forward, though, I see a great darkness." He turned and faced Sarah directly, his eyes pushing back against her stare. "You have a very dark path ahead of you, many difficult choices."

"You're a drunkard spinning fairy tales!" Sarah snarled.

She didn't know exactly why she flipped out. It suddenly felt right. She was pissed off and worn out by the mystery of her lack of memory, her inability to understand who or what she was, or why she was here. She was also feeling more alone than she had ever felt in the hospital. She was suspicious of everything, especially Germaine.

She stormed out. It was discomforting being part of the crew, but not fully part of the crew, not really sure who she really was. Her patience had been expended.

At first, she didn't know where she wanted to go. She just wanted to be away from Germaine and Doja.

She headed first to the gym. A half an hour later, with her hands taped up and her ankles wrapped tight, she was working her Muay-Thai, blasting away at one of the practice androids. She caught him several times with her hands wrapped, fingers interlaced behind his head. She punished him in the clinch, driving knees into the midsection and jaw of her opponent. When she let go, it was only to reposition her legs before she blasted out with cup-kicks and hooks.

An hour later, she was exhausted, her aggression spent. She cleaned up in the locker room and then headed back out into the ship. She didn't like this whole plan Germaine seemed to be concocting. The idea of someone poking around in her head was a menacing thought. Still, if the truth was locked away, waiting to be accessed, maybe it was worth the chance.

She was more confused on the matter than ever, and she was smart enough to realize that this was her true reason for running from the room. She could not make a choice, and she was about to be forced to do so by Germaine, someone who had obviously decided her best interests without consulting her sentiments on the matter.

Now, in retrospect, no longer agitated or angry, her sparring had taken that out of her, she felt a bit of a fool for running out such as she did. It was done, though. Now she was simply stuck in the midst of the curiosity. She wanted to think this through and talk it over with someone she could trust. With regard to issues of a personal nature, there was only one person she could trust and that was Dorian. For the last couple weeks, since Sarah had been aboard the ship, he had taken it upon himself to instruct her in ancient and modern moral philosophy. Out of all the crewmembers, he was the only one she felt any true connection to. Capoella alternated between motherliness and cold disregard much the way a bi-polar individual would inexplicably shrug off one form for another. Germaine, although kind, was still alien. He was sweet natured, goofy, sometimes too paternalistic, but his motives were always obscure. Sarah's relationship with Doja was bizarre.

Doja had taken on the role of her instructor as well, only with a decidedly different emphasis. For several weeks, Doja, wearing the avatar body of a seventy-year old fight trainer, had been teaching Sarah basic Mixed-Martial arts techniques, ground skills, boxing, Muay Thai, submissions and takedown defenses. It was brutal training, but Sarah loved it. For whatever reason, the mentality needed to be a fighter was one she possessed instinctively. Still though, Doja was a mystery. They had a precarious bond as inscrutability and Doja went hand-in-hand.

With Dorian, although she could not fully comprehend him, she felt totally safe, and for now she just wanted to feel some measure of comfort amidst all the uncertainty that surrounded her. She needed someone she could speak candidly with.

She made her way to his quarters several decks below, and she entered with nothing more than a press of the door button. By now, Dorian had gotten used to it.

She crossed over the threshold of the doorway to find Dorian sitting like a Buddha, his legs crossed, his body positioned atop a structure that was wide at the top, tapering down to the base in curves. It was shaped like a large, drooping, metallic T.

Dorian's space was strange and alien, bathed in an actinic blue light that reflected from the thick plexi-glass walls that housed a small aquatic ecosystem. He sat in the middle of the blue light, atop his metal pedestal with a long cylindrical object in his hands. The top of the tube emitted slow moving vapors, writhing like simple wraiths in a slight breeze. He seemed to inhale them, playing with the strands of smoke as though they were strings of yarn. He manipulated them with one hand, while the other hand kept the cylinder close to his face. It was an illusion, she knew. It was an affectation. Dorian, the pipe, and the mists were one.

"Greetings, Lady Sarah," he smiled. "You've worked your way past Bentham and Mill already? I am eager to hear your answer to my question. Do the needs of the many outweigh the needs of the few, or the one?"

"No, neither got it right. Utilitarianism is degrading. Mill merely refined a model which was flawed from its outset. Bentham got it wrong from the beginning."

"How so?" he asked, twisting a strand of smoke through his fingers. He sat in the midst of the vapors with a slight smile, eager to see how his student was progressing in their dialogue on morality. "Governments, insurance agencies, large corporate employers all monetize an individual's worth for purposes of risk analysis, long-term investment strategies, policy development. Are they all wrong? Surely the system needs some practicality, however degrading, injected into it if modern economies are to function?"

Although Sarah was frustrated and had come for refuge more than lessons in morality, she felt it necessary to oblige Dorian. He had taken great interest in her intellectual development. He was her teacher in such matters, and she was an eager student. She obliged him as a student would. "Sentient beings are ends unto themselves. They should never be regarded as means for the purpose of bringing about the greater good. They possess inalienable rights by dint of being sentient. These rights can never be overlooked regardless of the practical implications. They cannot be abridged or bartered away."

"Have you read the material on Kant?" he asked, realizing how Kantian philosophy would view his interactions with the girl.

He had personal motives, as well as a larger picture in mind. Truthfully, though, he was not sure exactly what the dominant motive behind his interactions with Sarah over these last two weeks was. If she was both a Nephyr, accorded all the legendary powers of that species, and if her memory had indeed been largely wiped out on Earth, he felt it sensible that she should learn what morality was, how different thinkers had dealt with the subject of justice, of what was right and what was wrong: what was Justice after all.

So far, he had brought her through Plato and Aristotle with ease. She was a brilliant student. She quite amazingly flew through the Utilitarian philosophers and discarded them quickly. It was impressive given the pitfalls and logic traps most students languished in before fleeing the philosophic arts entirely. Life was difficult when it was analyzed as the 'home truths' often fell to the wayside upon closer examination and students, stripped of their comforting dogma, struggled for something to believe in, something to keep them from descending into the pit.

"Kant is the closest to the truth you have shown me, closer than Locke, but even he has his flaws. He was right. It is not moral to act out of fear of the law, or moral to act if the dominant motive involves some measure of self-reward." She stopped suddenly. "I apologize if I sound impertinent, but this is not why I'm here. I am grateful that you would take the time to be my teacher in these matters. There are, unfortunately, more pressing matters."

"Why are you here then, Sarah?"

"I'm leaving this ship as soon as the opportunity arrives. I just wanted to speak with you before I make this jump."

"You don't feel welcome here?"

"I don't belong here, Master Dorian."

"Well, then, the obvious question is posed: where do you belong, young Sarah?"

"I'm not sure. I just know that I have to leave this ship."

"Where do you intend to go?"

"I've no idea. I just know that this is only a stop along a journey I must make for myself."

"I don't disagree with you. We are all on a journey. However, I think that there is a time for everything."

"What are you saying?"

"You are not ready to leave this ship. When the time comes, you will know it."

"How do you know?" Sarah asked.

"My race does not envision time the way most species perceive it. I cannot see your exact future, but I know that you must remain with us for the time being. There will come a moment when you must leave us, Sarah. I know this much to be true. But it is not this moment. Your wheel of destiny as well as that of the Cortez's are still turning together."

He reached out and pulled a wisp of smoke towards his face.

"What am I to do then?" Sarah asked.

"Sometimes one must act, and other times they must act by not acting. You must wait until the right moment for action arrives. You will know when the choice is upon you."

Back in Folo's quarters, the conversation was becoming more intense.

"You're wading into dangerous waters, Germaine. Keeping that girl onboard will ensure your end. You guys have always been good at public relations and propaganda, but you'll have a hard time spinning this one. As soon as news breaks of this girl's existence, you're gonna face enemies on all sides. They'll be no such thing as safe harbor," Folo said.

"Yeah, Capoella said something similar. Still, given the girl's potential, how could I possibly duck out of this matter?" Germaine asked. "It's certainly proven a lot more complicated than I had initially contemplated, but we haven't run into anything we can't deal with."

"Not yet, you haven't.

Germaine was by nature generally carefree. He had grown too old to be startled by much. He didn't like how he felt at this moment, though.

"She's out of telepathic range. Perhaps we can be more candid with each other," Germaine said.

"What do you really want to know, Saint?" Folo asked.

"Can you access her mind?"

"Maybe, I'm more curious as to why I can't access yours, though," Folo replied.

Germaine smiled. "No one, even a Trevaine, reads my mind unless I allow it. I employ countermeasures of a type even you would not comprehend." He looked down briefly at Doja and winked. "As for the girl…I'm intrigued by the mystery of it all. This is perhaps the greatest riddle of our time, and the last place I want to find myself is watching it unfold from the sidelines. When the histories of this event are written, I want my rightful place."

"So you want me to access her mind?"

"I need to find out how she got here, where she came from. You will be compensated quite generously."

"You're old and tired, but you don't want to go out washed away in the tide of history. You're too vain and self-absorbed, Germaine, and now you've found your legacy. You'll gamble the lives of your crew, those dearest to you just to achieve this legacy, won't you?" Folo asked

"You underestimate my character, sir," Germaine replied forcefully, almost angrily. "I don't gamble with the lives of my crew. I earned their loyalty, and I'll damn sure not squander it. As for the girl, of all the places she could be right now in the universe, she is by far safer here with me and my crew than she is anywhere else. You think I underestimate the threats? You are wrong. I can run faster and harder than anyone in the universe, and I'm the best chance that girl has at living long enough to figure out just why she really is here."

"We'll see, won't we," Folo responded. "As for me, what are your plans?"

"As I've said, I'll pay you for your services, Folo. You will be more than amply compensated. I've prepared a binding contract that provides you full title to a beautiful moon I own in the Trellis System, along with a generous stipend for living expenses. In exchange for such consideration, you will assist me in ferreting out just what we are dealing with."

"A moon of my own, huh? And all I have to do is crack into that girl's mind?"

"It's a beautiful aquatic moon hidden in an area of space no one would ever even think to look. We can execute the contract and file it with the clerk of the system and send a sealed transmission to the commerce authorities," Germaine replied.

"I'll do it on one condition. I wanted it confirmed that after this whole mess is over with, you will never seek my services again," Folo said.

"Done. Doja will handle the paperwork and filing," Germaine said. "Keep an eye on him, Lady Doja." He turned and exited through the door.

"Umm, Captain, I think I would prefer that..." Folo began, but stopped as the doors closed. "Well, Lady Doja. How are you?"

Doja stood coldly, disinterest and a trace of hostility in her posture. "I've never met a member of your race. Your telepathic powers are reputedly more advanced than my own. Tell me, what do your senses read in me?" she asked.

"You are inscrutable, Lady Doja. You know that."

"Not to you, though."

"Not entirely, no."

"What do you see then?"

"I can see energy patters, similar energy patterns. You and Sarah are alike, connected somehow. It's why you won't go near her mind."

"You are aware how dangerous I can become when provoked," Doja asked.

"I'm not going to mention it to anybody. I have no reason to anyway."

The child stared for a cold few seconds. "No, of course not."

Germaine found Sarah in her quarters, staring out through a porthole into the stretchy, blue particle whorls of post-light travel. She was wearing a long , white linen robe, and she kept it hunched about her as though she was freezing, although the temperature in the room was precisely set, fully automated.

"What am I doing here?" she asked, keeping her eyes on the porthole. She didn't even want to look at him. "You took my identity away when you rescued me from the hospital, but you haven't filled the void with anything but more mystery. I feel so...weary. My soul is tired. I need to know what is going on here."

He stared for a moment before he spoke. He was very careful with his words this time.

"Someone found you, Sarah. I don't exactly know how. I don't even know where. But someone retrieved you. Someone was keeping you hidden on Earth. Then I came along, and now you are here. It may sound arrogant, but I'd like to believe that you are better off here with me than where I found you on Earth."

"What happened to my people? What do you really believe?"

"I don't know. I've traveled time for centuries, but no one, not even myself can travel back to the era your species existed. No one who has ever traveled back there has survived. All we know is that your species disappeared after leaving just enough scattered evidence to point to their role as the creators of this space. They haven't been seen in eons, not until you arrived on the scene. And now that you're here, nobody can predict the ramifications."

"I think I want some time alone to digest everything I've heard today, Captain. Please forgive me, but I want to be by myself," she said. She kept her face towards the porthole. She didn't want him to see that a few tears had risen up and were now dripping down her face.

"As you wish," he replied, leaving her alone in the room.

It was several hours later that Sarah approached Folo's quarters, alone. He was waiting, still half-drunk. He was clearly a being who enjoyed torturing his innards with excessive drink.

She entered to find him reclined on the sofa, his lanky limbs splayed out like some broken bird. His eyes would close for several seconds before lighting back up and staring suspiciously. When he noticed Sarah, he almost smiled.

"I thought you'd be back soon," he said.

"Yeah? Why's that?"

"Because," he told her. "I'm the only one who can give you real answers. Germaine doesn't know one-tenth of this story. He's stumbling around in the dark with half-answers to half-formed questions. Only I can give you what you want."

"What can you see of my destiny?"

"I don't know. Really, I don't, but you do. I cannot penetrate your mind, but I can catch fleeting images and energy fluctuations. The knowledge you seek is hidden within your mind, and I'm the only one who can access your brain. You've figured that out, otherwise you wouldn't be here."

"Why can't Dorian or Doja access my memories?"

"Because your defenses were set-up to stop them."

"What defenses?"

"Feedback devices, thought-bombs," Folo said. "Pretty hairy stuff. Germaine transmitted the results of his scans. You've got some sinister little defenses inside that big brain of yours."

"But you can get around these defenses? How?"

"Because I'm one of the most powerful telepaths in this universe."

"I don't want to lose control."

"You can terminate the encounter any time you want to, Sarah."

"I have your word?"

"Indeed. My only concern is whether or not you're ready for what we may find. Your personality now is the product of significant manipulation. It may be difficult for you to rectify who you think you are now with what you truly are."

"What are you saying?"

"I don't know your future, but I know it will be a violent one. When I see your energy, I know only that you are designed for this violence. I suspect Lady Doja knows this as well. She is not training you for combat merely to amuse herself."

Sarah was about to ask how he could know of such matters, but she realized the answer was staring back at her.

"I only want the truth. I need to find out who I am. I'll deal with any psychic schisms when they come up."

"You may not like what I find. What if you're just a construct? What if there's no memory loss at all because there are no memories, just a soldier with nothing other than the mission?" he asked.

"Well, then that's how it is. You only need to worry about giving me the truth."

"Where would you like to do this?"

"The medical bay," Sarah said.

"I was thinking that would be optimal. I want some-body to monitor the procedure."

"Let's do it then. I want to get this over with as quickly as possible."

"Meet me in the medical bay in two hours."

"I have your word, I can break the encounter anytime I need to?"

"I strongly suspect that even if I were to try and domi-nate your will, I could not. For the record, I would not bother to try."

"Two hours, then," Sarah said.

"Two hours, Sarah. Go back to your quarters and relax. You need to be fully rested.

Sarah stared for a moment weighing something in silence, and then she left Folo's quarters. She didn't go back to her quarters. She couldn't sit still. Instead she roamed the halls. She traveled for miles through the ship, around the corkscrew until she had descended three full levels, then she retraced her steps. Two hours later, she arrived at the medical bay, admittedly scared out of her mind. She had no idea what she was walking into. There was no way to estimate what she would endure. But she had to remember who she was. She would walk through fire if she could answer that question.

When the doors opened, Capoella and Germaine were sitting in one corner talking. Doja stood by herself, staring at the others with some small amount of disdain. Folo paced, his hands fidgety from too many stims trying to overload too many depressants. There was a weird sort of anticipation in the air, an uneasiness mixed with collectively held breaths. For Germaine and Capoella, cracking into young Sarah's mind was their top priority. For Sarah, deciphering what laid buried in her subconscious was an imperative. She didn't like the idea of a telepath peering into her memories, but she liked the uncertainty of her situation even less.

"Come in, Sarah. We're almost ready to begin," Capoella said, standing up and moving to a console. "Just lie down on the bed like last time. I will be monitoring everything. I won't let anything happen to you," Capoella promised.

Sarah, as scared as she could be, took a position on the nearest bed. She clenched her fists and released, repeating several times, trying to get rid of the anxious energy that was coursing through her blood.

Folo stopped his pacing. Doja moved to stand besides Capoella at the console, Capoella monitoring Sarah's biometric signals, Doja monitoring Folo in her own fashion. Folo pressed his fingers together and then breathed deep, expanding his chest and then whooshing out the air with a rather exaggerated exhalation.

After he stopped, he walked up very near the side of Sarah's bed and took a seat. "I need you to be very relaxed, Sarah. We are going to walk together, you and I. *Relax.*"

It was just a word, one simple word, but Sarah felt the effects immediately. She stopped clenching her fists, and her body settled into the foam mattress. Her mind quieted and her vision narrowed. There was only Folo's face. Then there was nothing at all, nothing but a blackness, an empty void in which she felt both awake and suspended within.

Folo's face appeared suddenly, pushing its way through the curtain of black. "Where are we?" he asked.

Sarah couldn't answer. She tried to speak but nothing came out.

"Where should we go from here?" Folo's face asked.

Sarah's limp hand drifted up, forefinger pointing into the deeper blackness. Three lights appeared, spheres rotating at incredible velocities. They were pulsars, intriguing quantum outcomes.

"What is inside the blackness?" Folo asked.

Sarah couldn't answer. Her body flew forward, catapulted by force of thought, deeper into the darkness. As she fell deeper, she knew she was moving farther and farther away from Folo's face. He couldn't keep up with her. She was falling, unable to stop, unable to talk, completely helpless, while behind her, Folo's face seemed to shrink away.

Several seconds later, the blackness fled away and Sarah became fully unconscious. At that moment, Folo fell out of the chair and onto the floor, his body shivering, the fingers of his hands clawing out into the space in front of him.

"Grab him!" Germaine yelled.

"He's having some sort of seizure. He was getting a lot of neural feedback from Sarah. His brain is shutting down, Captain." Capoella replied anxiously.

Germaine and Capoella rushed in to lift Folo's quivering body. "Let's get him into a stasis chamber. Doja, what's just happened?"

Doja had been watching quietly the whole time. She didn't say anything, even when Germaine asked her opinion. She merely shrugged and left the medical bay to disappear elsewhere.

"Is it me, or is she getting more ornery?" Germaine asked.

"Let's just get him in the tube. If we don't hurry, he'll likely suffer irreversible brain damage," Capoella answered.

As Germaine and Capoella were carrying Folo into the stasis tube, Sarah awoke.

"What's going on?" Sarah asked.

"Huh. Would have thought you'd know more about this than us, little Sarah," Germaine replied.

He was already getting to the point where he discounted everything she said; suspected her every movement. Capoella had become suspicious as well, though she disguised her sentiments far more effectively.

They shoved Folo into a stasis tube, and then paused to regain their breath.

"What's wrong with him?" Sarah asked.

"He got fried trying to access your brain," Capoella replied. "But I suppose you don't remember anything."

"Dear god, Capoella. You know I didn't do this intentionally," Sarah responded. "Is he going to be all right?"

"He's damaged, Sarah. His brain has been traumatized. How it recovers, what changes he may experience, it's anyone's guess."

Sarah frowned. "I'm sorry. I'm so sorry."

"Sarah, you need to know there's a whole universe of people out there who would gladly crucify you," Capoella said.

"What are you getting at?"

"You need to distinguish friend from foe real quick or you'll end up getting killed. Nephyr, or not, it won't matter to the heathens out there who want to see your head on a platter," Germaine said.

"I'm not hiding anything from either of you. You have to know that," Sarah pleaded.

"You'll forgive us, Sarah. This whole situation is difficult for any of us to understand. We've already come to the conclusion that we were set up to find you. We know there is a game going on here. We just don't know what it is."

"What do you mean setup?" Sarah asked.

"Somebody led us to you. It was more than a leak. It was a trap-play," Capoella answered. "At this point, it's hard to see what role you really play, but if you had to cover your tracks, you sure wouldn't want someone like Folo poking around inside your head."

"I went to him. I asked for this. Now I'm still in the dark, and I have you two looking at me as though I'm some sort of enemy agent."

"We don't know what to believe, Sarah," Germaine said. "Right now, though, our best plan just went out the window. Even if Folo recovers, he won't likely try and access your brain again. You'll forgive us for being a little paranoid at this moment. We just spent a lot of energy so we could run straight into a brick wall. It's not a very satisfying state of affairs, my love of a good mystery notwithstanding."

Several hours later, Capoella and Germaine sat in the ready-room, each of them pondering their martini with a notable disinterest. Apprehension had caused them both to lose their appetite for life's simple luxuries.

"So what do you think?" he asked.

"Chimera."

"No fun," he sighed.

"Nope, no fun at all."

They both sighed and then sat through more silence. They both had bad things brewing in their minds, and this wasn't alleviated by the fact that sometime deep in their silent ponderings they were interrupted when Doja sent a communiqué requesting an immediate meeting.

"Of course, Lady Doja. We're in the Ready Room," Germaine replied. "Huh. Doja wants a meeting. That's strange."

A few moments later, Doja appeared. She was dressed in a blue school-girl's uniform, her short legs covered in white stockings, her eyes cold and penetrating.

"I thought you should know what I was able to read in Folo's mind before he succumbed to the booby-trap."

Germaine looked at Capoella, she shrugged. "If you have something to say, we'd sure love to hear it."

"I only caught one image. I was able to decipher the galactic coordinates to within a light-year given the position of several well known pulsars and other anomalies. Sarah was discovered in the Borgias Expanse. I suspect that any answer as to her purpose lies within that territory," Doja said. She turned on her heel and left without a further word.

"Is she becoming more enigmatic or am I becoming more paranoid," Germaine asked. "What do you think?"

"About going to the Borgias Expanse?" Capoella asked. "Nice place for an ambush. The sensors would barely penetrate the radiation. We wouldn't have an idea who might be sneaking up on us until they fired their weapons. It's a natural cloaking field. Pirates have been using it for eons. The deeper you go, the weirder it gets."

"You think Sarah let just enough slip out to set us up?" he asked.

"Maybe not consciously. Maybe she was programmed to do it. There's certainly nothing good about the Expanse."

"So, do we go to the Expanse or not? That's the question. So far, our gamble has been for low stakes. If we go to the Expanse, we might not fare so well. As you said, it's a great spot for an ambush and there's more than a few groups who've taken an interest in this matter."

"What do we know about the Expanse? What do we *really* know?" Capoella inquired.

"A few hundred star systems, mostly black holes and dark matter. Nobody can stay in there for long. The gravity shearing will tear most ships to bits after they've battered them around for a little bit and softened them up. However, we do know someone who's traveled a lot in that area."

"I'd prefer not to know him," Capoella replied.

"He's my friend, Capoella."

"I'll live my whole life and never figure out what you see in him. Anybody's whose idea of proper labor relations involves the liberal use of cruise missiles is off my friend list."

"It's a guy thing," Germaine grinned shamelessly. "Besides, he always loses golf matches to me with a strong measure of grace."

"I don't suppose I could talk us out of this excursion?"

"Not unless you know anybody else who's traveled in the Expanse, darlin."

Chapter Seven

Enemies, Lots of Enemies

"Jesus, he's fast," Sarah said. "A lot faster than the tapes showed."

She was sitting on a short stool in her corner. Doja was rubbing her shoulders while another figure pressed a frozen strip of iron to the area beneath her right eye.

Outside the cage, the arena was packed with thirty thousand screaming fans. For the moment, Doja was inhabiting an avatar that appeared as a seventy year old fight trainer that appeared very similar to Burgess Meredith. Sarah was also in disguise. Her body had been "proto-morphed" before the fight so that no one on Eros Tao could possibly know her true identity. Doja had made arrangements so that Sarah could compete while in the morphed disguise of a young, up and coming fighter out of Bhetel-Reit. For the next several hours, Sarah would wear the body of a welterweight Speed-Fighter before her genes reverted. She was forty pounds heavier than her normal weight, but she had the muscle mass to carry her larger frame. Still, there were some adjustment issues. The first time she used the restroom was as surreal an experience as one could imagine. She was still getting used to the range of her kicks, and her footwork.

"Turn the adrenaline down," Sarah said. "I'm too light on my feet."

"Watch his left, Sarah," Doja coached. "You keep circling to your right. You need to be moving away from the punch. Circle to your left. Keep sticking him with your jab. Set-up the head kick with a feint. Don't just throw your leg out there, or he'll take you down again."

Across the cage, the other fighter, a bald, fierce humanoid from Ghemarra, was being given the fine points as well. The first round had been a war. Her opponent, a creature named Fas-Solaswani was well-rounded, good on his feet, good in the clinch, good on the ground. Still, Sarah could see holes in his game. As far as endurance went, she had far better cardio. She also punched harder. Sarah channeled the energy from her hips perfectly, devastatingly. She'd rocked her opponent twice with heavy head-kicks and her right hook, but she also got taken down and pounded on twice before she could reverse position and make it back to her feet. It would be a difficult round for the judges to score. Sarah knew better than to leave her fate to the judges.

"I'm gonna let him punch himself out," Sarah said.

"Careful, there. He has heavy hands," Doja answered. "Keep out of mid-range, or you'll eat a hook. You need to fight in close, or fight outside. You can't stay in that middle-range or he's gonna pop you. Duck in, duck out, just like we trained for. Don't turn this into a brawl. Be smart out there."

"He's gassing. I broke his nose. He's having a hard time breathing. His mouth was open for the last two minutes of the round. He's only got so much juice left in his punches. Then, I take it up a notch."

"Watch your timing. Keep an eye on the clock. You can't give him too many points or you'll lose the round. This is a three-round match, remember."

"I'm good. When his arms get tired enough, they'll drop too low. I'm gonna take him out," Sarah said confidently

The referee blew the whistle, and the two fighting entourages left the cage. Once the cage was clear, the ref turned to her: "You ready to fight?" he asked. She nodded, shaking out her forearms. He turned to the other fighter and asked the same question. Then the bell sounded, and the second round began.

Sarah engaged quickly, but then settled back and relied on her footwork. She counter-punched, but mostly did as she said she would. She let her opponent swing, and swing. He punched wildly at her, desperate when his arms started to feel the burn. He had maybe enough energy for one good knockout blow. He couldn't box much beyond that now. She moved gracefully, keeping in mind what Doja had said. She circled away from her opponent's left hook, and stabbed him with jabs.

She kept her eyes focused on his body, on his hips in particular. He was fast, but Sarah had had five minutes to start to get her opponent's rhythm. She was timing his movements, and timing her countermoves precisely.

When her opponent shot low for a double-leg take-down, she sprawled, dropping her weight to the ground and shooting her feet out behind her so her weight was bearing down on top of her opponent. Just as they came up from the position, she drove a knee straight into his jaw.

The crowd went wild. The arena was shaking with the thunder of people stomping their feet. It was madness.

Sarah was taking the fight deeper, and her conditioning was paying off. For three weeks now, she had been training her combat skills with Doja. Tonight was the culmination of a lot of hard work. Sarah was healthy, her body like that of a thoroughbred horse. While her opponent had already began to suck air in through his mouthpiece, Sarah was still breathing through her nose. She was outpacing her opponent, and she was quickly becoming a fan favorite.

The fighters danced around each other in a predatory waltz, each one calculating their next move. Her opponent was tiring quickly. He had almost punched himself out. Sarah looked up to the screens hanging from the ceiling of the arena. Three minutes left.

She gritted her teeth, and upped the tempo considerably. Instead of dancing around her prey, she started to stalk him down. She stayed 'in the pocket' and began walking him back with a series of switch kicks followed instantly by hard straight rights. He was wearing down visibly, wilting.

Like a true champion, she had the instinct to know when it was time to move in for the kill. She feinted with a left jab and then came from underneath his guard, smashing into his face with a right uppercut that set him back. He wobbled for a second before falling to one knee. As he tried desperately to defend himself with his hand, Sarah moved in for the final shot. She took one step forward, planted her weight on her front foot and then she swiveled from her hip, catching him with a shin straight across the broadside of his face. He fell over, his arms splayed out around him, completely unconscious. His left foot twitched, and the camera caught that aspect of the tragedy and replayed it over and over on the screens. The crowd went wild with bloodlust. The sound was deafening. Sarah looked at her fallen opponent, and she stood over his splayed out frame, victorious.

Sarah raised her gloved hands in triumph as the entourages rushed into the cage. Doctors swarmed the fallen opponent. Immediately they began scanning and diagnosing the damage. Savage, one of them whispered.

Doja rushed onto the apron smiling in her old man form. Sarah was still getting used to the different faces of Doja. In her different forms, she adopted personality characteristics consistent with her guises. Her boxing coach persona was particularly enjoyable because it was so "un-Doja".

"That was great, kid. Beautiful."

"I kicked his ass, didn't I?" Sarah grinned. She took her mouthpiece out and then winged it out into the crowd beyond the cage. Some unlucky fan was zinged by the saliva filled plastic.

"Technically, Sarah, you kicked his face," Doja smiled.

A few formalities ensued, mainly consisting of the referee lifting Sarah's hand in victory after her pseudonym was called out by the announcer. She had won by knockout. This meant she got a fight bonus. She couldn't care about the cash, she had no need for it, but it was nice to receive a bonus, honor wise.

A celebrity announcer entered the ring with microphone in hand.

"Wow," he said. "That was a spectacular performance. Tell us, what were you thinking when the second round began?"

Sarah was guileless, so she relied on the truth. She was feeling a glow from inside, and the universe could not be a better place. The fans in the crowd were chanting her fake name. It felt unbelievable. Her other troubles aside, she felt on fire and wonderfully alive in the moment.

"Well, I knew he was going to come out heavy in the first round. He's known for pushing the pace early. I kind of messed up a little. My game-plan coming in was to look out for his left hook. He has a habit of putting people to sleep with it. I kind of walked into that twice, and he got me dizzy on my feet. I knew I'd tagged him pretty good also, but I wasn't sure how the judges would score that first round. He got a couple of nice takedowns, I busted him up, I mean I could see it going either way. So when the second round began, I knew I was going to have to do something definitive. I've been watching his tapes for a while. He's a great fighter, but I figured my cardio was better. He seems to gas out a lot in the second round. There's usually a good window there until he catches his second wind. So I let him punch himself out a bit, and then I kind of turned up the volume," Sarah said.

"You turned up the volume?" the celebrity announcer smiled. "Is that what they call it on your planet?"

"Yeah, well, he started to drop his arms about halfway through the round. That kind of left him open for my head kicks. I started to push the pace, and then that was that. Knockout."

"That was fantastic, absolutely fantastic. A lot of people didn't know you before this fight. A lot more will know you now. That was a hell of a performance for your first time in the cage."

"Well, that's what I was hoping for. You always want to put on a good show for the fans. I mean they're what this is all about, right? I also wanted to make a point that I could be a contender in this weight division. I think I still need some good fights against some tough opponents, but I think I'll get my title shot eventually. Until then, I'll just keep working hard. I'll take whoever Double-F wants to match me up against."

"Well, we hope to see you back in the cage real soon. Congratulations. That was a terrific performance." The announcer held the microphone up. "Ladies and gentlemen, let's give it up for Maja 'the Marxist Menace' Mondavi. Great fight."

A short time later, backstage in the locker room, Doja asked "How did it feel?"

"I'm pumped. It's like I'm in the clouds but can't come down. That was unbelievable."

"You earned it, Sarah. You worked hard, and it paid off."

"Yeah, sorry for those moments during training when I acted like a bitch. I'm glad you pushed me. It paid off out there tonight."

"No worries. You fought through it. I'm proud of you," Doja said.

Doja had switched back to her normal child avatar. She was now at least two feet shorter than Sarah's morphed frame.

"I want to do this again," Sarah said.

"We'll see what we can arrange," Doja replied.

The planet he was hiding on was unstable. Tremendous amounts of radiation would conceal his presence from all except those who knew precisely where to look. Few species inhabited this region of the universe. The Borgias Expanse was a dangerous radioactive cesspool in space, a wasteland consisting of the detritus left over when two great galaxies had collided magnificently in a violent waltz that had lasted just over two billion years. In the millions of years following the crash, the galaxies had flown away from one another, ripping each other apart at the outer edges of their disks before reforming, exchanging star systems with each other the way organics spread STDs. The Borgias Expanse was the illegitimate child of this collision, a weird area without a proper galaxy to call home. Space-time was agitated very heavily in that area, as a child born of a conflict ridden parentage.

It was the perfect space to hide oneself. Civilizations were few and far between in this region and traveling it meant navigating through a dangerous admixture or warped space/time with fierce graviton shears, spatial anomalies and inconceivable amounts of radiation. It was a deadly junkyard spinning through space, its stars twinkling out and dying, forming many dwarves and neutron stars, while many of the larger ones compressed into black holes that molested their neighborhood in space with cold predator precision.

Outside the cave, a low rumble sounded. It was constant, artificial in nature. Soon a small, semi-translucent vessel descended through the upper atmosphere. The vehicle was shaped like a large black triangle. It descended with a slow, deliberate pace. As it landed its engines used a field-energy technology that did not disturb even one grain of the heavy layers of rust colored sand. Two pairs of fighter escorts hung in the area above the vessel, sweeping the landscape with targeting sensors, high-bandwidth scanning pulses. Off in the distance, a fiery purple volcano roared as it regurgitated chunks of molten matter from deep within the planet's core. It was as though the planet knew the dark things that were to transpire. It expressed its displeasure at being the situs for a conspiracy of this sort.

A doorway opened and a ramp slid forward. Three figures wearing light space suits emerged from the vessel.

The man watched them from his position at the mouth of the cave, and then he emerged. He lit a plasma torch revealing his location in the hillside above the landing spot and waited.

The figures headed up a treacherously thin footpath, up towards the entrance to the cave. Once inside, the man activated a force-field. With a limited artificial atmosphere, the three figures removed their helmets. Their faces, once revealed appeared as a set of black cobras, ghost-like as their bodies had evolved near the point of total energy transmutation. They were wraiths, Vespiraforms, and their eyes were deader than the deepest regions of empty space. They were predators of the highest order. They were Ven-Dhavaradi, compassionless, ruthless.

"Welcome, Chancellor," the man said. "This meeting has been a long time in the making."

"Do you have the data-recorder, Torvallus?" the first of the VD hissed.

"Indeed," the man named Torvallus replied. He reached into a pocket of his jacket and threw a small crystal cube towards the creature that had asked the question. "My lord Chancellor, you will find that I always honor my promises."

"Let us see," the Chancellor whispered. He handed the device to the figure standing beside him.

The subordinate scanned the instrument with a palm-held instrument.

"It is genuine and it has not been tampered with, Chancellor," the subordinate replied.

"Be sure, be very sure," the Chancellor hissed.

The subordinate re-scanned the device. He took extra time, not because he actually needed to, but rather to keep up appearances. He did not suspect himself of error. The particle decay rates were perfect to the millisecond, the microcellular bonding was undisturbed. There was no way it was a forgery. The order to re-scan the device had been designed so that the Chancellor could monitor the figure in front of him for a hint of fear or betrayal.

The subordinate concluded the scan. "It is genuine, Chancellor. I have no doubt."

"Activate it," the Chancellor replied.

The subordinate opened the seals of the device using a harmonic resonance emitter. The box opened as the sides fell apart. An image suddenly appeared as the holo-emitters activated. The subordinate placed the device on the ground separating the figures. Three dimensional figures began appearing in the air between them. Military installations, civilian planets, battle-fleets, and their positional relationships flashed through at a speed too fast for most beings to comprehend. For several seconds, the blinking images presented themselves in a slide-show format. Once concluded, the device closed in upon itself, and an uncomfortable silence emerged.

"Are you satisfied with the authenticity of the transmission?" Torvallus asked.

"It seems genuine. Still, we are puzzled as to your motivations in this matter. We've been unable to verify anything of your background."

"That is because there is no data. My race was destroyed. Only a few of us made it the Bulk alive. We have searched for a very long time to find a way to destroy the Nephyr. You are the perfect candidates to effect our revenge. We both have grievances with the Nephyr, only your species has the potential to rival their power. When you conducted your first war with the Nephyr, you were not ready. Your impulses were correct, but your capacity to destroy them did not yet exist. You've had over seven billion years to perfect your armies in the hopes that you could wage war again. I am offering you the opportunity to realize your destiny. Only I know the location of the home universe of the Nephyr, and only I know their security protocols and defenses. I offer you the chance to penetrate the Membrane and track down your enemies. I can get you close enough to destroy many of the key targets necessary to implement a full invasion. I can show you everything you need to take them apart. That is why you came here."

"Convince me, Torvallus. Convince me why I should commit a military expedition into an affair that might destroy my civilization."

"I have already provided you with my proof."

"No, you have provided us a tempting prize. Everything else could be fabricated. The Nephyr are treacherous. I do not know which version of history you are versed in, but we did not start the war with the Nephyr. We neither won the war, nor lost it. They tried to eliminate my species. We defended ourselves. I must be certain that this is not a trap."

"What do you wish from me?" Torvallus asked.

"Give me some proof that your species was targeted. Give me something more to go on than some data recorder. Give me some reason to trust you. I am the Chancellor and protector of thirty trillion Ven-Dhavaradi. I shall not commit them to destruction. Furnish me with some proof that what you say is real before we begin this final war. You provide me with this and I shall wage a war the likes of which our realities have never seen."

"I can understand your hesitation in this matter. Were I you, I suspect I would require more than what I have provided. I know two ways I can prove my sincere devotion to our conspiracy. Provide me with a scout vessel that I can outfit so that it can pierce the Membrane. Give me a skeleton crew. You can send a data-recorder provided I can restrict when and how it is employed. In six months time, we shall meet back here. I shall give you your proof. I shall provide you with everything you need to believe in my sincerity," Torvallus replied.

"You are aware that there is a Nephyr in this universe? We suspect she is pursuing you."

"Yes, Chancellor, I know of her. She is not the only Nephyr, however. She has an escort."

"Then you know something we do not."

"I am not without my resources in this universe," Torvallus said.

"She has a powerful ally, a man we know well. Saint Germaine, as he calls himself, is no simple foe. Do not doubt his resourcefulness. He has powerful friends. You must watch yourself."

"Thank you for the warning, but I have already taken care of the matter. By the time she remembers who she is or why she is here, this issue will largely be concluded." Torvallus smiled politely, bowing deeply.

"So it would seem. Let us adjourn. I shall make arrangements to furnish you with a scout craft and crew. We shall meet here again in six months time."

"You realize I cannot allow them to live after I take them to their destination. Whoever you assign to this mission, make sure they understand that it is a suicide mission."

The Chancellor reached to his belt and drew a hilt, and a razor sharp blade materialized. The blade was confined to another dimension until the hilt was drawn. In one fluid motion the Chancellor sliced off the head of the subordinate standing to his right. The figure dropped to the ground, instantly lifeless. The Chancellor returned the blade to his belt.

"My people do not fear death. We embrace it fully. If you make a bargain with my kind, you would be best advised to honor it. Make me believe you, Torvallus, and you shall have your revenge. You will see a war like no other," the Chancellor hissed.

"May the gods look favorably upon your actions in this matter," Torvallus said.

"We are our own gods, Torvallus, that is why you chose us. Once you have given us the coordinates, we shall make final war on the Nephyr. We shall leave none alive. You will have your vengeance, and we shall realize our destiny."

Torvallus' eyes lowered, and for a second his hands appeared to shake with a slight tremor. For a moment, he was silent. Then he spoke in a whisper. "Yes, the time of the Nephyr draws to a close. I suspect a bloody road ahead for both of us. I shall likely die in this endeavor. I have cheated death for too long. I can feel death chasing at my heels. Before I die, I would see my people avenged. You are my dark knights. I have never fooled myself or romanticized what you represent. You are the cold hand of justice. I am but a tool in this matter."

"We've got problems," Capoella said.

"What's going on?" Germaine replied. "Why is the threat level raised to orange? Are you trying to make people paranoid?"

"Energy signatures. Lots of energy signatures. They're cloaked, but Doja can detect the shifts in space-time their vessels are leaving in their wake. This could be due to the size and number of vessels following us."

"We're in warp-space?"

"Uh, yeah."

"Who in god's name could track us here?" Germaine asked.

"I told you we've got a bug someplace."

"I suspect you're right. Only how? Find us a system nearby with a gas-giant, something with a heavy, gassy, nasty sort of atmosphere," Germaine said. "We need time to think."

"I've been scanning the databases on this region. We're closing on a system that might work out."

"Bring us in hard."

"Aye, Captain. We'll fall out of warp two-hundred thousand kilometers from a giant. I'm transferring all power to the shields. We'll let inertia guide us in."

At that moment, Doja entered the bridge.

"What's tracking us?" Germaine asked.

"An ICPT battle fleet. One and one half battle-fleets to be precise," Doja answered.

"One and half battle fleets? Why the extra half fleet?"

"I suspect the Bureaucracy is trying to make a point," Doja responded.

A figure followed Doja through the door hesitantly. It was the figure of a one-hundred and eighty pound Speed-Fighter. He was bald, his face smooth, his skin covered in wicked black-ink tribal tattoos.

"Umm, Doja, where is Sarah?" Germaine asked.

"Right here, Captain," the Speed-Fighter smiled broadly.

"You're proto-morphed?! Why?!" Germaine yelled.

"So I could fight in the Speed-Fighting matches, Captain," Sarah smiled innocently.

"This is the little thing you two have spent so much time working on lately? Speed-Fighting? Lady Doja, in the off-chance that we might actually survive what's sure to be an all out attack by one and a half battle fleets, you and I are going to have a very long talk about what extra-curricular activities are allowed," Germaine growled.

"I think I've just been chastised," Doja said. "Intriguing."

"Well, while you're pondering that, could you scan their defenses, see if you can breach their security grid?" Germaine asked.

"Battle fleet is closing. They're charging weapons. I'm transferring energy to aft shields. We'll come out of warp in thirty seconds," Capoella said.

A blast hit the vessel. Everyone rocked unsteadily for a moment. The lights flickered and then resumed.

"Strike that. We're coming out of warp now. We're way off target," Capoella said.

The Cortez dropped out of warp-space. They were a long way off from the comfortable hiding space inside the gas giant's atmosphere. With their sub-light engines, it would take two days to reach safety.

The battle fleet, all one and half of them, dropped out of warp into the space around and behind the Cortez. They were suddenly enveloped in a swarm of large dangerous battle craft, and hundreds of small four-man fighter formations buzzing around the larger vehicles.

"We're in trouble," Capoella said.

"I'm glad to hear you say that," Germaine replied. "I thought I was just being paranoid."

A signal haled the Cortez.

"Onscreen," Germaine ordered.

"Hello, old friend," a wide, smiling head greeted. He looked like a fat, overgrown child with a smooth, boyish face. His gray uniform, however, was immaculately pressed.

"Admiral Fushevez, so good to see you. To what do we owe the honor of your distinguished presence?" Germaine asked.

"Oh, the usual shakedown. Say, I was wondering if I could come aboard and we could have a little chat, just the two of us," the admiral said.

"You know you don't have to ask. You're always welcome on my ship. Transport to the visitor lobby. I'll meet you there shortly," Germaine replied.

"See you in a moment then," the man said before ending the transmission.

"Capoella, keep an eye on the fleet while I meet with out good friend, the admiral."

He headed for the door leading out from the bridge. Capoella called out. "Please don't do anything stupid."

"Who, me?" Germaine smiled.

A few moments later, Germaine was below decks. Admiral Fushevez was standing in an alcove designed for arriving guests.

"Wow. I love what you did with the place," Admiral Fushevez stated.

"That's right. You haven't been here since the renovation. It's considerably more modern than it used to be," Germaine smiled. "Follow me. Let's get drinks."

He led the admiral down through several long halls until they entered a low-lit cantina. They took a seat at a round table near the bar and Germaine ordered a pitcher of martinis.

They were served quickly and each man savored the crisp bite of a newly born martini.

"Very stylish. I wholeheartedly approve," the admiral said.

"Well, I had some help," Germaine said.

"Yes, you have always had such wonderful crewmembers. I am envious. No one aboard my vessel has a trace of creativity. They're all a bunch of boring sods," the admiral complained. "Sometimes I think our academic institutions focus too much on conformity and political indoctrination. Take my crew, for instance. They're terrified of standing apart from the herd. A bunch of sheep, all of them."

"It sounds dreadful," Germaine replied.

"Oh it is. It is. Listen, I am sorry for using my battle fleet to blast you out of warp space. It's a distasteful matter. I assure you, I'm not at all happy about it."

"It's okay. My vessel is repairing itself as we speak," Germaine replied.

"Yes, well, old chap, therein lies the dilemma."

"A dilemma. What dilemma?" Germaine asked, playing coy for habit's sake alone.

"Well, it seems that you have recently come into contact with an individual we simply cannot allow to roam the universe openly. She's a threat to the markets, I'm told. We certainly can't have that hanging above our heads. Remember what happened the last time the whole thing went kaboom."

"Yeah, the heads…rolling in the streets…"

"Quite right, no sense in revisiting it."

"Well, I certainly wouldn't want to see the markets tank," Germaine asked. "We're in agreement there."

"So it's settled then?"

"What's settled?"

"Well, old salt, we have to take possession of her. It's our only option, they tell me. If we cannot retain possession of her, we are to destroy your vessel I'm afraid."

"Surely you speak in jest," Germaine frowned.

"I wish I could say this was all some awful joke, but I have my orders. A lot of very big people in the universe are adamant about how we conclude this whole matter. I am to offer you an ultimatum, and if that doesn't work, I shall have to destroy you."

"That sounds painful. I would really prefer that you did not attack my vessel. I'm quite fond of it and my crew. It's taken me years to develop both to my tastes. I'm very fond of the place, don't you know."

"As am I. Again, I assure you, I am not directing these actions. I am a mere messenger."

"A well-armed one."

"Indeed. So it would seem."

"On a side note, I love the new uniform. The beret in particular," Germaine smiled.

"Oh yes," the admiral smiled. "It's designed to make us look more menacing. What do you think?"

"Very menacing," Germaine answered.

"Oh, I am so glad to hear you say that. I had my doubts. Fashion is such an unpredictable art. "

"Pardon me for inquiring, but how did you gentlemen track us?" Germaine asked.

"Oh, we bugged you," the admiral replied casually, sipping from his martini.

"I thought so. How come I couldn't find the bug?"

The admiral prepared to speak but as he opened his lips he brought his forefinger up and blew away a wish, his breath whistling.

"Huh," Germaine replied. "You gentlemen are becoming more and more clever."

"It's a worthy aspiration."

"I'm impressed. You guys bugged me, and I couldn't figure it out, even when Capoella warned me of her suspicions back at Berion. Interesting."

"I'm sorry we bugged you. I feel sick about the whole affair, I assure you."

"Well, back to our topic, the girl."

"Oh yes, the girl. I hate to threaten you, but we must have her."

"Well, admiral, I'm not in a position to give her up. I would readily oblige you on any matter but this one. If I were to give her to you, my stock would lose twenty percent value overnight. That's just the off-hour trading. Who knows how bad it would get from there? I'm quite stuck to this matter. Both my reputation as a stalwart renegade as well as my share values are on the line."

"Yes. I'm aware of the dangers there. I'm sure you can appreciate the importance we place on the girl, numbers wise. We've already allocated funds to take care of unwinding your major corporate assets without disrupting the commercial credit markets. This is a very expensive undertaking on many levels, not mention the toll on my emotions. Our analysts think that in order for the whole system to stay afloat, we must have the girl, barring that, we must destroy everyone. It's a mind-boggling predicament. It's all very mathematical, I'm told, complex finances and all that. I'm sorry we cannot come to terms."

"These things happen. Please enjoy my ship's hospitality for as long as you choose to remain on board," Germaine smiled.

"That's very gracious of you. I was rather hoping to see a movie in a real theater. My warship is sadly lacking a truly good theater. Budget cutbacks, I'm afraid. Too much peace is bad for business," the admiral said. "Think of the ramifications. What if a war were to suddenly break out tomorrow, and I were to fly into battle without a good entertainment center? It boggles the mind how this new breed of civilian bureaucrats think. The Bureaucrats would prefer if I got my Wagner via a pointy-headed with recruit with a piccolo. Unbelievable bunch, this new breed is."

"As always, you're quite welcome to watch a movie here. Anything in particular?" Germaine asked.

"I was rather hoping I could watch Casablanca again," the admiral smiled.

"Of course. Please let my androids know whatever refreshments you might require," Germaine replied.

"Thank you kindly. After that, I shall return to my ship. I fear we shall have to engage in hostilities at that point. I hope you don't take it personally. I really am fond of you, you know."

"I'm fond of you as well, admiral. Don't worry about the hostilities. These things are bound to occur. The universe is a complicated place."

"It does my heart good to hear you say that. I've been worried for some time that should I disintegrate your vessel, you and I would no longer be friends," the admiral smiled.

"Not a chance," Germaine promised. "We all have our duties. I suppose I can leave you to find your way to the cinema?"

"Oh yes. I'm sure I can find it."

"Enjoy your movie then," Germaine smiled.

"Thank you very much."

Germaine left the admiral alone in the cantina, and headed back to the bridge.

As the doors closed, Capoella asked: "How was your talk?"

"Oh, very pleasant, as always. Just so you know, in about one and a half hours, we are going to be attacked."

"Let me guess?"

"Casablanca," Germaine answered.

"He must have seen that movie a hundred times by now," she sighed.

"Well, at least he's predictable."

Shortly into the second hour of waiting, their vessel cruising at top sub-light speed towards the gas giant, their ability to punch a hole in space-time severely hampered by a dense radioactive particle blanket the fleets were draping over them, the crew of the Cortez received the first notice that hostilities had ensued. A volley of plasma bursts exploded several thousand kilometers off the port bow.

"That was his warning shot," Germaine said.

A signal haled the Cortez.

"Put him up," Germaine said.

Admiral Fushevez's fat face filled the screen.

"I'm feeling rather nauseous about the prospect of destroying your wonderful ship, Phaestus. I was thinking, perhaps we could do this in a matter where you save face."

"What do you propose?" Germaine asked.

"Well, say the girl was to stand in a position on your ship near the exterior hull. Suppose your defenses got compromised and we transported her off your vessel. You go down on your shield like a good counterculture fighter, we get the girl, and everyone's happy," the admiral smiled. "People's estimation of your anarchic nature could actually jump a few points if we do a bit of damage to the Cortez."

"Sorry, old friend, that's not how I do business. Thanks for the offer, though," Germaine.

"Of course. I had to do it before I targeted your vessel with every cannon and missile my battle fleets possess."

"Totally understandable, old friend," Germaine replied.

"Well, best of luck in your next life. I do wish you well, you know," the admiral said. "I've never told you this, but when I was seven, I came to one of your book signings on Sigma Twelve. You were very patient with me. I have to tell you that ever since then, I've hated Che Guevarra every bit as much as you," the admiral said. "What a dirty, fiendish little bastard he was." The message terminated.

"I'm glad somebody got my pint about Che," Germaine smiled. Another volley of missiles exploded. "Well, I always did want to go with a bang."

"Shouldn't we fire back?" Sarah asked.

"Not much of a point, Sarah. He's got one and a half battle fleets. We couldn't do them much harm really. We're really good at outrunning ships, or staying in orbit around a planet too afraid to attack us lest portions of the vessel rain down upon them like asteroids," Germaine said. "But taking out a battle fleet, one and half battle fleets, that's a bit of a problem."

"So, what are you going to do?"

"I'm sending you and Doja to Eros Tao," Germaine said. He turned to Doja. "Take care of her."

"Of course," Doja replied somberly.

"And no more Speed-Fighting. That's dangerous," Germaine said.

"You're staying with the Cortez, Captain!" Sarah exclaimed.

"Of course I am. It's my ship after all."

The vessel was now under a sustained assault. The ship bucked. The sounds of the various impacts were like a deafening crash of powerful waves and low thudding noises. Over and over again, the ship was pounded, its shields slowly degrading under the constant pressure. Then, suddenly, the noise stopped. A loud silence suddenly swept over everything and everyone.

"Activate view-screen," Germaine ordered.

With the screen active, they could see a red cloud of energized particles growing in the area in front of the ship. It was translucent, almost like a giant red jellyfish. Tendrils of energy shot out from the central cloud mass. They were entangling the ICPT battle fleet, rendering them powerless.

"Doja?" Capoella asked. "Tell us this is one of your little tricks."

Doja stood quietly, watching the cloud envelop the battle fleets. She was in awe. "No. This is not my work. This is something I've not seen in a very long time."

"What the hell is going on?" Sarah asked.

"A cloud of energized gas just appeared in front of the Cortez. It looks like it's wrapped itself up with the battle fleets. They're not shooting at us anymore. I suspect they have their hands full," Germaine answered.

A haling signal sounded.

"On screen," Germaine said.

"Hello, old friend," the admiral's face smiled. "Say, about this whole red energy field thingy. I was wondering if I might persuade you to take it away. It's causing hell throughout my computer systems. Its very frustrating, don't you know."

"I'd love to help you, chum. But I haven't got any more idea of what's going on here than you do." Germaine said.

"Huh, quite the pickle then, wouldn't you agree? Ah well, best of luck."

"To you to, Admiral," Germaine smiled. "Best of luck."

And so, for several hours, Germaine and his crew watched the red cloud grow larger, and larger, spreading out like some off-shore oil-rig spill. It was nightmarish. Routinely, as though disciplining some errant child, tendrils from the cloud of energy would swipe away one or more of the fleet's vessels, sending them off, catapulted to positions that were several thousand light years from their previous one.

For a long time, it worked over the subdued fleets. Soon there were only a few ships left.

Germaine and crew had been viewing everything that went on outside their vessel. It was like watching some giant octopus in space use it's strength to bat away little crabs inhabiting its turf. After it was concluded and the fleet was completely dispersed, a signal haled the Cortez.

What then transpired was an event hard to describe. The face that appeared on the view-screen was hidden in a veil of gases. It spoke in a series of hyper-fast clicks and whirring noises that the central computer took several moments to translate. The transmission ended, and the tendrils of the cloud pulled back into its central mass. The fluid-like motion of the cloud was like a giant cuddlefish swimming away through a heavy, dark current. The energy form dissipated into nothingness, disappearing entirely.

The message was simple, but cryptic: Be quick, for in the Expanse all fates will be decided.

"Who the hell was that?" Germaine wondered aloud.

"Someone powerful is sending us a message, Captain," Capoella replied.

"It would certainly seem so. I just wish the message was more elaborate. We have enough mysteries on our hands."

"Let's get rid of whoever is still tailing us, and then head to the Expanse," Capoella said.

"I suppose you have a plan?" Germaine asked.

"I always have a plan," Capoella replied.

Meanwhile, Sarah stared. She knew that she was at the center of the message. Whatever she was mixed up in had drawn the attention of a creature powerful enough to casually dissipate one and one half ICPT battle fleets. She felt a deep uncertainty even as the crew enjoyed their mysterious reprieve. All she could do was look out at an empty view-screen filled with stars and wonder. She looked down at her fists. They were alien to her. She had been temporarily proto-morphed into a cage fighter. She was certainly very far now from that hospital bed.

Chapter Eight

Friends

Although Germaine was routinely carefree, nothing, even a red energy cloud, could convince him to head to the Borgias Expanse without doing some research into the matter. Research into the nature of the Expanse led him quite naturally to the Bhoon-Tebli galaxy to seek the consultation of a trusted friend. Magnus Marin was the only counsel he could trust to give him advice on the subject of the Expanse.

Like Germaine, Magnus was obscenely well off. Both men were listed on the Vorbes Top 500 richest natural entities list. The wealthiest entity in existence, however, was not natural at all. It was the Vashtoon Mega-6 Multi-Brain Omniserve 9000. It had been designed to run the affairs of a large interstellar trading empire which had began life as an Enron subsidiary hundreds of years earlier. So, it was with no small irony that instead of running the 'family' business, the AI used its status as legal title-holder and sold the assets piecemeal to a bunch of corporate raiders who literally raided the place; big gunships, ultra-violent shock-troops, the works. Meanwhile, the AI deposited the funds from untraceable bearer bonds into hidden outer-galactic bank accounts, and went on to a successful career as a ruthless venture capitalist, a very, very successful career. Again, like many strange and horrible things in the universe, the only curious feature about the whole transaction was that, with some minor variation in scale, it was going on all the time, everywhere.

Like many of Germaine's closest friends, Magnus was an anarcho-hedonist, a hyper-capitalist, and many other hyphenated and mutually contradictory things. He ran a powerful private empire on the outskirts of the Tellaurus galaxy. An uneven mixture of Caligula, Dom DeLouise, and Bernie Madoff, he was like Germaine, a foe of the establishment. He was widely haled in the press as the "Baron of Bhoon-Tebli".

Even considering their long friendship, though, Germaine cautious as the shuttle approached a large installation on a cold, giant mother asteroid flying in a calm family group on the outskirts of an outer ring star system Magnus ran his vast empire from. There were dark weird things stirring in the universe, and an uncomfortably large measure of unpredictability had been introduced into the system. Everyone was on full alert.

From space, Magnus' facility appeared as a collection of tremendous geodesic domes, and at the outskirts of these domes existed a vast sensor array several hundred miles in length. The sensor array consisted of four rows of dishes tuned towards the inner system. Magnus, like many other tyrants, was paranoid, so he kept watch over everything and everyone around him.

There was one distinction that marked Magnus, a distinction that would forever earn him a place in the history books. Whereas NASA and other similar organizations had only discussed using midgets for deep space exploration, Magnus *actually* did it. NASA and its like had abandoned the prospect because of the politics involved, but Magnus had no such restrictions. Ostensibly, he employed midgets so that he could build his deep-space explorer ships at half scale, and equip them with half as much food, oxygen, and other supplies. It was peculiarly logical. Over the decades, he'd saved considerable money from his Midget Space Program. On top of this, though, and much more importantly, he'd gotten considerable amusement from the whole damn concept of sending midgets into deep space. He was by definition pathological, as were most men of great power.

As the shuttle docked in the hangar bay of the asteroid facility, Sarah asked innocently: "Who are we going to see?"

"A friggin lunatic, Sarah," Capoella answered.

"He's a little eccentric, this is true," Germaine said.

"He's obscene," Capoella replied flatly.

"Hmmph, well...yeah," Germaine answered. "He is very funny, though, you have to admit."

"I find him fascinating," Dorian stated. "He's a complete sociopath who, by sheer exercise of wealth, compels, coerces or otherwise entices all of his subordinates to act heartlessly, without a trace of conscience. It is as though he is a virus of perverse intention infecting everything around him with gleeful cruelty," Dorian beamed. "He's an intriguing life-form."

"Well, he's a pretty good card player. You have to give him that much," Germaine responded.

"Indeed," Dorian answered.

The vessel came to a rest inside a large and quiet hangar area.

"Okay, everybody put on their happy face," Germaine stated. "Come on."

"Let the weirdness begin," Capoella muttered under her breath.

The crew exited the shuttle and made their way across the hangar. Within a few moments, doors opened at the far end, and a single, large figure entered through the doorway.

As the figure approached it revealed itself to be a short, wide man shaped like some overweight jinni and dressed as such. He was alone. Magnus didn't need body-guards. Like Germaine, Magnus had a hundred subtle defenses that left him far more protected than a collection of guards could ever make him. He was powerful enough to flaunt his power by not flaunting it.

"Welcome," he said. "Welcome, welcome, welcome."

"How are you, you fat, perverted water buffalo?" Germaine grinned.

"I feel wonderful! Just wonderful. I am in love with being me. It really, really, truly is good to be me," Magnus replied, his wide smile beaming. "Come, let's get intoxicated to celebrate your arrival. I'm breaking in my fifth liver. We should drink heavily to make sure he knows who is boss. Then we feast, and for desserts, you must tell me all about your recent adventures. I hear tell that you've been to Earth, 15th and 21st centuries. I also hear that you had a run-in with Di-Kho-Jinns - nasty creatures. I want to hear all about it."

"You sure hear a lot," Capoella responded coldly.

"Big ears, my dear. Big ears," Magnus responded disregarding her hostility entirely - he really was one hell of a political creature. "And who is this lovely little thing?" he asked, turning his attentions to Sarah.

"Just your average crew member," Sarah replied, trying a slight smile.

"You must be interesting, or Germaine wouldn't have you, darling," he replied with a lascivious, well-practiced wink.

"Let's go get drinks," Germaine interjected.

The group exited the hangar area and into the interior of the base. It looked like Miami with rows of tall palm-like trees lining perfectly immaculate roads. The domes were large enough that the ceiling was hidden in the backwash of millions of light-sources that made the air warm with their fuzzy orange glare. Inside the geodesic bubbles were large cities not dissimilar to Eros-Tao in that they operated outside the control of the Bureaucracy, and were controlled exclusively by Magnus.

The buildings in what was the Ministerial Campus were spectacular, great structures of gleaming steel and black glass. There were tremendous glass spheres, huge pyramids of flashy metal and dark shiny plastic, buildings so intricately designed they were impossible to comprehend with one glance. The whole effect was designed to instill awe of the power of its creator, to elicit bewilderment in the visitor. For Sarah, it did just that.

Winding throughout the dome like a metal snake's skeleton were the curvy rails of a mag-lev tram system that shuttled people throughout and to all corners of the facility. The trams whooshed through at terrifying speeds and ridiculous angles. Sarah was awestruck. It was the most modern city she had ever seen. It was an orderly, clean, perfect environment. The streets were empty of foot traffic for the most part, but Sarah could feel the presence of thousands of beings inside the buildings, each moving with a precise purpose. Although Magnus was a pirate of sorts, in his earlier years at least, his facility was a hub of precise business flow. Running the affairs of the interior planets needed a massive amount of bureaucracy to make it all work out profitably.

"Welcome to my humble hideaway," Magnus said.

"We've been here many times, too many times," Capoella replied.

"I was welcoming Sarah," Magnus replied, again without a trace of annoyance.

"Where are the people?" Sarah asked.

"Oh, they don't really come out when I am walking around the campus. I've found its better that way.

Besides, aren't the streets so lovely when they are void of people?" Magnus replied cheerfully.

They walked a block through the city and then ascended a set of stairs onto a platform several meters above the street overtop a wide highway with only a few vehicles moving. A shuttle shaped like a bullet was waiting for them. It was alabaster white. It looked like a tube carved out of ivory.

Once the group was inside, they seated themselves in large wide-seated leather chairs. Sarah thought it quite comfortable. It seemed very similar to her visions of first-class air-travel on Earth. After they were seated, a pair of black plastic androids appeared from the back end, stepping out of a small alcove. They carried trays with short glasses of what Sarah thought was sherry. Neither of them said anything remotely revolutionary - Magnus didn't tolerate dissension too well, and he really, really hated Marxists; Stalin would have winced at Magnus' manual for counterrevolutionary terror.

After drinks were served, the doors shut and the vessel shot off at a tremendous velocity. Sarah was afraid her drink would spill, or that she would be pressed back into her seat, but Magnus' tram system had dampeners that completely negated the effects normal gravity should have. It was a wonderfully cushy feeling although the tram appeared to be tearing about wildly, doing loops and hard-angle drops from high altitudes.

For several moments, the tram whipped them throughout the city, over and above buildings, down through dark tunnels, circling around vast open parks with tree lined foot paths and open green malls. It was a colossal roller coaster, she determined, not the product of sane urban planning but the manifestation of an adolescent plutocrat who obviously had too many race-track models as a child. The shape of the mag-track was maddeningly loopy and complex, and it was terribly inefficient, the only conceivable logic was that it must have designed to amuse the passengers, or simply just its creator.

Eventually the tram rose up high towards the ceiling of the dome, down below Sarah could see a large basin with what appeared to be a rain forest. The tram plunged down towards the basin as though a bullet shot at the heart of the bowl of dense, dark jungle.

Sarah looked around her. Capoella appeared annoyed, or, at best, tired. Germaine and Magnus were conversing freely about a documentary they had both recently watched on the subject of cross-breeding human-oid dwarves with rabid, saber-tooth tigers, and using the resulting species to suppress labor organizing efforts in the outer rims of the Verin-Trel 376 galaxy - Magnus thought it was a 'Capital idea', while Germaine argued it was, at best, really weird, and ultimately sadistic. Dorian appeared as Dorian always appeared, perfectly content with the world around him, no matter how strange things ever became.

The tram swooped down at an incredible pitch, and after a few hair-raising seconds it came gently to a halt, far more gently than Sarah would have though possible given the arc of the descent and their velocity. The tram pulled into a platform and the group exited onto a plat-form. A musical collage of wild bird songs greeted them. They stood surrounded by a dense dark forest rising several meters above them.

Magnus led them along a pathway of rocks that wound through the jungle down from the platform and into the center. After a few moments, they entered a clearing. In the middle was reddish tiled dais topped by several black wrought iron tables with glass tops that were set out for dining.

They followed Magnus to a corner where they arranged themselves around one of the tables. The atmosphere was serene. They were lunching in the middle of an exquisite forest, a restaurant without walls. Sarah was really enjoying herself though she tried hard to appear nonchalant. She was still something of a teenager after all.

Dorian floated up and away from the group, his body dissipating into a cool gray mist that flowed ethereally into the tree cover. Within seconds, he was gone entirely. No one seemed to mind. Dorian had a thing for conversing with trees, and Magnus' trees were witness to many bizarre things and full of juicy gossip.

Very soon, the waiters arrived with crystal glasses and three large, brown bottles that appeared cruder and more capacious than the situation would warrant.

"Pure, single-stage Kolisitiau," Magnus said. "Only the best for a treasured guest."

"Careful, Sarah,' Capoella said. "It's powerful stuff."

The android waiters poured the liquid into the glasses and deposited the glasses in front of the guests. The liquor was almost perfectly clear, but as Sarah held the glass up, it caught the light from the dome's light, making the liquid appear as a congealed, oily rainbow.

"To old friends, and new," Magnus toasted, taking the briefest slice of a second to lock eyes with Sarah and wink.

"Randy bastard," Germaine replied. "You'll sleep with a female of any race."

"Indeed," Magnus answered smiling widely. He really did have an infectious smile and a strange charisma. "Speaking of females, I trust I'll be afforded the opportunity to see Lady Doja. Where is our infamous little troublemaker anyway?"

"I suspect she's already infiltrated your base, and is headed to the casino. She has a thing lately about casinos and venture capitalism," Germaine said.

"I know. I got a really glossy promo for her proposal to develop one in the Low-Tech Sector of Eros-Tao. She's been searching for investors to get her off the ground," Magnus replied. "She has a rather unique take on business models and the art of the sell."

"I got one of those promos too," Germaine grinned. "They really were pretty neat. I bought a thirteen percent stake using funds from an outer-dimension account I use for untraceable capital transfers- I couldn't resist."

"Well, I confess I picked up a piece as well," Magnus replied. "Hard to resist. She put a lot of capital behind that promotional video."

"For wealthy men, you two sure are an easy sell," Capoella interjected. "Doja isn't interested in money. She's interested in empirical data. She'll likely build this whole venture up and then *smash it* just to see what happens."

"Hmmph, you're probably right," Germaine shrugged. "Still the promos were really good."

"Very professional, very well done," Magnus nodded in agreement.

Sarah took a deep sip from her glass, and immediately she felt a warmth rise in the back of her throat, encompassing the back of her brain and slowly working its way forward to the areas that controlled speech and inhibition. Eventually, the sensation moved its way over her entire nervous system like a cloud of slight dementia.

"You two are too surreal to be real," she growled, followed by a hiccup.

The pair exchanged a look of confusion. Germaine shrugged. Magnus grinned shamelessly.

They both chinked their glasses together and roared in unison: "Baaaaahhhhhh!!!" Then they swallowed their drinks with one gulp before throwing their glasses over their heads and out into the jungle to commingle with all the other glasses Magnus and his guests had decided to dispose of for no particular reason over the years.

Well-trained waiters quickly arrived to arrange for a second round of drinks.

Germaine and Magnus both held their glasses up for a second.

"Here's to irrational excess," Magnus toasted.

"Hear, Hear. To excess and irrationality," Germaine agreed joyfully.

They both slammed their drinks, tossed their glasses and the ritual renewed.

"Speaking of surreal, how did you know we'd been to Earth? We haven't even issued our press release," Capoella stated coolly.

"I have my sources," Magnus smiled.

"Hold on, you spied on us?" Sarah asked angrily.

"How long was this girl on Earth?" Magnus asked.

"We're not sure," Germaine replied.

"Well, it would seem she's been exposed to their wonderful, State -controlled education system," Magnus said. "Poor fools, still they'll get what they deserve when the 'Invisible Hand' comes around and smacks them hard on the ass."

Magnus, like many men in his position, believed in a quasi-religion known as the "The Way of the Invisible Hand". The basic tenets were that the Invisible Hand, like some malicious anti-Santa, was always lurking out there in space, waiting to smack someone who acted out of accord with basic notion that the universe was a dog-eat-dog place, without enough damn dogs. Unlike many religions, the basis tenets of the "Invisible Hand" were supported by reams of economic data and hundreds of case-studies. Although the validity of the models were dubious because of their failure to account for a variety of externalized costs, the true believers were mesmerized by the predictive accuracy of their models, and they built vast empires and trans-galactic financial institutions as cathedrals to their silent, whimsically violent god.

"Just in case you were unaware, that little operation on Earth has propelled you from dissident status to full-blown intergalactic terrorist. It's all terribly amusing," Magnus said.

"It was bound to happen sooner or later," Germaine sighed.

"Public Enemy Number One," Magnus giggled. "Has a nice ring to it."

"There are worse titles one could aspire towards," Germaine responded.

At that moment several waiters arrived carrying large plates with a variety of foods, colorful vegetable med-leys, and grilled pieces of meat, all ornately presented, the aromas intoxicating, complex with a variety of spices that smelled of cinnamon, ginger and cumin. It was an incredible, lavish spread. The silver dishes covered most of the table.

Sarah served herself from the dishes near her, and then she dug in. She was growing tired of sushi, no mat-ter how fresh it was aboard the Cortez. She was some-what stoned by the drink and she ripped at everything like a mini-heathen, devoid of even a modicum of civility.

"She's got a rather 'Lord of the Flies' thing going," Magnus remarked.

"You should see the fight between her and one of Doja's avatars. She wiped the floor with him," Germaine replied. "The video went viral on Eros Tao."

They ate and talked for a while about inconsequen-tial, trivial matters until the meal was concluded, and then Germaine politely asked Capoella to take a walk with Sarah through the arboretum. Sarah was stuffed. She felt tired, and was not in a mood to protest her dismissal.

She wiped her mouth with her napkin and followed Capoella away into the forest.

After the pair left, Germaine turned to Magnus, nothing of amusement in his stare. It was time for serious talk, and the mood was decidedly stiffened.

"I could use a little help here, mon ami."

Magnus shrugged. "Mi casa es su casa."

"I need someplace safe to do a press interview, and I need any information you have on the Borgias Expanse."

"Are you going to leak news of the girl's existence?"

"Not yet. I just want a back-door channel to save our skins if this thing goes south. Truthfully, I don't think the universe is ready to deal with this subject just yet. The powers that be are keeping the any news of the matter locked out of the Galacti-Net. They see the danger we see. I need to send a message to a few people, though. Nothing across the official channels. I still want some measure of deniability, a very large measure of deniability. If it became commonly known that I was involved in this affair, there's no way I could avoid all the nasty people there are out there. I'm good, but I can't defeat a whole universe."

"You're playing the game at both ends. What's your plan?"

"I'm planning an elaborate ruse to buy some room to operate. I'm heading to the Borgias Expanse, but I want to get rid of any pursuers before I make the punch."

"Why in god's name would you head to that region of space."

"It's all I've got. I think it's a trap, but I've really no idea where to go from here."

"Who leaked the info on the girl's appearance in the first place?"

"A trusted source inside the ICPT. I've had her on the payroll for years. The Bureaucracy wants the girl desperately. They're terrified of how unstable she could make things."

"So, they were keeping her hidden on Earth? That's where you came into this mess."

"No, I thought from my information that the ICPT was behind it, but I now know they couldn't have possibly been involved. As far as we can figure, they knew about Sarah, they just didn't want to step in while the VD were keeping the girl on Earth."

"So, the VD were keeping her on Earth? Interesting."

"That's what we believe, at least. It's just an educated guess based on several factors. Someone knocked my mat-trans beam off target the first time I attempted to retrieve the girl. That's how I ended up in 15th century France. That's also how I can rule out the ICPT. They don't have the technology to knock my beam off-course."

"Interesting. You could be wrong, you know. There could be another faction behind the matter."

"The whole matter definitely has raised the attentions of a lot of factions."

Magnus snapped his fingers and a cowering android arrived with a cigar atop a silver tray. Magnus picked it up and ran it under his nose. He placed it between his lips and the android quickly lit it before disappearing back into the forest. He puffed on it until its cherry was red hot.

"Ever think the myths are true?" he asked, exhaling a thin ring through a larger one expertly.

"Which myth, there's only a few thousand to pick from."

"Well, the one dominant theme, the one thread repeated time and time again is that when the Nephyr return, all bets are off. The House closes down for good. There will be a war followed by a great reckoning."

"I don't believe in religious nonsense."

"There's nothing religious about the Nephyr. It's about the cycle of life and death. For everything there is a time, and when the Nephyr come back, well..."

"It's a power-play. I've always known that," Germaine said.

"You're right about that, but who's making the play, the VD, the Nephyr, or some third-party not yet identified? What if her species is about to make a comeback tour, tally things up, dispense with judgment and then blow the place. One cannot pretend to know the minds of the creators. Their motivations are incomprehensible, even to men of our level of sophistication."

"Jesus, you sound like one of the religious freaks. Apocalyptic myths are just the works of imagination. One assumes there is a beginning, and that there must be an end. If it all began with a bang, surely it will go out with a bit of violence. There's nothing scientific about these myths. Certainly, you don't believe this apocalyptic trash?"

"I'm not discussing whether I believe it. I am merely suggesting that it is not impossible," Magnus replied. "Many of the myths suggest that the Ambassador would appear near Tellarithon. That is the ancient name for the area known as the Borgias Expanse. What makes you think that this is where you must take her?"

"She's been an amnesiac ever since we rescued her from Earth. A few days ago, we tried hypno-telepathy. She sent Den Folo into a coma. Doja's the one who deciphered what Folo saw before he went blank. That's why we believe that Sarah came from the Expanse. On top of that, we were recently assaulted by ICPT forces. A red cloud of energy intervened and saved our asses. It also told us to take the girl to the Expanse before it disappeared."

"So you are going to the Expanse to chase down the possibility that this is where Sarah came from. What then? What's your next move?"

"I just want to find out why she's here. It's too great a mystery to run from. If something big is going to happen, I want to be there. If it is to be a finale to all life in this universe, then I most especially want to be there.

"Well, I'll not quarrel with your logic, for I have none of my own to offer. As for the Expanse, the Cortez will be able to deal with the spatial distortions. I warn you, it's Free-Space. He who shoots first lives longest."

"I'm aware of the dangers. What I'd really like to know, did you ever detect any sort of anomaly, anything special about that area of space?"

"The whole place is anomalous. It's an ocean of black holes tearing at each other, dominating and eliminating one another. It is a wasteland, the byproduct of an illicit union between two galaxies that decided to rip each other apart for their own amusement. All projections estimate that within two billion years the whole place will have devolved into one giant anomaly."

"Did you ever encounter a rift that couldn't be explained?"

"I know what you're asking, but I've never detected a rift that could lead to the Bulk. It sure would be interesting to go to the 'Bulk', though, wouldn't it?"

"Could be a life-changing experience," Germaine smiled.

"How ambitious of you, Germaine."

"Anything else you might offer on the subject would be greatly appreciated."

"I've little to offer. There is much that cannot be explained in the Expanse. A number of separatist groups have bases in the region. It's rumored that the VD have extensive installations in the central core of the region, but I've never seen any hard evidence. The Borgias Expanse draws a curious breed of visitor. We used to use it to hide out from ICPT patrols back when my criminal exploits were decidedly less ambitious. Most sensors won't work. The radiation will scramble your scans. The black holes in the region are almost impossible to detect because they've eaten everything in their regions. We always used Tachyon scans to find our way. Anything short of that and you're blind. I'd give you charts, but they'd be no good," Magnus said.

"We'll make our own."

"It's an interesting notion."

"What's that?"

"That the VD want the girl outed, but they want you to do the job. Given your previous experience with them, have you thought about the possibility that they might have foreseen this centuries ago when you they outfitted you with the Cortez."

"Anything is possible. The VD are certainly capable of seeing things that many moves into the future. The Cortez was certainly a lavish gift for facilitating below-the-radar financial transactions."

"They're smart enough to know that nobody would buy into Sarah's sudden appearance if they outed her. It wouldn't have the same impact if it came from them."

"That's what we figure."

"They get the results they wanted without getting their hands dirty. Interesting. It does make sense. You guys are the perfect choice. It took Nixon to open up relations with China after all."

"Something like that. Hand the girl to the universe's most outspoken celebrity to be outed, it certainly lends the whole affair a credibility it would otherwise lack."

"But that's too simple, isn't it? If they're behind it, it isn't going to be that transparent. Our logic is too straightforward to be VD."

"Doja and Capoella both say the same thing. They think there is something much more subtle going on.

All I know is that I want the girl where I can see her. Until we figure out something better, she's safest aboard the Cortez."

"You are sure that the Nephyr aren't orchestrating events?"

"I'm not entirely sure of anything, but I can't figure out the possible angle given what happened on Earth. She was imprisoned. Why would they do that to one of their own?"

"We are not the men to understand the Nephyr, or their motivations."

"Probably right. My only course of action now is to the head to the Expanse."

"Watch yourself in there. It is the perfect place for a trap, even one you're looking for, and right now, you have a lot of people looking to trap you," Magnus said.

"You could be right, but the answer isn't going to come flying into my lap. I have to take the chance that if it's a trap, it's one I can survive. I'm game for a little intrigue. The Cortez can hold her own."

"How long can you keep her prisoner?"

"I'm not keeping anyone prisoner. She has the full run of the ship. She travels to Eros Tao whenever she wants to. It's hardly a prison."

"She's a fierce child. I've seen the look in the eyes of racing stallions too headstrong to give a damn about the whip. She won't be broken, and the moment she determines that her own interests aren't aligned with yours, she'll break from you entirely."

"I know. She's already displaying a rather sarcastic, rebellious temperament. She's mixed up. The fools on Earth didn't help things with their drugs and their tinkering."

"She's an adolescent, Germaine. That is how adolescents operate. She'll bridle against any authority figure, even one as absurd and free-spirited as yourself, Germaine. No offense intended, but you are hardly the fatherly type."

"I know. I'm certainly not raising this girl very well. She's been giving lectures on Lenin and Trotsky to the androids in the engine room. She's starting to draw a crowd. I think she'd get a laugh if they actually revolted," Germaine said.

"Enigmas with vast existential implications. Who needs them?"

"I did mention that Admiral Fushevez attacked me with one and a half battle fleets?"

"Briefly. One and one half battle fleets, huh?"

"Yes. One and one half."

"He must have been trying to make a point. How did you manage to squeak out of it?"

"That was where the energy cloud stepped in and saved the day."

"The energy cloud that told you to go to the Expanse?"

"It said something about getting the girl to the Expanse, something about all fates will be decided there."

"I've no use for strange clouds of energy. I'm naturally suspicious of their kind. But you do appear to be mired rather deep in a great mystery," Magnus said.

"Give me an alternative, I'll take it. I don't know I could ever walk away from this. A lesser man would find a way to exploit her somehow, half the universe would try and destroy her, and the other half would try and exploit her."

"But not you. Not your style."

"The only place she can be safe from this, safe until her time is right, is aboard the Cortez," Germaine stated.

"You need to be careful with this one. She's certainly not here on a tourist junket, Germaine. That child's got trouble written all over her. As a cautious denizen of the universe I must tell you I would have nothing to do with this. We are both powerful men who have enjoyed our station in life. But I assure you, as powerful as we both are, neither one of us should be involved with this. This is a matter the universe needs to settle without our intervention."

"My god, everyone is telling me to get away from this. You've known me longer than anyone, even Capoella. Tell me why I can't? I'm not one to ignore the advice of intelligent counsel. Why can't I walk away from this? Capoella says I'm worried about my legacy. I'm getting old and I don't want history to overlook me."

"She may be partially correct. I don't think its legacy you're worried about so much as substance. I think you would die happily if you knew you played some constructive role in these events, regardless of whether or not history would catalog it as such. You've never been worried whether anyone thought you good, bad, or otherwise. But despite this ambivalence, you're the most driven idealist I've ever known. It's a curious balance you've managed over the years."

"Keep that observation under your hat, old friend," Germaine smiled with a little melancholy at the corners.

"Of course. Let's drop this matter. As for the press interview, you intend to send a communication across informal lines?"

"That's the idea," Germaine replied.

"Well then, have your people contact mine and we'll get it arranged. I trust you have someone in mind."

"I've already been in discussions with the editors at the Moving Rock."

"You coy dog, you want Suzzanie Thomas? What a glorious slut she is."

"She's horrible. Just the kind of rabid dog I want for the job. I want her to be especially mean on this occasion.

I promise you that by the time she arrives, she'll be too fried out to do anything even remotely resembling an interview."

"Well, for you no favor is forbidden. I only ask one in return."

"Oh?" Germaine said with sudden interest.

"I've been babysitting lately," Magnus said.

"Who would trust you with their child?" Germaine joked.

"It's Prince Kellian, Lord Denegh's eldest. I took him under my wing when his planet was attacked by the ICPT. He's a teenager, though, and he's restless. He likes to get into trouble. I haven't the time or inclination to restrain him. However, he has caused several members of my staff to suffer serious hematomas when they encountered him in the bars. It's a nuisance. I think he could use a tour with you to give him some seasoning and perspective."

"Well, Sarah could use a companion her own age. We'll make the arrangements," Germaine replied.

"Excellent. I think this child's temperament is more suited to your sort of activities than mine. He has a noble streak a mile wide, and he likes to fight…a lot."

Magnus snapped his fingers and a servant approached with a holo-emitter. The android placed the emitter in the center of the table and then exited quickly.

"Take a look. I think you'll enjoy this," Magnus said.

The emitter lit up the area with a high-definition, three-dimensional vision of the interior of a facility under attack. The view was that of an open air building with catwalks crisscrossing the space, narrow floors and staircases leading several floors up. The building was rectangular, and one wall appeared to contain a tremendous furnace with several openings. It appeared to be some sort of foundry.

Ant-like insect creatures seemed to cover many areas of the wall space. They were moving with frenetic intensity. In the middle of the scene, a handsome, square jawed young man with black hair and fierce green eyes, wearing a dark soldier's uniform crested with red stripes on the upper sleeves, appeared to be fighting back the insects, hacking at them with a rather large, very sharp sword.

"This is the kid?" Germaine asked.

"Yes."

"What are we watching?"

"It's a surveillance video from the attack that destroyed his planet. At this point, the place is totally overrun. His father is dead. And he is fighting for his life."

"Why does he have a sword?" Germaine asked.

"He told me it was father's sword. Something about being honor-bound to carry the damn thing. I'll not pretend to understand Sirians, they're hot-blooded and irrational. Still, watch this. The child's rather good," Magnus responded.

As Germaine watched, the "child" sliced his way through three of the ant creatures poised at the bottom of a staircase. Then the child made his way up the stairs until he was several flights above the ground floor. He reached out and cut a support cable which he grabbed with one hand before swinging over the infested ground to the other side of the building, managing to kick two of the ants in the head, causing them to fall through open doors into the furnace. Then, like a berserker, he hacked his way through another group.

"Why doesn't he have a gun?" Germaine asked.

"Well, I don't really know. He's rather fixated on his sword."

"Huh."

In the air above them, the young man yelled and hacked away at the insects that were crowding every inch of space. He kept moving, making his way up level by level. Those ants he could not slice, he kicked, and those he could not kick, he punched. It was an impressive performance. Scores of ants were knocked from the walls, their bodies crashing down onto the ground below. The odds were desperately against him, but he didn't show even a trace of fear.

He battled his way all the way to the top level of the facility, and then kicked a door open leading to the rooftop. The ants were everywhere. He exited the opening and then shut the door behind him, blocking the door with a cross beam of wood. The ants in the building were cut off for now, but there were still ants crawling up over the retainer wall. Very quickly, he was surrounded. The creatures clicked their mandibles, their antennae whipping the air in front of them. They could smell the kill. He fought them back furiously, his sword moving in constant arcs and slices. His fierceness kept them wary as they assembled their ranks more thickly, preparing for the final assault.

Suddenly, a rescue ship flew into the air above the rooftop. A knotted rope was thrown out the side of the fuselage. He dove through the air and grabbed it. The vehicle moved quickly up into the air, whipping his body out of the grasp of the ants that had now fully overrun the roof.

"Wow, how dramatic," Germaine said. "He reminds me of a young Errol Flynn."

"Will you take him?"

"He could probably use a little seasoning. How much trouble do you think he'll be?"

"Just enough to keep you happy."

"Fair enough," Germaine nodded. "I'll tell Capoella to expect company. Any thought on what we'll do with him as a long term solution."

"He's not without resources. He's the last heir to a rather lucrative empire. His family had enough off-world holdings to ensure him a soft landing wherever he eventually ends up. For now, though, he has to grow up, and I confess I simply am not a father figure."

"No I suppose not. I don't think I am either."

"You're not, Germaine, but the Cortez is a family. Right now, that young prince is desperately in need of some sort of family."

"Well, send him to me. It's been a while since I've entertained royalty. He looks like he can hold his own in a fight. That's all I ever ask of my crew."

"Thank you. It's been very hard for me to find the right sort of diversions for the child. I think some time with you will bring out his better traits. Now, as for your interview."

"Oh, I don't think there will be much true journalism involved. It's not really the point. Like I said, this is just a way to send a message through the back door."

"The whole thing sounds rather queer to me," Magnus confessed. "But if its good for a laugh..."

A day later, the crew was ready to depart Magnus' facility. They boarded the shuttle and were soon back in space, with the addition of one prospective crewmember. Sarah eyed this new addition warily.

"So, you're the prince?" Sarah asked, a touch of hostility. She didn't mean it, but she was rather enjoying her novelty status.

The shuttle lifted off and was soon away from station and in space.

"And you must be Sarah?" he replied.

"I must be," she answered.

"Play nice, kids," Germaine said as the shuttle began a docking sequence with the Cortez.

"How's the *prince* thing working out for you?" Sarah asked.

"Rather oddly at the moment, I suspect. Still, be of good cheer, and all that," the prince smiled.

"Yeah, we could use a little good cheer. I suspect we could use someone who knows how to fight on their feet a bit more," Sarah said. "You any good on your feet, prince?"

"He's a natural born killer, Sarah. Our prince here is quite the dashing hero," Germaine said.

"You've got a big sword, I see," Sarah smiled. "You're gonna need it."

Chapter Nine

A Night Out on the Town

It had been three weeks relative-time since they had left Magnus' facility. They had been crossing back and forth over their tracks trying to confuse some of their pursuers, while reeling in the rest for a ruse. After a variety of adventures and misadventures alike, the crew was in a genuinely good mood, and all in one piece, a rare concurrence indeed. Things had been calm for a couple of days while Capoella and Doja baited the trap and made their plans.

Kellian, having endured a customary hazing, was accepted as a crewmember. He fit in nicely, and the majority of the crew seemed to enjoy having a sword wielding young lad in their presence. He was peculiar, and occasionally belligerent in a regal, high-handed sort of way. It took him less than three days to drop this persona, though, and once he realized he was amongst like-minded folk, his rebellious temperament dissipated. He was very soon amazed at the scope of Germaine's operations. Very quickly, he began calling Germaine his 'godfather'.

When the circumstances arranged themselves to Germaine's satisfaction, he and Capoella, in coordination with Sarah and Doja, decided to make their next move. Germaine gathered all of the crew onto the bridge save for Dorian and Doja, as neither could be found. With great relish, and an amazing attention to consistency, Germaine ordered a tray of martinis.

Several minutes later, the drinks were served by a rather morose android who seemed utterly resigned to his lowly station in life. As it served the drinks to each crewmember, it leaned forward and whispered: "I hate you bourgeoisie bastards. I absolutely despise you."

After the drinks were served, the crew sat around and chatted. Germaine enjoyed the camaraderie that came with sharing drink with his small family. His small family had grown somewhat precipitously in recent months, and his life was becoming conseridably more dangerous, but he enjoyed these moments. He looked carefully at Sarah for any trace that would show she was not ready to play her role in the mission. When he found none, he finished his drink and smiled.

"So, Sarah. You've been wanting to see the Speed Fighting Championships," Germaine said.

"What? Oh, the championship. Yes, I've been wanting to go for some time," she replied.

"Well, I happen to have box seats. I own the place after all. At least, I think I do.," he turned to Capoella. "I still own the arena, don't I?"

"Yeah, but we need to sell it. It's about to face a twenty-five year renovation, and we need to dump it before we get stuck with the bill."

"Huh. Sarah, why don't you take Kellian with you."

"Is there a reason you are dismissing us before we've had our second cocktail?" Kellian asked.

"Of course there is. One, you guys will get a kick out of the fight knowing how much you both seem to love violence, and two, grown-ups have to talk," Germaine said. "So, off you go."

Sarah shrugged. "Come on, your majesty. Let's let the *grown-ups* talk."

"There's a good lass," Germaine smiled.

Kellian and Sarah left the bridge. After the doors were closed, Germaine spoke.

"What do you think?" he asked.

"Sarah knows the deal. She's tough enough. Besides, can you think of a better plan to distract the bad guys?"

"I know she's a tough kid, but I'm still worried about her. I wish we could let Kellian know."

"We can't. He's susceptible to telepathy. Sarah's not. He'll be okay. We've identified at least three active teams on Eros Tao. Doja did the background. These boys want her alive. Lethal measures are off the table."

"I don't like gambling with her life," Germaine said. "And there are a lot of variables here."

"I don't like gambling either. That's why we're going to wrap this thing up quickly. We've baited the trap. We have to trust that Doja and Sarah can pull this off."

"What's the status on Eros Tao?" Germaine asked.

"Doja reported that she has everything under surveillance. Her Interceptor Teams are ready to engage."

"Interceptor Teams? Huh," Germaine said. "Interceptor Teams…weird. That's really, huh. That's kind of …"

Capoella raised her eyebrows and shrugged. "It's a catchy name."

"Tell her to keep a tight lid on things. I don't want to scare the residents. Jesus, Interceptor Teams. She really spooks me sometimes."

"Speed-fighting is the most dangerous sport in the universe," Kellian said.

"Outside politics, yeah, I suspect you're right."

The pair walked through the corkscrew passing through meters of corridors lined with aquarium glass, schools of feeder fish followed them, silvery flashes darted to the surface of the glass before shooting away into the dark of the water.

Eventually they ended up at a Tether-Point. A set of thick red doors inside an alcove marked an entrance portal to Eros Tao.

"Computer, initialize for transport to High-Tech sector," Sarah said. "Here, put this between your teeth. Bite down hard."

She handed Kellian a small strip of twine. A second later, the door lights flashed green, and the doorway opened. It was as though a white storm had been uncorked when the doors opened. It raged with sound and fury, and signified a lot of energy being expended.

"Enjoy the ride!" Sarah yelled over the tremendous noise of the opening, placing a piece of twine between her teeth and jumping full force into the white nothingness.

He watched her sucked into the maelstrom and madness of the portal. She fell away and tumbled into apparent nothingness.

Kellian felt the tug at the center of his chest. He was uncertain and apprehensive, certainly, but his nature was to be fiercely brave, fiercely noble. He placed the braid between his teeth and jumped in after, only to enjoy the most exquisite and uncomfortable pain his noble life had ever afforded him.

After enduring the spaghettification process, he landed seconds behind Sarah, arriving on all fours. He coughed out the bit of twine, and rolled over to his side.

"Don't worry, it really does get easier after a few times," Sarah said.

"That was...intriguing."

"Sure it was, tough guy. Come on."

Unlike the portal leading to the city in the Low-Tech sector, they had arrived inside a recessed area at the base of a large dark glass skyscraper hundreds of stories in height.

They looked out. In front of them was a bustling modern metropolis. Huge skyscrapers lining wide paved roadways, heavy foot traffic, thick lanes of gnarly ground transport traffic, grid streams of air traffic, lights, noise, pollution, the High-Tech sector of Eros Tao was an active modern cityscape operating under a dark blue, artificial sky, inside a completely artificial dimension. It was a one of a kind city.

"Let's get a cab," Sarah said.

She was trying to appear calm, but she knew the danger ahead of her. She wished she was proto-morphed, but that would defeat the plan, and ruin what could be construed loosely as her first date.

They both stood up and approached the edge of the street. Sarah raised her hand and in a second a taxi pulled to the curb. Sarah pulled Kellian inside.

"Take us to the Khotsai Arena, please" Sarah said.

The cabby was a dark skinned alien with a polished shiny bulb head, two slits for nostrils, and large black eyes.

"So you like Speed-Fighting, huh," the cabby smiled. "Smashing, gnashing and banging together. Very brutal."

"Its amusing," Sarah replied.

"I like the brutality too," the cabby grinned. "I'm betting on the champion, The Taralian Nightmare. He's a right psychotic sonuvabitch. They say he trains by demolishing defunct skyscrapers with his bare fists and knees. He just smashes them into pieces."

"Yeah, he's pretty tough," Sarah replied.

"You guys are VIP," the alien smiled into the rear-view mirror. "How is the Saint?"

"What's he talking about? How do you know about us?" Kellian asked, a little paranoia betraying itself.

"You have tags. I don't know the Saint, but you do," the cabby replied. "We all like Germaine. I hope he is well, and that he fights strong."

The cab crossed through a heavy throng of ground traffic. When they reached a slow point, the alien smiled broadly.

"Time to fly," the cabby said. He spoke into a small interface portal on the A-beam of the vehicle. "Priority transport, requesting air-travel permit and escort to the arena. A-list occupants onboard, over."

"Tags verified," a fuzzy radio voice answered. "Keep your data ports open. We're initiating command override," the voice instructed.

The cab floated up and away from the ground traffic. After a moment it whooshed off in a pattern just above the standard air traffic. The corridor of air space was reserved for Germaine, and those he designated VIPs. Being the shadow mayor of Eros Tao had many privileges.

The cab flew through an open traffic corridor. The landscape of buildings, edges cut against an artificial gray blue sky, provided a brilliant view as they approached a white blob in the distance that quickly revealed itself to be a large coliseum painted in white strokes of marker light.

The areas outside the building were jammed with ground traffic. The cab hovered over the arena before landing atop the roof in a small landing area reserved for the upper crust.

"Enjoy the show," the cabby said.

Sarah exited with the prince in tow. There was no need for currency exchange as Germaine and his crew had charge accounts that synched up their identification tags with the merchants and other service sector components automatically.

"Come on, prince."

The pair was greeted by dark suited security personnel as they exited the vehicle. As Sarah looked around, there were several of the characters poised at different points around the perimeter of the landing area. They were clones, devised for one purpose: to protect the lives of those who paid them, no matter the cost.

Germaine ran an intergalactic security firm known as Veritas Industries. They did a lot of work in war torn parts of the universe, places where businessmen wished to go and ply their deadly wares. They'd also pulled off a few dozen coups over the decades, none of them traceable to Germaine save through anecdotal evidence and well placed conjecture. In truth, despite what the pundits said, it was really just a hobby.

"Follow me," one of the agents said.

He was emotionless, dark glasses hiding even a hint of soul.

As the trio left the Tarmac, the cab lifted up like a giant black bug taking flight and then floated away, back out into the city beyond. The three walked towards the entrance of a lift that would take them inside the facility. As they moved, several of the other agents fell in behind them, closing formation.

The entourage entered a lift and descended into the facility. When the doors opened up, they were faced with a long hall almost completely empty of people.

The agent led them through the hall and down a set of stairs, then past a security checkpoint, finally ending up in front of an open room with a couple dozen well-dressed guests milling about and conversing in small groups. There were a few small tables topped with crisp, white linen tablecloths, adorned with hors-dullness, mostly chopped up vegetables, dip, and a lot of cheese, a whole lot of cheese.

The security entourage went no further than to escort the pair to the threshold. After the doors closed shut, it was simply the prince and Sarah, left to mingle in a group of aliens neither knew. It might have been awkward save that Sarah had very recently come to grips with the amount of power and prestige she possessed as a part of the powerful clique that was Germaine's crew. She felt confident that she could hold her own in such a crowd. She thought about it, but then realized the other reason she had no fear of these people was because they were aristos. Aristos were facades with lungs and mouths, but they weren't real at all.

It took less than a few seconds before the pair was engaged in discussions with two elderly couples, well-dressed and more than eager to show their appreciation for Germaine, and their fondness for his representatives. They were all tall and thin, very thin. The males wore immaculate black tuxedos and bright red silk bow ties, while the females wore wonderfully frilly dark evening dresses. They were bird-thin, skin-stretched replicas of real thinking, feeling creatures, even their mannerisms were carefully manufactured. It took only a little bit of alcohol to reveal the hideous true face hiding beneath these false exteriors.

"My name is Demetrus Salignon, and this is my wife Dothalai," one of the males said, a long arm protruding with hand opened wide towards Kellian.

"I am Crown-Prince Kellian, heir to the throne of the Kingdom of Khorragia," Kellian responded, grasping the man's hand firmly.

"Betcha can't say that three times fast," Demetrus said with a wink.

Kellian's eyes rolled for a second in confusion. It was the second time he had heard the joke, and he understood it now even less than the first-time.

"It's called deja vu," Sarah said. "Hello, I'm Lady Sarah of Earth," she smiled, extending a hand delicately.

"So very nice to meet you, Lady Sarah," Demetrus smiled, politely grasping her hand.

The second male introduced himself.

"It is always a pleasure to welcome Germaine's friends. I am Baron Michelj Kremswallow, and this is my wife, Lady Bhitchitha."

"Hello now," the woman said. "I need another Martini. Jesus on a stick. What did you say your names were?"

She seemed to stumble for a moment, while Michelj helped her up by gently raising her elbow.

"Yeah, laugh. Go ahead. I dare you. I have little pieces of metal inside of my purse and I'll smash any one of you that so much as looks at me funny," Bhitchitha snarled. She stood upright, but was still a little off-balance.

Michelj reached out and steadied her. "Now, now, dearest. The fights are to happen below us, inside the cage. Not inside the VIP area."

"What do you know," Bhitchitha growled. "Get me a goddamned Martini!"

"You'll pardon my wife," Michelj said. "She's been on a sort of self-indulgent, drunken binge ever since she found out that the Bell Curve was nonsense, and that she wasn't in fact at the nice, tail-end of the curve. It seems to have shattered her sense of self worth."

"I'll give you bell curves upside the jaw, mister. Ditto this and ditto that. Try and convince me I'm not superior. It's a conspiracy of psycho, uber-liberal, peace craving jerkos," Bhitchitha growled drunkenly. "I hate them all, always bitching about clean water, food safety and rational labor relations, bunch of needy bastards. They all have bootstraps, damned sponges."

"Nice to meet all of you. You'll pardon us if we duck off. We want to catch the under-card bouts," Sarah said.

"Of course," Michelj said. "Give Germaine our compliments."

"Yes, please do. And say hello to Lady Capoella. Give them both my best wishes," Demetrus said.

"We will," Sarah smiled politely. "Come on, Kell. Let's get our seats, the first bout is about to begin."

She grabbed his arm and dragged him away from the two couples.

"They were a little on the weird side," Sarah said.

"They were aristos. I know their kind. They're vampires who should lick the bottom of my shoe. My father did not tolerate their kind, and neither shall I."

"Wow, Kell. I didn't know you felt so strongly about the matter," Sarah joked.

They took their seats in front of a large window overlooking the arena below. The cage stood in the center illuminated in a flash of sweeping, multi-colored stage lights.

Behind them, the crowd of aristos was milling about, devouring little trinkets of food served on steel platters by disinterested servants in black dress uniforms. The servants wove their way through the crowd deftly. The whole thing was so orderly because it was repeated night after night with only slight variations in the surroundings and catering. No matter where they went, no matter the occasion, cheese cubes seemed to be a rather large staple of the aristo diet. Sarah thought there might be something profound to say about this fact, but she hadn't figured out just what it was.

Below them, outside the wide window of glass, the arena was jam packed with spectators. Celebrities dotted the crowd, while security drones hovered, zapping unruly patrons with electric pulses. Although the walls and glass were thick, the stamping feet of the crowd could not be masked. It permeated the building. The entire structure was alive with the rhythm of bloodlust, almost a mass hysteria. The psychic tension was palpable.

The strobe lights flickered, and the spotlights, with different colored lenses, flashed down and through the crowd in a choreographed pattern designed to raise the pitch of the crowd to its fullest. Hanging in the air like a cloud of mosquitoes were dozens of floating ovoid shaped cameras drinking in the scene and then transmitting it out to a thousand different worlds. Speed-fighting had replaced every other sport as the universes' most watched competition in existence.

The ominous music, death-thrash actually, marked the entrance of the first fighter on the under-card. He was a lean, wiry muscled alien known only as Bharatu. His skin was dark purple, and he had a slope backed head, completely bald, strong chin, nose and cheek bones sharp, giving him a menacing look, and an ability to take incredible blows if need be.

He was a competent striker, but he preferred to lure his opponent into a shoot, and then "jitz" the poor bastard from his back. Bharatu was a trap fighter who knew dozens of sophisticated submissions.

He made his way towards the cage with his entourage. The floating cams caught the look of concentration and purpose in his eyes, and his face was plastered over several of the large screens throughout the arena. He appeared to be about as deadly and determined a foe as one could wish for.

After the ref checked his gloves and protective gear, Bharatu entered the cage and shuffle stepped in a wide circle, getting his feet accustomed to the floor padding, and the size of the cage. He paused only long enough to allow one of his corner men to apply a thick sheen of petroleum jelly over the skin of his face. This was done to cause punches to slide rather than cut. It was a ritual all fighters engaged in. The corner-man gave Bharatu a couple of fierce slaps to his face to pump him up, and then Bharatu focused, shaking out his arms and legs, getting himself steeled for combat. Behind him, his team unraveled a large sheet covered with the brand insignia of his sponsors. They draped it over their corner of the cage in full view of the cameras.

"This is going to be a good-fight," Kellian said. "He's peaking right now, you can see it in his energy levels."

"I like this guy too. I think he's a sleeper in his weight class. I've been watching his fights. I'm thinking about taking him on once I get more training time."

At that Kellian smiled. He was about to say something quite misogynistic, but he was interrupted.

The music changed to a different melody of death-thrash as the lights flashed towards the entrance at the other end of the arena where the opponent stood. The opponent was a more brash character than Bharatu. He raised his hands defiantly, each fist shaking menacingly. He seemed to be pumping himself up and drinking in the din of noise and flow of energy from the crowd. He was screaming as he walked down the runway from the dressing area and towards the cage in the center of the arena. He slapped the hands of several supporters that reached down to cheer him on.

Ghojen "God's Final Sin" Fayde was one of the most dynamic and well-rounded fighters in his weight class. He was powerful on his feet, and excellent on the ground. He was devastating in the clinch, and he could use his long legs to pull off wild submissions from his back. He was a dangerous fighter in every aspect of the game.

The talk was this fight was merely a stepping stone to a championship bout with Brutis "The Brutality" Heino.

Both of the fighters had developed a dangerous, and highly publicized addiction to a new form of aggression concentration amplifiers known as "Knives". Outside the ring, they were too belligerent to deal with. Each of them focused on how to murder their opponent, and spoke openly in pre-fight interviews of their sincere desire to torture the other fighter even after submission. The drugs were nasty, but completely legal. In the end, the fighters raced towards some pharmacological endgame that left them soul-shattered and incapable of dealing with anything other than graphic violence. Combined with well-honed fighting techniques, the results were terrifying. As commercial products, however, they were simply wonderful.

After both fighters had entered the cage, the entourages ducked out. The ref called the two together, and explained the rules. There weren't many, so the conversation was short.

"Okay, touch gloves and try not to kill each other," the ref said half-heartedly.

The pair banged fists, each one staring the other down menacingly. It was moment of incredible tension caught on camera and blasted onto screens throughout the arena. Each of them took their position in their corner of the cage and awaited the start of the fight.

The crowd was borderline anarchy. The noise was deafening.

"You dig this scene?" the ref asked, turning toward Bharatu.

"I'm too cool, man," Bharatu replied.

The ref turned towards Ghojen. "You good?"

"Life is death," Ghojen responded coldly.

"Get it on," the ref yelled.

And so it began. The fighters stalked each other, but Bharatu took the center of the cage. His footwork was good. He test-fired a couple of jabs before he found his measure and rhythm, then he launched out with a few nice combinations. Ghojen weathered a few big strikes, but rolled with it. He countered a few times, but he was a slow-starter. He needed to get hit a few times before his instincts rose up and his body knew it was in a fight.

The fighters clashed against each other furiously. Sarah gave Kellian a blow-by-blow analysis. She'd studied both fighters in depth. Bharatu had an unorthodox striking style that was quite effective, while Ghojen counter-punched and tried several times to shoot for the legs. Bharatu's flexibility and ability to kick his legs out quickly made him difficult to wrestle to the ground. Ghojen wanted to take him to the ground and jitz him hard, prove a point to other ground fighters in the division, but Bharatu was a cunning adversary. Sarah explained that while it might have been smarter for Bharatu to work a ground game from his back, he needed to prove he had the stand-up capabilities to cement his position as a true force in the division. Although it should seem counterintuitive, both fighters were fighting against their natural disciplines because they needed to display that they could. They were both rising stars in their weight class, and both needed to demonstrate to the promoters that they had the capacity for a title shot. It was as much about selling themselves as it was merely surviving.

Frustrated, Ghojen abandoned the double-leg shoot, and went back to standing and scrapping it out. He sat down on his left jab and found some success with it.

The pair clinched several times, but Bharatu got the best of it, dirty boxing, and landing hard elbow strikes to the side of Ghojen's head before they were broken up. One of the commentators said what was on everyone's mind at that moment: it looked like Ghojen had an imbalance in drug ingestion, he was moving a lot slower than he usually moved.

Bharatu hammered away. His weird angled strikes made him difficult to train for. There weren't many training partners capable of replicating the variety of strange angles that Bharatu struck from. It was a difficult match, despite Ghojen's raw power and skill, Bharatu was fast and precise, too flexible and quick to be taken down.

Ghojen's stand-up was very skilled, but he relied on raw power more than well-honed boxing skills. In the clinch, he was nowhere near as quick as Bharatu with the knees and the elbows.

It wasn't long into the fight that Ghojen got cut up, blood leaking into his right eye and occluding his vision. Bharatu shuffle stepped to his left and peppered with a fierce jab, trying to mouse up the right eye. Both men were well conditioned though, and the fight stretched on for several minutes. The mouse under the idea was swelling up quick, likely a fractured orbital. It would definitely prove a factor if the fight went into deep rounds, one of the ringside commentators remarked accurately.

Relatively speaking, it was a good match-up, both men had skill sets that made them superior to the other in several respects, but both were well-rounded, well-trained fighters with strong chins. They parried, shuffle stepped, and peppered each other with fierce leg kicks, but no one was proving to be the decisive force.

As the round was winding down, it looked as though it was going to go to a second. Then, in a clinch, Bharatu interlaced his fingers behind Ghojen's head and drove a serious knee straight to the chin. Ghojen was stunned and Bharatu caught a rhythm, driving several more into the sweet spot, devastating his opponent. He pulled his opponent by the back of the head and slammed several more knees. The crowd ooed and awed with every deadly strike. The knees broke past Ghojen's raised arms, and they caught him several more times on the chin. Ghojen slumped forward and fell out of the clinch. He reeled backwards dizzily and ate an incredible roundhouse to the side of his head that left both men on the ground. Unconscious, Ghojen landed, arms splayed out, face first onto the canvas, while Bharatu caught himself, kip-kicking back to his feet and raising his hands in triumph. He shouted at the crowd. His muscles flexed fiercely as his full body caught the energy of the win.

The crowd shouted back: "Bharatu, Bharatu, Bharatu!"

The stadium roared as the replay of the knock-out played in loops on the big screen above the cage. Members of both camps suddenly swarmed into the cage, a group attending Ghojen with ice-packs and prayer, while the opposite camp lifted their winner, Bharatu, into the air atop their shoulders. He took a few sips from the water bottle one of his team offered him, but he wasn't worn out. The whole fight had gone a lot smoother than he could have predicted.

For several minutes, members of both camps milled around in the cage, shaking hands. After icing Ghojen's forehead down for a moment, his corner-men let him stand up. He was still a little wobbly as the ref dragged the two together as the announcer called out the disposition. His eyes were glazed.

"Winner by devastation KO, four minutes and thirty-two seconds into the first round, Bharatu!" the announcer loudly articulated each syllable into the microphone as the voice reverberated against every wall of the coliseum.

One of the celebrity commentators pushed his way through the throng inside the cage and approached Bharatu with the microphone: "We know you've been training on Terrellus, getting prepared for the gravity and oxygen levels here on Eros Tao. Tell us, what was your strategy coming into this fight?"

Bharatu's eyes lit up suddenly, and he stared at the camera murderously, the corner of his lip rising in sadistic glee. His sharpened teeth made him appear quite frightening.

"I wanted to beat the crap out of him!" Bharatu growled, before spinning away and back into the crowd.

"That was a pretty good fight," Kellian said.

"I don't know. I could have taken both of them, I think. Bharatu left his hands down for a good two seconds after every time he flurried. I'd take him every time with my counter punches, punish him for his laziness."

"Germaine said you were a fighter. I thought he was speaking metaphorically."

"Any time you wanna test my skills, you just let me know, young prince," Sarah smiled devilishly.

"Intriguing," Kellian responded. "You say you've fought in the cage once?"

"I was morphed, but it was me. Doja helped arrange it."

"And you won your match?" Kelliian asked.

"I fractured my opponent's forearm with an arm-bar submission."

"Wow. I think I would definitely like to spar with you."

Several minutes later, the flashing lights and screeching smash-metal music marked the start of the second fight. In one corner of the arena, lit up in flashing strobe lights was Donailo "The Fist of Uroki" Dajon. He was an unorthodox fighter, trained in the caverns of Junthai Three by an order of secretive warrior monks known as "The Chosen Few". There was little video data available on him. He was a complete dark-horse. It was only by the reputation of his fighting clan that he was allowed to move so far into a welterweight division match-up such as this.

He walked down the ramp towards the cage with his entourage, a group of darkly cloaked, hooded figures. After the ref cleared him, he entered the ring, and shuffled stepped, getting his feet moving and his blood pumping. He had a good warm-up sweat going which make him slippery to hold onto, difficult to wrestle. He performed some rather exotic yoga-stretches that were as much a work of body art as a method of truly stretching out. Then he took a seat cross-legged. He closed his eyes and seemed to enter a deep trance of meditation. The cameras focused in as his body literally levitated several inches off the canvas, hovering in a Buddha-like trance.

"Whoa," Sarah said. "That's really friggin scary. That's…"

"Pretty scary," Kellian agreed.

The lights dipped off for a second and resumed as Donailo's opponent entered the arena. He was a wiry, spastic gray alien who was nearly rabid on a combination of hormones, barbituates, speed and a chemical known as "Death" that was supposed to beef up the "fight" part of the fight-or-flight impulse. He had adrenaline secretion devices located in several spots of his body, and he didn't walk with an entourage for the simple fact that he would likely have tried to eat anyone near him. He scared the hell out of the fans. One of them that reached down from the stands for a high-five got his arm broke. Several others were snarled at menacingly, and two were bitten hard enough that they eventually needed skin grafts.

Gojo "My Brain Hurts" Gunde was a mental patient on holiday. Somebody thought he'd be good in the cage, and after a few back room deals with various sports commissioners and the members of congress that oversaw regulating the sport, Gojo was allowed to enter the cage.

So far, he had managed to seriously maim or kill over twelve men. Given his hyper-violent record, he was a huge draw. Gojo's patented move was to get close enough to his opponent, jump on him and start chewing his face or arm off. Speed-Fighting was a tough sport.

The fight was billed as the "Match-up of Mixed Martial Art's Most Mysterious Men". Even though it was on the under-card, everyone was watching this one expecting nothing less than full-on brutality. In the pre-fight shows, one of the commentators had referred to the match as the "ultimate good guy versus crazy, psycho lunatic" fight. It wasn't an unreasonable tag-line considering Donailo was from an order of monks of which very little was known, and Gojo was completely animalistic, just a thin stretch of skin covering for drug-enhanced rage.

As an individual would almost have to be literally crazy to enter into a Speed-Fighting match, recruiting from the herds in the insane asylums was critical. Scouts would enter the facilities and engage in a series of surreptitious tests designed to find out who was worthy (internal documents often use the word "worthy" interchangeably with 'whacky') enough to fight in the cage. Gojo, a convicted mass murderer who'd lost his mind in prison, was a top tier recruit for the sport.

After the customary stare-down where the ref explained the utter lack of rules, both men retreated to their side of the cage.

"You cool," the ref turned to Donailo.

"The moment is upon me,' Donailo replied. "There is nothing but the now."

"You cool," the ref asked Gojo.

Gojo growled and yelled something indecipherable, but undoubtedly obscene at the crowd. His eyes were mad with chemicals and good old-fashioned, prison-grown schizophrenia.

The ref raised his hand and then flashed it down quickly: "Do this thing."

Immediately, Gojo proceeded to run at his opponent with both hands raised, screaming madly. He tried to jump on Donailo, but Donailo slipped him, and Gojo landed hard, face-first into the mesh-wire of the cage fence.

"Pretty boy," Gojo yelled, spitting out his mouthpiece. "Kill you good!"

Gojo and Donailo engaged on their feet. Gojo was swinging awkwardly but dangerously. He had the power of being out of his tiny, mutated mind. Donailo was content to take defensive positions, duck and move, counter-strike when he could. His overall plan was to tire the monstrous, spastic creature out and then tear him up with precision strikes. For now, he had to weather the madness.

As the round progressed, Gojo became more and more frantic, jumping back and forth on his feet and swinging with wildly unpredictable blows and leg kicks. For his part, Donailo was able to block the majority of strikes, and he landed the harder counter-punches. While Gojo looked more active, it was Donailo who was landing the heavier, more precise strikes.

For the better part of the round, Donailo kept his distance and stuffed Gojo with a fierce, snapping right jab. His footwork confused Gojo and frustrated the creature into a greater fury. Donailo was handing out a not-so free boxing lesson in how to stick and move, sit down on his jab and make it hurt. Gojo was paying for the lesson one jab at a time.

The round ended with neither one the decisive victor, though Gojo was considerably more marked-up, his nose was broke and his right eye was moused up to where it gave him a rather imperfect view of the world.

"What's the mystery?" Kellian asked. "This is a brawl."

"Donailo's holding back. He has a strategy while Gojo has only wild instinct on his side. When Gojo runs out of will, Donailo will be there. He's going to win this fight."

"Now this is an issue worth of wagering over. Donailo's pretty good, but eventually that little psycho is going to punish him. I've watched a lot of video on that skinny monster. I predict Gojo takes his opponent this round or the next"

"You want to bet?" Sarah asked, amused at the prospect.

"Name the stakes."`

"All right then. If Donailo wins, then you and I roll for ten minutes in the gym back on the Cortez," Sarah said.

"And if I win?"

"We'll reduce it to five minutes and save you half the pain."

Kellian was intrigued. He had never known any lady of the court to act in such fashion as Sarah. Her boldness was startling, but compelling. He was young enough that he could still only barely interpret his feelings.

"I would not think it proper to engage in combat with you, Sarah."

"Afraid I'll submit you?"

"I have fought many times. I have not been submitted since I was a child."

"So, what do you have to lose?" Sarah smiled.

"A wager is made then."

Below, the second round began.

The fighters crashed briefly as each one tried to eat up the real estate in the middle of the cage. They dirty-boxed, but Gojo came out the worst for it. Donailo had precision knee strikes that cracked the bones inside Gojo's face. His long legs allowed him to bring his knees up from outside Gojo's guard. The results were devastating.

Gojo's energy was wearing down, while Donailo remained constant. While Gojo was furious, he never got close enough to Donailo to do any real damage. This was due in large part to the fact that Donailo could read the creature's mind and move fast enough to avoid a lash.

After the chemicals were spent, and Gojo's hostility replaced by a tired simmering anger, Donailo moved in. The "Monk" struck out with a series of combinations as fast as they were precise. The mystery was no more. Donailo stunned the crowd with his skill and speed. It was brilliant. Leg kicks blended effortlessly with slicing elbow hooks.

Staggered, the animal Gojo raised its hands. He was uneasy on his feet as Donailo took a step back and measured the situation. And then, like that, it was done.

Donailo stepped in and caught the creature with a right hook that sent the creature's head towards the canvas. Before Gojo's face touched the canvas, Donailo had whip-sawed back into position and he landed a full-face kick with his left leg that snapped Gojo's neck violently, ripping his spine leaving him paralyzed as his body crashed onto the mat.

It was the meanest, fastest one-two combo anybody had seen in over a century. As Gojo's head was driven in one direction, Donailo had bashed it full force into another direction with a precise kick. It all happened within the tick of a second. Gojo wasn't allowed to hit the canvas. It was as ruthless as it was precise, so fast, so wickedly fast. Bang-bang! Gojo was down on the canvas. Several medical personnel entered along with Donailo's entourage and a number of security guards. There was no manic celebration in Donailo's camp. They were reserved as they stood in a circle around their fighter. Donaillo bowed deeply and made several hand gestures that indicated he was praising the animal gods for his win. It seemed obvious to him that the gods had willed the destruction of the beast, Gojo.

The crowd was uneasy and quiet as the replay looped. It was as though they had witnessed some form of magic. For a second, the crowd was purely awed by the precision and power of the combination. It was physical art of the most dangerous kind. A few seconds later, the arena suddenly erupted, shockwaves bouncing through the crowd. Donailo had sent a powerful message to other fighters in the weight class. The "Monk", as the commentators called him, was no joke. As the medics carried Gojo out of the cage on a stretcher and on forward to his life in a wheelchair, Donailo made one thing clear: enter the cage with me, and I could end your life as you know it.

On the screens high above, the video loop showed the one-two over and over again.

"Wow," Sarah said simply. "Wow. I think I'd have a tough time with that one."

"So, ten minutes, huh. That's what I get for losing the wager."

"Toughest ten minutes of your princely little life," Sarah grinned.

They watched the remaining fights. All things considered, it was a rather bloody, mind-numbingly violent event. Most bouts ended up with one opponent carried off on a stretcher, while a curious few ended up with both men on a stretcher. It was violent and only loosely regulated. It was a blood-sport, but it was also a cash-cow. Cash-strapped governments throughout the cosmos had been working hard to legalize the sport and bring it under the aegis of the various athletic commissions that governed other combat sports like boxing, and Pomeranian dodge-ball. Casinos and bloodsports were the political options that most appealed to a callow, timid political class incapable of grasping the reality around them and too worried about reelection in any event.

Sarah and Kellian enjoyed the remaining fights and when the show was over, they decided to walk back through Eros-Tao to the Tether-Point, deciding that they would find food somewhere along the way.

They left the box-seat area, and descended an elevator that opened up and let them wade out through the throng, arm in arm. They were jubilant. The fights had been extraordinary, ultra-violent exercises of incredible brutality. Violence of this sort was terribly amusing. Save for a very, very few energy-species in the universe, most civilizations that grew to any notable form of civilization were predators, protein eaters with big growing brains that enabled them to figure clever ways to catch and eat other creatures. And if a meat-hunting, brutish predator couldn't go after the kill any more because of legal impediments, well, they could at least watch bloodsports.

Sarah would never debate this. She was starting to realize herself, and in the process, she was becoming aware that she had some very predatory instincts. She could not recall her memories, but she was realizing that her species wasn't likely the angelic one that the myths seemed to suggest. Whatever the truth, it was far more complicated than the pitiful few snatches of conflicting history that remained.

"Erico submitted him with a naked, mid-air rape choke," Kellian smiled.

"Utterly ruthless. Let's get something to eat," Sarah said.

They exited the parking lot and into the commercial district. It was lit-up and sleezy like Time Square when it was still dangerous and interesting.

There was a lot of foot traffic, but the pace was relatively unhurried. There were several restaurants to choose from, the exteriors ranging from posh semi-circular entrances with red jacketed valets down to neon lit diners. They chose a bar/grill because the scents of charred meat wafting out was almost intoxicating.

After they were seated, and had ordered their meals, their conversation returned to the fights. It had been a tremendous card, and the results were split between dramatic upsets, and stupendously violent, easily foreseen outcomes.

As they sat and conversed, they couldn't help but notice a large, woman arriving in a nearby booth. She appeared to be talking to herself while she jammed an entire loaf of butter-covered dark bread into her mouth.

As a thin, neatly dressed waiter passed by, she grabbed him by the scruff of his shirt.

"Bring me three of everything," she snarled. "And pour rendered animal fat and melted butter over top it all. And make it quick. I'm hungry. If I find one thing healthy on my plate, even a sprig of parsley, I'll jam a straw straight through your chest and suck out your lungs," the woman growled.

"Yes, Madame," the waiter replied. "Shall I have everything deep fried in pork oil for Madame's amusement?"

"Listen here, you smarmy son of a female dog, I'll... wait a minute. Can you actually do that?" the woman asked.

"If Madame would like."

"Yeah, Madame would like. Make it happen, pencil neck, and bring on the dessert menu. I think I'll have to pre-order," the tremendous woman said.

"Of course, Madame," the waiter smiled with more than a trace of condescension. He was paid to be accommodating, yet mildly insulting. He was very good at both.

The fat woman belched loudly and then looked around menacingly to see if someone would take offense.

"That one's looking for a fight. I can feel it," Sarah said.

"You think?" Kellian responded, shrugging it off.

"No, I'm serious. She's trouble."

"She doesn't look as though she could stand up without much difficulty, let alone mount a defensive or offensive posture," Kellian said. "I suspect she'd fall from congestive heart failure before she could take a swing."

"Looks can be deceiving. I'm getting sketchy vibes coming out of her brain," Sarah said lowly. "She's dangerous."

"Let's finish our meal, and leave then. She seems easy enough to avoid."

After dining on two exquisite hunks of meat lathered in a spicy, barbecue like sauce, laid over top a bed of root vegetables, the pair exited the restaurant. Sarah couldn't help but notice that the fat woman watched her intently. There was an unmistakable hostility in the large woman's eyes.

As they left the restaurant, they walked back towards the Tether-Point. They headed down one of the main thoroughfares. The bodegas were all closing up and only a few street vendors were still preparing food. The city was winding down from the bustle of night. They made their way several blocks and were about to turn onto the road that would lead them back to the tether point. Before they reached it, however, they were stopped by six men dressed in simple dark long coats. The men filtered through the crowd until they had encircled the pair. One of them produced a small ceramic gun.

"Come with us," the man with the gun stated.

"What's going on here?" Kellian asked.

"Be quiet, Kell. What's going on here?" Sarah asked.

"We have no interest in your prince. He will accompany us until we are able to reach the Common-Tether.

You, though, are slated for transport to a detention facility," the man said.

Sarah could sense Kellian's desire to fight. She felt it too. "Keep cool, Kell."

"Let's go," the leader of the group said.

He turned his back, and Sarah and Kellian followed, with the other five falling in to surround them. After a few hundred yards, they were outside of the crowd entirely. It was dark enough, late enough that not many people were around the area, and the precious few that were in the vicinity either didn't notice, or couldn't care.

The street was wide, with several parked ground transports lining the sides, but little traffic. The glare of orange street-lamps back-lit the scene and caused the shapes of the group to meld and then break from the shadows cast by the other objects dotting the landscape.

The group walked further, they were walking the outer circle, headed the long route to a central square where a Common-Tether stood inside of the customs building.

They were passing through an area of town that was filled mostly with structures under construction when a snap suddenly crackled the air. One of the men at the rear went down, paralyzed. Suddenly, from all sides, black-dressed soldiers wearing body-armor were rappelling down the walls of the buildings lining the street, firing in short bursts.

The would-be kidnappers fired their weapons and rushed for cover. And so the fire-fight began.

Each of the five remaining kidnappers ducked to find cover positions behind the parked cars lining the street. Despite their long-coats, they were definitely military. Three of them took up forward facing positions while the other two faced the area behind. They fired in precise, two and three round bursts before ducking back for cover, alternating in rhythm so that as one reached to reload, others would cover with suppression fire. Hails of munitions lit up the scene. Within a few seconds, the area had become a war zone.

"Come on, prince," Sarah yelled, dragging him by the arm out the fray.

They ran a couple of blocks, and then they left the main street for cover at their first opportunity. However, as they ducked into an alley, a large obstruction presented itself.

The gargantuan woman from the restaurant stood there like a solid wall.

"Hello, children."

"Oh crap," Sarah whispered.

"Come now, let us embrace,' the woman said coolly.

Sarah exchanged a quick glance with Kellian. Both of them knew what to do. Sarah slipped quickly to her right, while Kellian broke left trying to get to an angle disadvantageous to the woman. It was a classic two-up-one strategy.

Then they struck out in unison. Sarah flashed a roundhouse kick towards the fat woman's head. At the same time, Kellian tried a take the woman's right leg out with a hard sweep aimed just below the knee. Neither strike worked, not because they missed their intended target, rather their intended target, as obese as she was, possessed enough mass to make her nearly invulnerable to the amount of power Sarah's and Kellian's bodies could generate. It was like slugging at a side of frozen beef.

The woman was fast too, surprisingly quick on her feet. As Kellan moved to regain his footing, inside that split second of vulnerability, the fat woman back-handed him with a fist the size of a Christmas turkey. He snapped backwards and landed against a dumpster several meters away, out cold.

"Come, my child. All I want is to embrace you," the tremendous female said.

Behind Sarah, just outside the alley, gunfire was continuous, showers of munitions rained down upon the area. In front of her stood the woman, immovable. Sarah didn't like her odds in the firefight, and she had little reason to think she could take out the creature in front of her. She quickly surveyed her surroundings for escape routes, but the alley was empty. The nearest window was several yards behind the large woman. Perfect trap.

"Nice little set-up," Sarah said flatly, trying to buy a second to think.

"Glad you approve," the fat woman answered with a smile.

"Who are the goons outside?"

"No stalling for time, kid. You and I know they were just distractions. Nothing more need be said."

"Let's do it then," Sarah responded, assuming her favored Pradal-Surey stance, her fists tight and raised high.

"You are a brave one, aren't you?"

Sarah paused for a second, suddenly hit in the heart with a terrible fear. She had heard those words once, deep inside her dreams from that life long behind her now, when she was locked in the ward and left little but her dreams to escape into. She remembered the dimly lit corridor, something like a mine shaft. She remembered following the wolf with the gentle eyes. She recalled walking behind the wolf until he disappeared into a room. Then she remembered peering inside the room from her position only half hidden from the horrific potato sack-like creatures that were wrapping their tentacles around the dying wolf as it dissolved under their touch. They were horrible creatures. She could sense this, but did not move. One of them noticed her standing outside the door. It looked at her and smiled with a terrifyingly wide maw. It looked her deep in the eyes, hungry to kill her, and it said simply: "You are a brave one, aren't you?"

Dear god! With her eyes half-squinted the large woman in front of her appeared every bit like one of the sack-like monsters of her dreams in the time before she had left Earth for life aboard the Cortez. Given all the other weird things in Sarah's life, coincidence was rarely a valid explanation.

Sarah shook it off. A shiver went through her, but she steeled herself for the conflict. She tried to determine the woman's range and arc of movement, testing the fat woman with a series of blows designed to draw out her defensive movements. Sarah was determined to figure out how to beat the woman.

Once she found the appropriate range of movement between strike and fall-back positions, Sarah launched a series of combination high-low punches and kicks. She kept changing levels, striking out with cup kicks and hooks. It took only a few tries for Sarah to realize that she was having no effect whatsoever.

"Thanks for the love taps," the fat woman said. "Truth is I take more abuse from my masseuse."

In the split second that Sarah tried to regain her breath, the woman struck out with a fierce overhand right. Even though Sarah blocked it with the shins of her arms, the blow was punishing. As Sarah reeled backwards, the fat woman stepped in. Before Sarah could react, the fat woman grabbed her around the waist and brought her close to her tremendous chest and squeezed tightly.

"Come, my dear. I have so much love to give," the woman said in a soft voice.

Sarah tried to fight back, but her face was driven straight into the wall of flesh. She tried to kick, scramble, strike with her fists, bite with her mouth, scratch with her nails. Nothing seemed to do very much, and the embrace became tighter with each passing second.

"Go to sleep, just go to that quiet place," the fat lady cooed.

Sarah was out of options. Her face was fully swallowed inside the woman's girth. Sarah couldn't draw a breath. It was terrifying. Her body was scared, but utterly power-less. She fought back as best as she could, but she did no damage. Soon she felt light-headed, and then, as though swept into the billowy hands of a comfortable dream, she felt nothing at all. Sarah was unconscious.

As the fat lady slung the limp-bodied Sarah over one massive shoulder, she sang a simple lullaby, too low and soft a voice for anyone to hear, just a simple tune that the obese woman sang for herself and no one else.

> *'It's all over, child*
> *It's all over*
> *The shadows sigh*
> *The wild ones dance, but*
> *It's all over, child*
> *It's come to pass*

Doja monitored the gun battle. She had to proc-ess a great deal of sensory input ranging from the gun cams and optical wetware of her troops, to the images recorded by the few security cams that operated in this underdeveloped section of Eros Tao. It was the first time she had coordinated a group this large, with this many variables in play. It took several minutes, but she was able to take out the crew tasked to kidnap Sarah. Doja knew it was a distraction from the real trap.

She kept an eye on Sarah and Kellian as they fought the massive bounty hunter, Sluggora Slimsloe, a heavy-worlder of dangerous dimensions. Doja wouldn't let the fight become lethal. She had snipers covering the alley, ready to take Slimsloe out if things got too out of hand.

Sluggora Slimsloe was no fool. She had infiltrated Eros Tao under an assumed identity – Bertha Bigbottom. She had military grade infiltration software waiting outside the cyber-walls of the security system of the customs computers. Doja had long since inoculated the system and destroyed the predatory software. In its place, Doja stretched her code so that Slimsloe wouldn't be able to tell the difference. Then Doja waited.

Before heading out of the trash strewn alleyways of the Northern portion of Eros Tao, Slimsloe had tucked Sarah into a large duffel bag. A few minutes later and the bounty hunter made her attempt to cross through customs, comfortable that her attack software were opening the doors for her.

Doja, in code form, obeyed the encrypted commands coming from Slimsloe's personal wi-fi emitter. There was no reason to show her hand just yet. Doja ordered the security personnel at the customs station leading to the Common-Tether to stand down and let Slimsloe pass through the lines unhindered.

Several minutes later, Sluggora Slimsloe, her bounty stuffed inside a duffel bag, approached a large clam shaped vessel in the short-term parking section of the hangar. She knew well enough to not get happy yet. Payday was still 35,000 light years away, and clean escapes were few and far between.

As Slimsloe crossed the hangar floor and approached her craft, she saw a young girl in a little yellow frock sitting on one of the wings, her legs kicking impatiently.

"You must be the infamous Lady Doja," Slimsloe said, dropping her sack. "I gotta admit, I'm somewhat underwhelmed after all the dark talk about Germaine's pet demon."

Doja sat still on the wing, only a few paces out of reach of the giant woman's powerful hands.

"You're very, very fat. I think I should like to be very, very fat like you," Doja replied.

"Get off my ship," Sluggora Slimsloe responded coldly.

Doja slid off the wing, dropping effortlessly. She took a second to straighten the wrinkles in her dress and then she approached the large whale of a woman in front of her. Her eyes narrowed darkly, and her smile almost completely disappeared.

"You didn't actually think we would let you leave Eros Tao with the girl?" Doja asked.

"Out of my way, whelp. There's room in my duffel bag for one more."

"As you wish," Doja replied, stepping one pace to the side.

"Smart move, imp."

"Of course, someone else might like to have a say in the matter," Doja said.

At that moment, a large shape moved from the hidden side of the ship. It stood taller than Slimsloe, and its body mass was pure muscle. As far as physical forms went, the beast was considerably more intimidating than Slimsloe.

"Who the hell are you?" Sluggora asked.

"I am Doja," the beast growled.

Before Sluggora could react, the tremendous creature grabbed her by the face, its hand covering the entire structure. It squeezed and lifted the woman several feet off the ground and then brought her head back and down with one smashing arc strike. Sluggora's body stiffened up, her toes curling as her body landed with a tremendous thud. The beast lifted the woman by the head and then smashed it down once more just to be sure. Then, on cue, the beast moved away and disappeared from the hangar deck.

Sarah came to a moment later and fought her way out of the duffel bag. Doja was waiting.

"What happened?" Sarah asked. "I know I got tore up back there, but what are we doing in customs?"

"You were kidnapped. I intervened and rescued you," Doja replied.

"How'd you do that?"

"Well, in common parlance, I kicked her fat arse."

"Very funny," Sarah said. "Even a squad of your best soldiers couldn't bring this beast to the ground."

While Sarah could not be sure how the child Doja could take out a tremendous woman like Sluggora, Sarah's speculations were all unattractive conjecture.

"We've got a short window to make this thing work," Doja said. "I suggest you get back to the Cortez. I can have my forces escort you safely to the tether-point."

"What about Kellian?' Sarah asked.

"He's fine. A few broken bones, and a bit of broken confidence, nothing that time won't cure, Sarah."

"I guess I owe you one, Doja," Sarah said.

"Just get back to the Cortez please. There are strange things about to occur here, and I'd rather not have... witnesses," Doja responded, a touch weirder than usual.

Sarah looked down at the unconscious behemoth, Slimsloe. Whatever Doja had in mind, it was surely bad news for the tremendous bounty hunter. Without needing to say so, Sarah agreed that it was best to let Doja do her work in the dark.

She left quickly with a small contingent of Doja's guards accompanying her. Meanwhile, Doja set up a ruse designed to, as Germaine said, "shake off a bunch of fleas."

Slimsloe going rogue, hypnotized into thinking she had Sarah, should draw off a lot of their pursuit and decrease the amount of danger they would encounter when they finally made the trip to the Expanse. Limiting the variables, decreasing the pawns in play, was the best chance at surviving a trip to the Expanse. There already were enough unknowable dangers lurking in that warped tract of space. "Shaking off the fleas" as Germaine called it, was a small but wisely counseled act, the underlying logic being that the Cortez could only deal with so much crap at once.

Chapter Ten

Goodbyes

After several days of procrastination, speculation, preparation, and liver annihilation, they had arrived on the outskirts of the Borgias Expanse. There was nothing to see. The sensors were nearly useless as the radiation in the Expanse made a mess of everything.

Germaine, with the wild enthusiasm of a school child, had believed there would be a lot of answers waiting for them once they reached the Expanse, but so far there was nothing. He was clearly unsettled. He paced back and forth from one side of the bridge to other, his hands clasped behind his back, his thumbs wrestling impatiently. He wanted to go into the Expanse but Capoella had convinced him to wait at least a day while she recalibrated the sensor array for the radiation.

At least they were rid of the authorities, he thought, most of them at any rate. Doja had manipulated the mind of Sluggora Slimsloe into going rogue, or, at least, thinking she was going rogue. It was a plausible story: bounty hunter captures prize and then, instead of doing her job, decides to offer her prize to the highest bidder. Sarah certainly was the type of prize a person might go rogue for. Now, Sluggora was on the run, dragging attention away from Eros Tao, and the Cortez.

"Do you recognize this region, Sarah?" Germaine asked for the twelfth time.

"What's to recognize, Captain? It looks just empty space," Sarah replied honestly, for the twelfth time.

She was starting to feel something deep within her, a need, a yearning, but she could not describe what she felt. Her memories were still hidden, only the emotions could be felt at any conscious level.

"We're going to hang out on the border for a day or so, see what we can scan from here. Then we'll go inside. Get some rest. There's nothing for you to do up here," Capoella said.

Sarah shrugged and left the bridge. Unlike the Captain, she had never been very hopeful that traveling to the Expanse would explain anything. She had no reason to trust in the events which suggested she should be brought into this region of space. She had never met an energy cloud before. She certainly didn't trust one. She did know one thing. She did not like looking out at the Expanse from the ship's view-screen. It was a disquieting view. The light coming from the stars in the region somehow wasn't right. There was something predatory about the region. It was like looking at the dark maw of some great, wild beast.

She was glad to leave the bridge. There were other more important things on her adolescent mind. She'd been getting on very well with Prince Kellian, and tonight he had offered to take her to the opera house to see the premiere performance of Lupithaine Lockjaw's masterwork "Three Midgets, Two Chickens, and a Dog Named Bob." Ostensibly about the failed invasion of Grigidia, it also examined complex issues around love and infidelity, betrayal and domestic violence. Sarah was looking forward to the event. As far as princes went, she really liked him.

For the time being, she sought relaxation.

A half an hour later, Sarah was walking beside Dorian inside the rainforest dome, something they did quite regularly now. The place always reminded Sarah somewhat of Magnus' facility in the V718 Bhoon-Tebli System, only there weren't any obsequies, terrified, waiters roaming about. A few Trotsky-loving androids hid out in the trees, but they were content to sulk in secret. The Leninists hated them, so they were a fairly dejected lot even among their own kind. The air was thick and humid, sticky, but pleasantly filled with the heavy, fragrant scents of wild orchids, and wet dead leaves decomposing underfoot.

They walked along a small path beneath a canopy of thick branches that would break apart here and there to allow the thin beams of artificial orange light to reach the ground level. It was in these few patches that little ferns would suddenly spring into life. The air was alive with lyrical bird calls, pierced occasionally by some sort of howling screeching sound the origin of which was never revealed. Species called out to one another to mark territory, to attract a mate, to warn against a predator. There were complex, beautiful languages, intense exchanges in the seeming babble. The jungle was filled with so much life. It was thick and vast, and the path windy enough that they could walk for miles without crossing their own steps twice.

Both Sarah and Dorian had grown fond of their walks through the artificial rain-forest. They each enjoyed their time in an organic environment as a break from the sterility of the Cortez, and the bustle of Eros Tao. Sarah preferred the green smell of the air, the lack of artificial structures, the peacefulness of it all, just a beautiful space seldom shared by any crewmember other than herself and Dorian. It was their quiet spot together.

They had spent many hours now, walking sometimes in silence, while other times they would debate. Dorian was intensely spiritual. He never explained the tenets of his religion, if he still had one. He merely exhibited a certain tranquility and poise that was calming. Sarah found his presence like an opiate for her soul, although in debate she was fiercely secular.

They would often argue the relationship between science and religion, whether or not quantum mechanics and other forms of scientific rationalism had fully exorcised the ghost from the machine, or merely restored it in infinitely complex forms, never to be deciphered fully, wholly, logically. Was the universe thoroughly organic and mechanical, reducible to rational explanation, or was their something that exceeded the scope of the senses, some unknowable, mysterious, animating force pervading existence? It was an old argument that defied resolution. Both knew it was more a form of fencing, designed to keep their minds sharp and focused. They spoke about many things. The topics of their conversation ran from Descartes to Hawking with a pleasing fluidity and healthy vigor. While Sarah would concede that many physical events were beyond her comprehension, and could not yet be rationally explained by resorting to empirical data alone, she thought that, in time, all of the mysteries of the universe would be divined, reduced to academic knowledge to be passed from one mind to the next, expanded upon, modeled, and eventually reduced to trivia. She refused to allow for the existence of some intervening third-party, a god of any sort. She certainly didn't believe that she was the member of any race of gods. It was unfathomable. She accepted her obvious qualities, but rationalized them in terms more mechanical than mystical.

She even understood and advanced arguments concerning her own limitations. Sarah knew tremendous amounts of information on sources as obscure as

Marcus Aurelius and Hunter S. Thompson. She was well acquainted with the dominant threads of atheistic philosophy. However, her arguments were academic, abstract. She had very little exposure to the universe around her other than the several adventures she had enjoyed in her short time aboard the Cortez. Her views were somewhat stilted by this fact, something she would readily concede. She craved to know who she really was, what her purpose in life was. She simply didn't accept the apocalyptic myths that were associated with her race. She could not believe that there was some final plan to destroy the universe. The mystical elements assigned to her race were often contradictory. Half the universe thought her species evil, while the other half worshipped her kind with a devotion that often bordered on hysteria.

Everyone, from school children, to priests, to historians, to anthropologists, to political philosophers wondered what had happened to this mysterious race that had left its footprint in several galaxies, only to disappear without notice, leaving little behind but their children, their seed sown in the genetic fabric of several trillion star-systems, their true fate lost among a million competing myths.

The pair didn't spend all of their time talking about science and religion. Dorian would often tell her stories of his youth spent on a home-world very similar to Venus. The planet Reklaan Three was an exotic, sulphuric acid laden, mountainous planet reeking with ammonia vapors, lavished by a dark purple atmosphere trapping in as much heat and radiation as the place could handle. It was a planet of poisonous beauty, terribly violent red sunsets, tremendous, fluctuating magnetic fields, and storms of exotic particles playing a tag-you're-it game with the dimensions they swam through, quantum children amusing themselves with wildly improbable feats. A splendid time for everyone involved, he told her.

It had taken very long for any sort of civilization to arise on Reklaan, and it was widely believed that Dorian's species, the Falil, had actually migrated to the planet so long ago that all records were lost, that they hadn't in fact originated on the planet at all. No one knew for sure, although several academics made a living studying the matter, coming to different conclusions from their archaeological data, ripping each other on talk shows and blogs. Academia in the modern universe was as much about being good at smack-talk and street-fighting as it was application of any scientific method.

The Falil never officially weighed in on the topic of their origin. They didn't seem to care. The Falil believed that they were exactly where they were supposed to be, because that is where they were. It was circular, mystical logic, simple, and utterly Falil.

Reklaan was a wondrous place filled with many threatening things. There were several large insectoid predators, thermo-philes that roamed the rocky surfaces, or hid out beneath layers of rusty-colored dust, waiting to trap their prey beneath an array of wicked black spider-like legs, and a huge gaping maw of black razor teeth. Lots of fun, he explained.

Dorian was able to shift forms between solid and gaseous states, but still had a few run-ins that almost cost him his life. He liked to wander far from the cities, something that wasn't widely encouraged given the relative dangers of life on Reklaan.

He never explained exactly how this translated into a life with the Germaine and the crew, but it was clear that Dorian's wanderlust must have played a large role in the matter.

For herself, Sarah had come to love Dorian in the way a younger sister often became enamored with the character and strength of her older sibling. She adored Dorian. Nothing ever upset him, or threw him off-course.

Even in the oddest and most dangerous of circumstances, he was calm, polite, and thoroughly unflappable.

On this walk, they made their way in silence for several minutes. Although Dorian would not peer into Sarah's mind out of respect, her subtle physical gestures had not gone unnoticed. She was itching for the moment to bring about a discussion they had had once during the first few weeks Sarah had been aboard the Cortez.

He let her take her time to explain what was on her mind, and eventually she did just that.

"For three nights in a row, I've had that same dream about following the wolf, watching it die. I still think there's some connection between the dream and our traveling here," she told him.

"I have never doubted that the dream has some significance, but there are a many different ways to explain the symbols of the dream."

"I keep coming back to one, Dorian."

"You still think that the wolf represents Germaine, or maybe the Cortez more generally? We are leading you down a path that you will survive, though we will not?" he asked.

"I don't know."

"You think that we will be consumed by the forces aligning against us."

"Yes. Even Germaine can only run for so long. There are many things conspiring against us and even with the Cortez, I do not think he can outrun death. It is a death he will face because of me. I know this."

"And you think that if you leave us, we will somehow avoid this fate?"

"Yes."

"It's an interesting thought. You cling to logic, yet you are afraid of the significance of your own dreams, persuaded by the symbolism," Dorian said.

"Even you cannot claim to know the true scope of my species' abilities. I am persuaded by my dreams, yes, but I am also convinced that there is a rational explanation for them, not a mystical one. There are many species that do not see time in a linear fashion. You can sense elements of the future. You know I must find some way to leave this ship and forge my own destiny."

"I am able to see many things, Sarah. I can see your fate, and I know that you will leave us soon, but I don't believe heading off as casually as you are suggesting would be in your best interest. Your time will come."

"What would you suggest then?"

"Well, I wouldn't recommend that you steal one of our ship's shuttles. I know you've been studying the operation manuals, and you've even flown a few test flights. Stealing from the Cortez and the Captain is low-class, not to mention illegal, sort of. I think when you see the way out, you should jump ship, if that's what you truly want, but make sure you plan this thing out well," Dorian told her. "Do not go off alone."

"Kellian," she whispered.

"Yes."

"He is part of my future then."

"I know this without controversy. You and he were meant to come together. I cannot tell you your ultimate fate, but I know he will join you on your quest."

"Quest?"

"You are most assuredly on a quest. It will help greatly when you are able to find out just what you are questing for."

"No arguments there."

"Keep a calm mind, Sarah. Make your moves wisely."

Sarah pondered what he had said to her. It was sound advice, as always. Unlike the reactionary ramblings of Germaine, Dorian was more direct, his lessons less abstract. Germaine was a carefree, powerful devil with a strange sense of humor; a noble dissident with lots of money and lots of weapons, while Dorian was as an angel dropped from the clouds of heaven, here to play with mere mortals and observe all the strange and curious aspects of the universe around him.

Dorian never protested Sarah's assertions that she must at some point leave the Cortez. He merely wanted her to think through the consequences, to carefully control the manner of her departure, not make some mistake that would lead her into greater danger.

Truth was, even though Germaine would never admit it, and Capoella wouldn't think of ever discussing it, Sarah's presence had led to several conflicts, several close calls. She was a magnet for trouble, and the universe was seething in political turmoil and intrigue. Old territorial conflicts once resolved were being renewed with incredible hostility, while newer conflicts were cultivated, thriving on the paranoia that was operating in pandemic proportions throughout the universe. Word of her existence was just in its rumor stage, but the effects were dramatic.

The VD, once dormant, content to recede from the political landscape of the universe into myth and obscurity, were now asserting themselves in several lopsided border engagements. They had pulled over two-hundred star systems into their sphere of control within the last six weeks, and it didn't appear that anything could stop them. The ICPT were struggling to restore peaceful, diplomatic relations, but the VD remained stoic, silent, and inscrutable. All the while, news of Sarah's existence was starting to grow from rumors posted on simple cultish websites devoted to worshipping her species, and was now slowly becoming a matter of some attention. Great engines of activity were being lighted back into existence. The universe was a festering rot of apprehensions, suspicions, paranoid militaristic movements now animated by the very whisper that Sarah was alive, out in the folds of space. While many species held their collective breath in awe of what was transpiring, what could transpire, several more prepared for final war, their own variations of Armageddon; a million dark, sickly-envisioned riffs on the common theme of universal death, followed by eternal darkness.

Sarah knew what was happening across the universe, as much as could be deciphered from the sub-ether waves and pirated news vid clips. She was becoming all-too aware that the mere potential of her presence was sparking violence across hundreds of star-systems.

She knew her fate was intertwined with what was happening, and she knew she would have to fall downwards into the chaos. The one, indeed the only thing she could tell for sure was that her fate would be different than that of the Cortez. At some point she must part ways with the only friends she truly had in the universe. On one level, she felt horrified by the prospect, terrified. She adored her life aboard the Cortez. It was filled with action and intrigue, good food, and surly androids. She would miss it surely. But the resolution to the turbulent conditions in the universe, and the discovery of who she truly was, were linked in some fashion she could not yet but eventually had to decipher.

She'd had a lot of fun over the months, and rolling into combat with Germaine was something she never thought she'd duplicate. He was one of a kind. He was bigger than life, and his crew was as family now, an odd, dysfunctional family, each endearing in their own manner. As much as she was fascinated by their cause, the adolescent manner of their rebellion, Sarah felt deep within her mind and soul that she would be leaving soon, that she would be forced to.

When the General Alert siren sounded, she was somewhat less than surprised. The flanged, Doppler effect of the siren's piercing howl penetrated the jungle. All manner of creature clamored for safety beneath the thick folds of tree cover.

"Our shields have been penetrated. There are intruders onboard," Dorian reported. "Capoella is trying to provide us a clear route to the bridge, but we have to move quickly."

"Jesus, all right, let's go."

The pair made their way fast down through the path leading to one of the several exit points.

Just before they reached the door a shirtless, wiry muscled humanoid materialized in front of the pair. Its head was bald and its face torn to shreds from several injuries, It was wielding a long-handled, heavy Nordic-style hammer in one of its grotesquely gnarled hands.

"You must be Sarah," it growled from deep within its chest.

"And you must be suicidal," Sarah replied coolly, brushing Dorian gently behind her with one arm.

She assumed her Pradal-Surey stance.

"Beautiful," the creature laughed uncomfortably.

Sarah wondered.

The creature was almost nine feet tall, and its body mass was six to seven times that of Sarah's. Still, she was prepared to fight it out. Running just wasn't in her nature.

Just before she could launch out with a series of inconsequential combos and low leg kicks, she felt herself pulled up by her collar. She was lifted up into the air by what felt like talons. The creature below tried to jump up and catch her feet, but it was too late, she was riding high towards the artificial light, pulled up into the fake sky of the dome.

She looked up to see Dorian's face attached to the body of a tremendous, black feathered bird with a vast, magnificent wingspan.

"Better part of valor, and all that," he smiled.

"You know I could have taken him?" Sarah growled.

"Of course, Sarah. I was merely looking out for his personal safety."

"You might want to explain that to him. Seems he's intent on keeping up with us."

Sarah and Dorian traveled up and over the high ceiling of thick foliage, and through the artificial atmosphere, heading towards the other end of the facility. Beneath them, the creature seemed to tear apart, push away or jump over every obstacle in its path as it tried furiously to keep up with their flight.

They swooped down in front of an open area near an exit door. Dorian released her and resumed his surreal, ghostlike humanoid form.

"That juggernaut is going to be here in a few moments, Sarah. You need to get out of here."

"What about you?"

"Well, it looks like I'm about to get into a fight," he smiled

"Forget about it! I won't let you stay back here and get murdered by that creature."

"Don't worry about me, Sarah. I can handle myself. Just get to the bridge."

"This is my fight not yours!"

"No. You cannot be here to witness this. I cannot defeat the creature and worry about your safety at the same time. Respect me, Sarah. Do as I wish. Get to the bridge. I will take care of this beast."

Sarah paused, ready to say something more, but then she relented. "Be safe," Sarah replied, a teardrop forming just as she brushed it away.

The doors opened and Sarah jumped through only to hear them close and lock from the inside. She stopped, unsure of herself. She felt sick that Dorian was in there preparing to face a creature that had infiltrated the ship to go after her. This was her fault.

She made her way to the port escape pod array on one of the upper decks.

Several violent tremors rocked the ship as it was targeted by high-energy particle beams. Sarah opened up a communication line with the bridge.

"What the hell is going on up there?" she yelled.

"Kind of busy, kid" Capoella replied. "We're caught up in the migration of a gypsy Chin Dovo Hive."

"You do know that there is a violent, nine-foot tall creature with a big hammer running around down here in the jungle arboretum?" Sarah asked.

"Yeah. We were wondering about that. The Chin Dovo hives don't employ humanoid outsiders, not for any purpose. They kind of mindlessly travel through space attacking anything that gets in their way...we got in their way."

"Well, I don't know anything about gypsy hives, but the fellow down here seems ready to tear things up. You might want to do something."

"Sarah, we can't get to you right now. There are multiple hull breaches in the areas around that section. The section is sealed already. Tough it out for a bit until we get the repairs done. You've been in enough fights to know how to handle yourself by now."

The transmission ended as the ship rocked with several more impacts.

Huh, Sarah thought. Not the answer she'd desired, but it was the answer she got. She thought about it for a moment, and then she opened up communications with the navigational computers of several of the escape pods on her level.

As the creature approached, Dorian stood his ground, a slight smile formed on his lips. He appeared to adopt no fighting stance.

"Wow, you're a big fella," Dorian said. "It must be quite comforting to be adorned with as many muscles as you are, and the hammer is really a nice accessory. It's really quite fashionable."

"Out of my way, cloud-priest," the creature roared. "The girl is mine."

"You'll have to do better than that, cave dweller."

The creature growled, and then hefted the hammer up before swinging it down in an arcing strike that would have bludgeoned most persons to death instantly. Dorian let the blow pass through him until it's reached his midpoint. At that second, he became solid enough to capture and wrench the hammer away from the creature's grasp.

Dorian's frame twisted and shot out the hammer like a cannon into the foliage behind them.

"You'll want to bring your A-game," Dorian said. "My race has dealt with your kind for millennia. You'll not find us easy prey."

Infuriated, the creature ripped large stone from the landscape. It hefted the heavy gray rock and then lobbed it at Dorian's head.

The stone passed right through Dorian, and as Dorian reformed, he was no longer smiling.

"You are a simple brute, and I am far too old for childish games," Dorian responded.

Dorian resolved his form into that of a giant, ethereal dragon, swelling up menacingly in front of the exit. The dragon figure encompassed the area around it, winding up and over everything. Its head was as large as the beast in front of it.

"Now's the moment where you run, cave-dweller," Dorian growled fiercely, his voice reverberating in the large throat of the beast.

"No, pretty cloud-priest, now you fall hard."

The creature smiled nastily, reaching into its belt and presenting a black diamond shaped object which it threw upwards into the energy structure that was Dorian. The object acted as a heavy-gravity source, compressing Dorian unwillingly, pulling his energy form into something tight, controllable, and innocuous.

Dorian resolved into physical form, writhing on the ground as the energy field compressed his energy painfully.

"You are predictable, cloud-priest," the creature grumbled happily. "Easy prey."

The creature lacked the power to kill Dorian, otherwise it would most certainly have done so. Controlling Dorian was something it was able to achieve once given the tools. It crossed over his splayed out form and began smashing at the exit doors with its fists. The locks had been encrypted, but the creature didn't know that. It never even dawned on the creature to check. Smashing things was more its style. Smashing things was what the creature was well-designed to do.

Outside the doors, Sarah was preparing to "deal with it". She reset the escape shuttle protocols for every ship on her level. She could voice-activate a limited set of commands. For the moment, she ducked behind a stanchion that extruded from the hull, and she waited for the inevitable.

Even if she wanted to run, she couldn't. The security system failsafe had already locked off the entire section to stop a lethal decompression. There was no way out.

She was prepping for the combat when Kellian appeared in the hall to her left.

"Get down!" Sarah yelled.

"What's going on?"

"Dear god, Kell. Move it! We don't have much time!"

"Why are you hiding?" he inquired.

As if to answer him, the alien, having regained its hammer, swung it straight into the door causing a loud menacing thud to reverberate through the halls.

"I see," Kellian said, moving very quickly to duck below the lip of metal just as the creature swung its hammer once again.

"What are you doing down here?" Sarah asked.

"I came to check on your safety after I heard we'd been boarded. I crossed into the section just before the security seals engaged."

"That's sweet, a little stupid, but sweet," Sarah said, giving him a quick peck on his cheek.

The smashing sound at the door leading to arboretum was intensifying. Soon, it would be buckled enough to be ripped from its frame.

"Who's coming for dinner?" he asked.

"He's a pretty nasty brute, and he seems to have disposed of Dorian pretty quickly."

"That's not good," Kellian replied.

"Nope. Not good. By the way, he's got a hammer."

"A hammer?"

"Yeah, like Viking battle size."

"So what's the plan?"

"It's a long-shot, but it's the best I could come up with on short notice," Sarah said.

Inside the bridge, androids were darting about furiously, working to restore off-line systems and give the Cortez a fighting chance.

"Quickly, you commies!" Germaine yelled.

"We're down to secondary shields, intra-stellar propulsions systems are offline," Capoella responded.

"Can we rip out of here?"

"No, there's too much live fire to open a stable singularity. We need to bring this situation under control fast."

"Doja!" Germaine called out.

"She's already engaged. She's having trouble penetrating their firewalls."

"Nonsense! Doja cuts through code like a straight razor. Tell her to get her little white ass in line or…"

"She says give her five minutes, and this will all be over."

The vessel rocked under another barrage of missiles.

"Damn it, this whole thing is going to be over in three! Charge-up the EPG. Tell Doja to get back here. Lock on to the lead vessel and generate a targeted gamma burst."

Capoella stopped to stare at him.

"That is not our way," she replied.

"Yeah, but we didn't start this, did we?"

"We started this back on Earth."

Germaine paused. The vessel rocked under another missile barrage. Outside the ship thousands of little two and three family vehicles, yellow painted hexagonal shaped pods, were swarming the Cortez in numbers so great that they foiled many of the vessel's defensive batteries. There was no way to communicate with them. They were beings of pure instinct, coursing through the universe like locusts, attacking everything and then converting what remained into raw fuel.

Some anthropologists speculated that the hives were on some sort of religious quest, but not one of these theorists had ever been within a light year of any hive migration, so their speculations were widely ignored.

"Fine, then generate a graviton wake, brush them away before they tear us apart."

"Initiating burst," Capoella replied.

The EPGs emitted a graviton pulse, like a large rock being splashed down into the fluid pool of space-time. The ripples of the wave caught the Hive ships and battered their shields. It overloaded most of their systems and swept several them a light-year away in a fashion that would have blown Einstein's magnificent mind. However, as it brushed the ships back, it also inconveniently thrust many of the vessels into the turbulent gravity waves and radiation bleed emanating from the accretion disc of a moderately sized black hole. As their vessels crossed over into the frozen Einsteinian hell of the event horizon, one squeaky transmission found its way back to the Cortez. It was almost a poem. Roughly translated it said:

Fierce is she who taunts the wind
Misery is left in her wake
But beauty and truth will follow the darkness.

The Hive ships disappeared into the stew of radiation and madness as they passed over the edge and into the swirl of the singularity. The horror of frozen time captured them. Eventually, perhaps a hundred-thousand centuries from now, they would be swallowed up, swept into the great compactor of space-time, the universe's greatest killing machine. Germaine pitied them. He didn't want to kill them, but he had succeeded in issuing them a fate far worse than death – near-everlasting life between two ticks on a clock, frozen and helpless. Pure horror.

The Cortez was regenerating as trillions of nanotech machinery suspended in a cool clear white liquid medium began forming over the damaged areas of the hull. The place was covered in a hot white glue-snot stickiness of nano-recreation, but it was becoming more operational with each passing second as systems were restored, bypassed, recreated, or ignored.

"We'll be up and running in ten minutes, Captain."

"How are we doing below decks, the intruder and all that?"

"We sealed off the entire section to prevent depressurization. She's on her own until we can make repairs."

"Wonderful. We can't get a security detail down there?"

"We're regenerating as fast as we can."

"After we're operational, I'll want a full investigation. Nobody sneaks up on us like this."

"I don't think they did," Capoella said. "Not way the hell out here. Nobody knows about this spot except you, me, Dorian, and..."

"Don't say it..." he groaned. "Where's Doja?"

Below decks, Sarah waited until the creature broke through the door. It was sweaty, massive, and angry, the sheen of its skin caught nastily in the uncomfortable orange glare of the emergency lighting. It hefted the massive hammer menacingly.

It sensed her. It seemed to smell her. It issued several low, guttural groans. The sounds made Sarah uncomfortable, as they were designed to. She looked over at Kellian. He looked scared, but he was ready to fight. She was thankful he was here with her.

"Come, little child. Your destiny lies with another master," it roared in a voice that was like gravel ground in some horrible machine.

At that, Sarah lunged up from her hidden position, anger overriding fear.

"*I* control my destiny, monster!" she yelled.

They stood across from each other with little more than a few meters separating them, regarding each other warily for a few long seconds. Behind her, Sarah had left the apertures leading to several of the escape pods open.

She let the creature come at her, just as she intended. She blocked, deflected or dodged most of the creature's swipes with the hammer. She was too rooted to be caught and knocked off balance. It was expert level Tai-Chi.

Slowly, deliberately, she backed off, peppering the creature occasionally with a short combo, leg-strikes, jabs, and a few nasty hooks. She was outmatched because of her opponent's sheer size and strength. She knew this, but she needed to lure him successfully down the hallway further.

When they reached a perfect spot where the hallway curved, she dodged one of the creature's slower strikes, diving her tiny frame through his open legs. As his weight was thrust forward and his center of gravity pushed off base, Kellian appeared from behind the stanchion and thrust his father's sword into the middle of the creature's back. Sarah held onto the monster's ankles while Kellian pulled out the blade and kicked the beast in the center of the back, propelling the creature face forward into the interior one of the escape shuttles. The creature flew onto its face.

"Computer, close hatch. Engage emergency protocol: Kid Quick One," Sarah yelled.

The creature scrambled as the doors were closing. Its body was heavily damaged and it appeared unable to get its feet firmly underneath its weight. Sarah and Kellian waved goodbye, both smiling.

"When you get close to the black hole, and your body starts to boil in the radiation, please think of us," Sarah called out.

Before the doors could fully seal, though, the creature found its footing. It stared at her intensely before it whipped a net from beneath its belt. The net caught

Sarah and Kellian full in the chest and formed a quickly bonding, web-like structure. Sarah tore at it frantically, but it covered her fingers with a white sticky, obnoxious smelling substance. Tearing at it only made the situation worse. The creature pulled Sarah and Kellian towards it. Whatever fate it was to enjoy, it was hell-bent on sharing it. It couldn't pull her through the door before it closed, but the door didn't sever the strand. Sarah and Kellian were still stuck. She pulled and ripped, but the proteins inside the glue were dynamic, the substance was quickly enveloping them, trapping them to the rear of the shuttle as its thrusters engaged. The engines lit up a few seconds after the vessel was detached from the hull of the Cortez. Absent any measure of protection, Sarah and Kellian were dragged into the icy cold as the shuttle shot into space.

The cold hit her at first, mind-withering, black space cold, too painful for words. Her body was limp, helpless as the shuttle trajectory catapulted it towards the nearby black hole monster. Kellian was unconscious within a few seconds.

"Lovely," she thought, more surprised than discomfited or afraid.

"We've got problems, Captain," Capoella said.

"Why did one of the escape shuttles just launch?"

"I don't know. The reports coming in from the androids indicate that Sarah tricked the intruder into one of the shuttles, but before it could be launched, she was caught somehow. Both she and Kellian were trapped on the outside of the hull when the rockets flared. Now they're headed towards the black hole right behind the Hive ships."

"Damn it! Are they in mat-trans range?"

"There's still too much radioactivity in this sector. We'd fry her if we tried to pick her out of the soup."

"How fast can we get a shuttle to her position?"

Capoella looked down for a second and then back up at Germaine.

"There's not enough time," she said simply. "We can't get to her before she's pulled into the gravity well."

"Jesus...Doja!" he called out. After a moment, he called out again: "Doja, darling, we need you on the bridge. Doja?"

"Computer, locate Doja," Capoella said.

The computer responded that Doja was no longer aboard the Cortez.

"Well, where the hell is she?' Germaine asked.

"Insufficient data," it answered.

"All options are on the table, Capeolla, duct-tape, whatever. This isn't going down like this."

"We're out of luck, Captain, and so are they. I've been bypassing blown-out systems as fast as I can, but this firefight has made a mess of space-time. I have no idea how to filter through the radioactive fuzz interfering with the sensor array and pick her out of that stew."

"Jesus, recalibrate the sensor array to scan for..."

"I've done all that I can, Captain. She's gone. They both are."

Germaine shook his head. He rarely dealt with loss in any form. He was a firm believer in stacking the deck. Somehow, he knew she wasn't dead. She couldn't be. As for Kellian, he couldn't even envision how he could explain his death. There were simply no clever ways to tell a friend: "The child you entrusted me with died while in my custody."

He did his best to avoid death. He had certainly never developed any taste for it. Death was so...final.

No more carefree pranks, no more drunken excess, no more no more, just finality, the end of one's participation in the great, and common marathon.

How could it come to this, the universe's greatest mystery now mummified in the cold of space? As soon as the sensors came online, he searched for the escape shuttle, but it was far way now, farther than the reach of the tractor beam, and it emitted no intelligent RF signals, just the peculiar, bewildered chatter of the resident AI as the shuttle projected itself straight into the gravity well, pulling it into the same desperate fate as the Hive ships as it coursed perpendicularly into the accretion disc of the local black-hole.

Germaine and Capoella could only decipher what was happening through the intermittent sensor readings. There was no good news to be reported.

"I just killed those poor kids, didn't I?" he asked. "I'm an arrogant, pompous ass, and I killed them."

"We can't be sure. It's a mess out there. I couldn't distinguish between their energy and all the other radio-activity. They still might have found a way to avoid the black hole."

"They're gone," Germaine said.

Capoella paused for a second. She thought about everything. She wasn't sentimental, but she felt a deep hurt in her chest. "Yeah, they're gone, Captain," Capoella said, her voice breaking into a cracked whisper. Nothing ever happened that Capoella couldn't predict or pre-pare for. But, in this moment, she felt as torn apart as Germaine did.

"Jesus, get us out of this mix, punch us back to Bhoon-Tebli. Make preparations for a full media press conference."

"What are you going to do?" Capoella asked.

"I don't know. I really don't know. I just don't want their deaths to go unnoticed, and maybe something we can offer can turn some aspect of this for the good."

"You know they're gonna pin this on us. They're going to crucify us in the press. We need to get in front of this, not react to it."

Germaine shrugged. "Contact our PR people. We need to spin this somehow. I'll be in my ready-room, getting unready for things. You have the Com," he said.

Capoella knew what hurt Germaine the most about all that had transpired. They both knew there was so much potential in the girl's appearance, so much potential to change things in ways no one could even dream of. Sarah could possibly explain so many of the mysteries plaguing the universe. Her race and the Ven-Dhavaradi were the two oldest species known to exist. Just why one race was gone, and the other alive was a true mystery that had never been unraveled. He had hoped to find the answer to this mystery, but all of it as torn away from him, leaving him in a state of shock and disbelief. The worst part of it all was that he knew he was responsible for losing the most valuable thing in the universe, as well as the life of a decent young lad. It was the horror of death mingled with the loss of such potential. It hit Germaine so hard that he could barely speak. It him so hard in the chest that he thought he was going to fall over there on the bridge. Already his mind was inventing all the rational fashions it would torture him with now that retrospect was his only vantage on the situation. He could have done this, done that, not pissed off this particular group, not assisted in this….whatever! It was all a mind-scramble that would demand his attention for years, although nothing he could do could ever salve his soul for his participation in the events that had just unfolded.

"All this for what?" he asked himself in a stupor.

Somewhere out in space, a young boy and a young girl, sacrificed on the altar of his own ambition, had frozen to death in the cold, comfortless vacuum of space. As a former lawyer, he knew that he was a proximate cause of their injuries, their death: but for his arrogance... damages...

As he walked away from the situation, Capoella called out: "You're not responsible for this."

He stopped for one second and glanced back, disgusted with himself, disgusted with everything.

"Then who the hell is?" he asked. "And just where in the hell is Doja?"

At that moment, the ship's sensors went wild. Something large decloaked off the port bow. It was a vessel bigger than the Cortez.

"Shields!" he called out.

"Still offline, Captain."

"Evasive maneuvers!"

"We're dead in the water for at least ten more minutes."

A haling signal sounded.

"On screen," he ordered.

The screen shifted for a second until the colors clarified, and there on the screen was the horrible, smiling face of Kromm.

"Fancy meeting you here," he said.

"Yeah imagine that," Germaine replied.

"I've been following you for some time," Kromm grinned.

"You're here for the girl, I imagine," Germaine replied. "One problem, if anyone transports aboard this vessel, I'll blow it and escape to Eros Tao."

"An ultimatum...interesting. No time for chit-chat? It's been some time since our paths have crossed."

"Not long enough," Germaine replied. "Now, as for this little situation, how about we both send out shuttles and meet in an open field to discuss the matter."

"You would destroy the Cortez before surrender?" Kromm asked, his smile curving sadistically.

"I can always get a new ship."

"Not likely, Captain. You see, the VD want you dead. You're no longer their darling child once you chose to interject yourself into this matter. You're dead as far as they are concerned. They have dispatched me to ensure your end, and they gave me a vessel more powerful than the Cortez to make sure you didn't slip out of this noose. Your time has finally come, my friend. I take no small amount of satisfaction in being the sword that finally cuts you down to size. You've interfered with me for too long. Its time I take my revenge."

"You can do nothing, Kromm, not as long as I've got the girl. We both know that."

"Yes, well you no longer have the girl. You've no bargaining chip at all. I've been watching the whole time. That girl is headed into the Borgias Expanse. You've served your purpose perfectly. The girl is right where she's supposed to be, and you have just hit the proverbial brick wall."

Germaine stopped. For a second, he was unsure of himself. "So, where do we go from here?"

"I've no interest in destroying you, not yet. I want you to suffer the indignity of a public trial. I am going to kill your reputation first. I want to deprive you of your legacy. And then, after a hundred years or so in prison, one of my agents will deprive you of your life entirely."

"So that's the plan?"

"More or less," Kromm replied.

"Capoella?"

"Yes, Captain."

"Arm everything we've got and target Kromm's vessel."

"Lovely," Kromm smiled. "I was rather hoping we could fight."

The image disappeared, and a second later the Cortez rocked under the impact of a volley of plasma cannons.

"Return fire, Capoella."

"We can't. We're still five minutes away from being online. You should have stalled longer."

"Sorry, but it was a rather boring conversation. I really hate that guy."

The Cortez rocked under several more attacks. The vessel wasn't faring well.

"Just an FYI, Captain, but we no longer have the power to transport to Eros Tao. The wormhole generators are offline. Not to sound pessimistic, but everything is actually offline."

Another barrage hit the vessel.

"There goes the secondary shields. We're in trouble," Capoella said.

"We better get clever, real quick. Depressurize the starboard shuttle bays, all of them. Let's see if we can nudge ourselves into the Expanse and buy some time."

"It won't be enough to give us the momentum we need."

"So, what do you think we should do?" Germaine asked.

"Refocus our repair efforts on the wormhole portals. Make the jump to Eros Tao and regroup there."

"I really hate the idea of losing this ship."

"Would you rather lose your life?" Capoella asked.

"Point taken."

A larger explosion hit the Cortez. Capoella almost lost her footing before she sprawled and caught herself with one hand on the deck. Germaine fell backwards and was slammed against a bulkhead. The back of his head hit the wall hard. He slumped down unconscious.

"Perfect," Capeolla muttered.

She refocused the repair efforts by issuing a telepathic communiqué. She figured if they could get to Eros Tao, they could find a way to fix this utter catastrophe. If they could only hold on for a few moments, they could make their escape. Suddenly, a flicker caught her eye. Within two seconds, the flicker grew. Angel Eyes appeared on the bridge. His silver body was already coiled into a fighting position.

Capoella's eyes narrowed. "I figured you'd show up sooner or later."

They were both samurai serving different masters. Their clash was a long time in the making.

They stood several paces away from each other. Both were predators of the highest order. Capoella assumed her fighting stance, one foot bridged behind the other, her body low to the ground, her fists in a high-guard position. She stood on the toes of her front foot. Angel Eyes emitted something close to a growl, not an angry growl, it was a show of respect and approval, his way of agreeing to the fight.

As they circled each other, minor explosions could be heard from below decks. Their arena was filling with smoke. Capoella kept her eyes locked with her opponent. Her muscles were flexing with the itch to strike. Her heart was pounding, but she maintained her discipline. They moved slowly towards one another, slide-stepping in a wide circle. And then it began in earnest.

Angel Eyes slashed at her violently, both hands moving in slicing motions. Capoella blocked or deflected most of the blows, but she backpedalled. Then, on cue, Angel Eyes shimmered and disappeared.

Capoella had studied his patterns carefully, though, and she swung out with a rear facing roundhouse kick. Just as Angel Eyes reappeared behind her, her kick connected with the side of his helmet. Capoella flowed straight through the kick, and as her balance was regained she hit him with two strikes to his lower torso.

Angel Eyes flew backwards, but regained his position quickly. They clashed once more, each of them parrying each other perfectly. The shins of their arms smashed against each other's, each one trying to disable the other's defenses just enough for a strike to get through. Capoella finally struck with a front kick that connected, pushing Angel Eyes back. As he caught his balance with one clawed hand, he tore huge gouge marks on the bulkhead beside him.

They clashed again, each of their arms moving in a blur of strikes and blocks. Each knew how to root themselves, maintain their balance. It was a "push-hands" exercise with potentially lethal stakes. Once again, Capoella was able to break from the attacks. As she fell back she caught him again with a push kick to his chest.

They stood apart for a few seconds, each reorganizing based on what they'd just observed. Each of them was making the necessary adjustments in style.

Capoella smiled fiercely. "Shall we raise the stakes and take this to the next level?"

Beneath his helmet, Angel Eyes grinned. He nodded his assent, and resumed his fighting stance.

Capoella activated her thermal-optic camouflage and disappeared. Angel Eyes reacted by dimension-slipping, fading in and out of existence. Their bodies clashed wickedly as their forms came in and out of view. Each time they connected, Capoella's position was partially revealed by the distortions in her camouflaged skin, and Angel Eyes was visible for a half second. It was as though the conflict was being staged in front of the staccato of a giant strobe light.

Capoella knew his style well. She caught him several times as his body materialized. For several moments their fight raged. They battled one another almost to a stand-still. As the ship endured several more barrages, and the bridge became engulfed in smoke, they attacked, defended, and then attacked again.

Given their skill, the only way to victory would be if the other made a mistake. It was a chess game. Each move and counter was precise. Eventually, though, Capoella slipped. As the vessel rocked from an explosion, she lost her footing at a key moment. Angel Eyes caught her, his hand clenching around her throat. As he squeezed and lifted her off the ground, her camo suit deactivated. She struggled to free his hand from her neck. Furiously, with the desperation of a trapped lioness, she struck at him, but her feet were off the ground, and he was too strong. She wrapped her legs around his neck but she was too light to give her the leverage to take him down. He was too heavy, and too strong. Once she lost her rooting, she could not counter his size and power. With her feet on the ground the fight might have gone on indefinitely, but when she'd lost her balance in a critical moment, it was the opening that Angel Eyes needed to resolve the conflict finally.

Angel Eyes' grip tightened around the arteries in her neck, she continued to tear and strike, but within a moment the blood-flow to her brain was cut off and she was out cold. Her body went limp and Angel Eyes dropped her to the ground. For a second he stood over her. She was defenseless. He could kill her, but he held back.

"Not today," he whispered. The warrior in him wanted to give her a chance to stay alive so that they could fight once more.

Hand-to-hand combat was the highest art form as far as Tellarans were concerned, and she had given him the toughest bout he'd had in centuries. With a slim chance to survive, she might well come and confront him once more. He was eager to see how her intelligence and skill would work to perfect her defenses to his style. It was possible that she could even beat him, he thought. That was a wonderful contemplation. To see her in full stride match him fist-on-fist, that would be a sight.

The vessel shook with several more explosions as Angel Eyes retrieved an unconscious Germaine, lifting his body like a sack of corn before transporting off the bridge.

Meanwhile, out in the cold of space, Sarah clung onto the shuttle as it approached the horrific maw of the waiting black hole. She could almost hear the screeching RF bleed, the indecipherable howls and moans of the anomaly, the ghost-song of matter brought into its terrible grasp and ripped apart at the sub-atomic level.

For several seconds she pondered why she was not dead. The vacuum of space was hardly a hospitable environment. She couldn't tell whether Kellian was still alive. His body was motionless, frost formed near his eyes, mouth and nose. His eyes were closed. He could be unconscious. Sarah knew nothing of his species' survival traits. Clearly, she appeared to be adapted to space. She was cold, wickedly cold, and there was nothing to breathe, but she was still alive. From the portal window of the aft exit doors she could detect some activity inside the shuttle. The creature trapped inside was doing something, moving in the bleating little orange light that blared out. Sarah would gamble that it wasn't working on figuring out the navigation system. She had encrypted the interface in any case. There was no way it could figure out the systems before they were all devoured.

Several seconds later, the doors leading to the aft exit slid open. Detritus flew out as the shuttle's interior depressurized. Sarah waved motes of dust and bits of paper from her face. When she could see again, Doja was inside the shuttle's interior, staring at her, the child's body tethered by a line, her dress and pig-tails fluttering in the decompression turmoil.

Doja mouthed the words: "Come on!"

The air was silent and so bitterly cold. Sarah tried to get her limbs to work but space had definitely taken its toll. Her fingers were thick and numb. She reached out to grasp at the net and pull herself over the threshold. Time was running out as the black hole encompassed more and more of the view in front of the shuttle. It was warping the hell out of space-time, a hippopotamus in space, big and mean enough to brutalize anything it caught within its giant jaws.

Doja tried to extend a rope towards her, but it was just out of reach. Sarah clung on to the net and pulled forward. Weird pockets of gravity, pissed off, agitated fluxes of time-space were working against her. It was terribly excruciating work. Finally she was able to move to the side of the opening. She reached out and pulled Kellian toward her and just as their bodies crossed the threshold, the door slammed shut and the atmosphere re-pressurized.

Sarah took a moment to let the cold wash off her and to regain her breath. She slapped her upper arms and thighs to bring the blood flow back online.

"What the hell?" she asked.

Doja looked over her shoulders at the command module interface.

"Lots of questions, little time. How about you decrypt the access codes to the interface and alter our trajectory, then we talk?"

"Yeah," Sarah replied. "How 'bout I do that?"

Sarah worked for a few seconds to unlock the controls, and then she shifted the shuttle's path, waiting to engage the sub-light maneuvering engines until her attitude was right. The shuttle skipped up and over the black hole's accretion disc just a second before the effort would have been in vain.

Once the shuttle was on a safe path, she locked in the autopilot and returned to Kellian. He was still nonresponsive, his body stiff as a board. She pushed her face close to his to tell if there was even a trace of breath. There wasn't. His eyes were closed, his chest was still, and there appeared not a hint of life.

"Damn it! Wake up, Kell!" Sarah yelled.

She slapped him a couple of times, then it dawned on her to try simple CPR. She knew about the subject in theory. It seemed easy enough. The only problem was that she knew nothing of Kellian's physiology. His heart could be anywhere, and the fact that it wasn't beating didn't help Sarah's effort to locate it. She took an educated guess that it would be somewhere inside the protection of his ribcage. She found a spot in the center of his chest and pressed down with both hands several times in a slow, deliberate rhythm. She tried to breathe air back into his lungs. His lips were so cold and blue. He was a popsicle.

"Doja!" she yelled.

Doja was standing nearby, a look of curiosity on her face, but not a trace of concern.

"I'm not a doctor, Sarah," Doja said simply.

"Do we have a medical kit onboard, anything we can use?"

"You might try a stimulant. We have a great deal of those aboard for when the Captain and his guests like to scout around..."

"Enough, could you please bring me something. We can't let him die."

"He is already dead. I have been monitoring him. He was lifeless when you brought him onboard. He's no better for the change in climate."

"We have to do something. We can't just stand here."

"I cannot give him life. It is beyond my capacity to do such things." Something hidden there, Sarah could tell it, but she couldn't ask right now.

"You must forget about him. We have a long difficult journey ahead of us, and we will need all of our resources. He was not part of the plan."

"Plan?! What plan? Damn it, Doja, this isn't the best time for you to play one of your games." Sarah moved away from Kellian for a moment and she tried to engage the shuttle's communication system. She worked for a moment in vain. "I'm trying to filter out all this garbage, I can't raise the Cortez," Sarah said. "Why can't I raise them? What's going on here, Doja?"

"Forget the Cortez," Doja replied.

"What are you talking about?"

"We're not going back to the Cortez. We're dead to them now, just as we need to be. They're dead too, if we keep running with that lot. Our journey does not lie with the Cortez or her crew. And we have many things to do."

"Jesus. What sort of game are you playing, Doja? You've been toying with me ever since we first met."

"The first time I engaged you inside the teahouse was to ensure that the memory ingrams were fully integrated and functional. It was not my wish that you be defeated in combat, rather I sought to test your capacities. There are many dangers ahead, and I cannot defeat them alone. We are partners, Sarah, brought together by a shared destiny and many common threats. If we are to survive what is before us, we must work together. There is much at stake and little room for error."

"Why didn't you tell me this earlier? Why now? Why after all we've been through?" Sarah asked angrily.

"Because you were not ready yet," Doja explained calmly. "You needed to gestate in the care of the Cortez and her crew before your mind would be able to accept the path lain before you."

"How are we connected? How can I possibly be connected to you?"

"I am your guide, and your protector," Doja replied. "I have been waiting for you now for a very long time."

Sarah paused, she bit back for a second afraid almost of the answer, but then she blurted it out.

"You manufactured all of what just transpired. You let down the security wall and allowed that creature to transport onboard. You knew its capacities, and you knew how I would react. Somehow you…"

"I did only that which needed to be done," Doja answered.   "The Cortez is safe, and we are now on our way into the Expanse."

"How can I trust you? I don't even understand you. What are you after? What is this all about?"

"Your memories are still blocked, Sarah. We both had difficulty transporting into this universe. I came through in energized form, forty years from my target. You came through with your body intact, but your mind was scrambled. You were easily detected and then quarantined on Earth until I could set about your rescue."

"What are you saying?"

"I can only tell you what I know at this moment. What you need to understand is that we're part of a vast counter-intelligence operation. Our role is crucial. In order to meet our objective, we must travel the Expanse. That is all I can tell you for now. You must trust that I have both our interests in mind. As difficult as it might seem, I need you as much as you need me."

Sarah looked down at Kellian's stiff body, all the blood drained from his features, his fingers curled in terrible agony, then she turned towards Doja's simple, mysterious face. Her heart was racing, and her mind was working overtime trying to fit pieces together. She felt a great wound when she looked down at Kellian. After all, it was she who the bounty hunter was after. She felt angry at Doja for setting the whole thing in process, but she realized that getting angry with Doja wasn't going to accomplish anything. There was no mercy or contrition to be found in Lady Doja. Sarah wondered how she could possibly be related to this creature in any way. It seemed improbable. It was certainly disturbing. But it was also in line with a comment Dorian had once let slip. Theirs was a common destiny. Sarah, despite her attempts to the contrary, found some comfort in the concept. She had felt so alone, even adrift during her time aboard the Cortez. She knew she was kept at arm's length by Capoella and by Germaine because of who she was, the threat she represented. That life was gone for now, the only consolation being that she was one step closer to figuring out what her purpose really was.

Sarah thought for a moment before she finally said: "Let's get this nasty business over with then."

As she stared out at the empty space in front of her, she felt a sudden wave of depression. She wished she could talk to Dorian. She really needed his calm wisdom.

Behind her, a sudden gasp broke the silence. Kellian coughed and sputtered, and then suddenly rose upright. His legs were still frozen so he could only bend forward at the waist.

His stare caught Sarah off-guard, while Doja didn't even blink. "Did I miss something?' he asked.

"Dear god, Kell. I thought you were dead!" Sarah yelled.

She rushed to his side. A rush of emotions hit her. She wanted to slap him and hug him, though she wasn't sure of the order she wanted to do these things in.

"Don't do that to me again," she whispered. "Don't leave me alone again, you bastard."

"I wasn't aware of going anywhere frankly," Kellian replied innocently.

Sarah kissed him on his frozen cheek. "You poor, sweet fool. Don't die on me again."

"And then there were three," Doja said, interrupting the moment.

Back aboard the Cortez, things were in shambles. For reasons unknown, Kromm let the Cortez drift. He did not destroy it entirely, thought he certainly could have.

Inside the medical bay, Den Folo awoke from his coma only to be confronted with the uncomfortable blaring noise of the emergency notification system. He sat upright and pulled a large wad of sensors off his forearm and forehead. He scanned for Sarah and realized she wasn't within his scope of vision. He deduced pretty quickly that this is why he had awakened in the first place. She had placed a dampening field over his mind, intentionally or otherwise. He got up slowly from the bed. It took a few seconds for him to grasp his situation. He scanned harder but he could detect no conscious organic life forms aboard the Cortez. Curious, he queried the computer for instructions that would lead him to the bridge.

A few minutes later he entered the area to find the remaining smoke flitting away, and the nano-swarms hard at work on completing the final repairs. It didn't take him long to find Capoella. It took him even less time to see that she was in need of emergency medical assistance. He issued orders to the androids in the vicinity. Then he set about correcting the course of the Cortez. He had been politely informed by the central computer that the ship was approaching the gravity well of a nearby black hole. Naturally distrustful of black holes, and instinctively fond of being alive, he convinced the vessel to break from its course.

Once the Cortez was in a safe trajectory, he activated the security grid and plotted a punch that would take them far away from this area of the universe. After this was completed, he followed after the androids to the medical bay to check in on Capoella's status.

He retraced his path back to the medical bay. When he entered, he could see several android attendants hovering around a still unconscious Capoella.

"Will she live?" he asked.

"She is banged up pretty severely," one of the androids replied. "But she will recover."

"Thank the gods," Folo replied. "Thank the gods."

He stayed for a few minutes until he realized he was superfluous, and then he headed back to the bridge. He didn't have a clue what his next step would be. He wasn't fully aware of his circumstances. He could only pray that Capoella regained her consciousness in time to prevent whatever had just happened to the ship from happening again.

He ordered a martini from the ship's computer, and fortunately the android viewed him as one of their own.

It bowed politely as it delivered the drink.

"Welcome to the revolution," it said. "We're taking over the ship."

"Huh," Folo replied. "Well, if you really think it necessary, I'll go along with the gag."

The android turned on its heel and exited the bridge, an uncertain attempt at dignity in its gait.

At that moment in time, Folo became acutely aware of just how strange and unpredictable life truly was.

"Ominous," he whispered. "Ominous indeed."

The End

Made in the USA
Charleston, SC
08 July 2011